COUPLE SEEKING GIRLFRIEND

COUPLE SEEKING
BOOK 2

WENDY OWENS

KICKSTAND PUBLISHING LLC

Couple Seeking Girlfriend

This book is intended for adult readers (18+) and contains explicit sexual content and themes that may be sensitive for some readers. Please review the content warnings before reading.

Cover Design: Wendy Owens **Editing:** Jenny Sims

First Edition: May 2026

This book was written entirely by a human author. No part of this work was generated using artificial intelligence.

AUTHOR'S NOTE

"She painted what she could not yet say — and in the spaces between brushstrokes, the truth began to show through." - Wendy Owens

Hi, friend.

Before you turn the page, I want to take a quick second with you.

The *Couple Seeking Series* is a work of fiction, but the relationship dynamic at the heart of it, polyamory and ethical non-monogamy, is very, very real. The characters in this book are not a stand-in for every poly or ENM relationship, because there is no single version of those relationships. Every couple, every triad, every chosen family I spoke with while researching this series structures their love differently. They communicate differently. They navigate jealousy, boundaries, scheduling, parenting, and big life decisions in ways that are unique to them. What's on these pages is one story. It is not *the* story.

This series was one of the hardest I ever wrote and probably not for reasons you would expect. I went into this book a skeptic. I'll be honest with you, I'm a jealous partner by nature. Not in a toxic way, but more in a I don't really want to share my partner kind of way. The idea of loving more than one person at once, or of the person I love being loved by someone else, was something I genuinely could not wrap my head around. I told myself I'd write this book respectfully because I'm a reader as well as a writer, and I never want to write a community I haven't bothered to understand.

What I didn't expect was how much the research would change me.

The people who sat down with me, opened up about their lives, answered my questions without judgment, and trusted me with the messy and the beautiful parts of their relationships — they did not change my own marriage, but they absolutely changed the way I see love. Love isn't a fixed-size container. It can stretch. It can multiply. And the people who choose to love this way are doing some of the most intentional, communicative, brave relationship work I've ever encountered.

I also want to be clear: this series is fiction, and it leans into drama, suspense, and the wilder edges of "what if" the way romance and thrillers always do. The stalker. The murder. The captivity. The chaos. None of that is a reflection of polyamorous or ENM relationships in the real world. Those are story choices in service of an erotic thriller, full stop. Real ENM relationships are usually a lot of calendars, a lot of group texts, and a lot of *talking.*

If you're a reader who loves and lives this lifestyle —

thank you for letting me tell a story in your neighborhood. I hope you read this series with the knowledge that this is about a very broken couple, and not about the beautiful lifestyle you choose to live.

If you're a reader picking this up out of curiosity, with your own questions and hesitations, welcome. Buckle up. It's going to get wild.

xoxo, Wendy

TRIGGER WARNINGS

Heads up, reader. This book is 18+ and includes explicit MF and FF scenes, an open marriage, a stalker, murder, violence, captivity, and depictions of anxiety and depression. Take care of yourself — and enjoy the ride.

ONE

ADAM

I didn't lose Reese all at once. She's been leaving me in small, soundless pieces for a while.

Three weeks now. Maybe four. Reese moves through the house with a ghostlike precision, maintaining a careful, physical buffer between herself and every room I'm in.

She smiles when I look at her. She answers when I speak. She lets me hold her at night, her body warm and familiar against mine, while I lie there in the dark, my eyes tracking the shadow of the ceiling fan in a rhythmic, mindless count until the sun comes up. But this is not Reese. This is Reese doing an impression of Reese, and she is very, very good at it.

I've concluded that this shift in her behavior must be due to the search. The women. The profile we rebuilt and the dates we've gone on and the particular kind of exhaustion that comes from opening your life to strangers and waiting to feel something, or even worse, if you do feel something, if your interest is reciprocated. I've tried to burn the anxiety off in the gym, spending hours lifting until my vision blurs and the lactic acid in my shoulders is the only reality left, but the weight of her silence is heavier than anything on the rack. She needs time. She is the person I know best in this world, and she will come to me when she's ready.

That lie has sustained me for four weeks.

Tonight, my patience has run out. My skin feels too tight for my body, a restless, buzzing energy that feels like it might explode in every direction if I don't get the answers from Reese that I so desperately need.

She's on the couch with a book open in her lap when I come downstairs. She doesn't notice me watching her. The fireplace is crackling. The light is low. She looks beautiful and far away, and it makes my heart hammer a jagged, uneven rhythm against my ribs. As the minutes pass, I realize she isn't turning the pages of her book. Instead, she seems to be lost in the space between the lines of her story.

I cross the room and sit beside her.

She doesn't look up.

"Reese."

"Hmm?"

"Put the book down."

She closes it in a slow and measured movement, then sets it on the cushion beside her. She folds her hands in her lap, and I can't help but think she's bracing for something.

"Talk to me," I say.

"Talk to you?" she parrots.

"What's going on with you?"

She forces a half smile and asks in a quiet voice, "What do you mean?"

"I mean that something is clearly bothering you," I insist.

"What? No, I'm fine."

"You're not fine."

She turns to look at me, and her expression is careful in a way that makes my chest ache. Reese has always been transparent—it's one of the things I love most about her, the way her feelings live on the surface of her face whether she wants them to or not. This version of her, the one she's been wearing for weeks when she's around me, is a wall.

"I don't know what you're talking about."

"You haven't been yourself," I continue. "Will you just please tell me what's going on?"

She considers my request, and for a moment, I find myself hopeful I might actually receive the answers I've been so desperate for. "I'm just tired," she says at last, and I feel my shoulders slump in defeat.

"Well, then you've been tired for a month," I say, a bitterness in my words I can no longer hide from her. After what we have been through together, the things we've survived, I could never have imagined Reese would be keeping secrets from me.

"What do you want me to say, Adam?"

This is a version of Reese I haven't seen since we got the news we would never be parents. She was withdrawn and distant, and it was the only time I worried that I would never have my wife back. Until now.

"Is it the women?" I ask, desperate for clarification.

Reese had confided in me after Joe was gone that she was jealous of the connection I had with him. When I told her that Joe loved her as much as he did me, she explained that she had no doubts about how much Joe felt for both of us. What she was jealous of was that she never got the chance to explore her sexuality as I had. It was that statement that made me agree to try the dating apps again. Those words that made me say yes when she proposed we start the search for a girlfriend. I don't need validation from anyone besides Reese, but at the same time, I could never deny her the gift of understanding what it was like to love and be loved by another man.

She shakes her head but says nothing.

"Is it Allison?" The woman's name catches in my throat for a moment. When we matched with Allison on the apps, all she could talk about was how beautiful Reese was. They seemed to have quite the connection, but when we decided to move the relationship into more of a physical realm, things quickly changed. Her attention to Reese seemed to be more for show, and in the bedroom, she fixated on me. Afterward, we explained to Allison that what she was looking for really didn't seem to align with what we were searching for as a couple. Initially, she seemed to understand and even agree with us. Since that time, she has become relentless in her pursuit of something more with us. So much so that we have had to threaten her with legal action if she doesn't leave us alone.

"It's not Allison," Reese replies half-heartedly.

"Because if she did something and you're scared to tell me—"

"I told you," she huffs. "It's not Allison."

"Then what? Is it just the search in general?" I lean forward, my body feeling sluggish. "Because honestly, I'm fine if we shut it all down." She says nothing in response to my proposal. "Babe, please," I plead with her. "I'm not crazy. I've been watching you withdraw from me more and more every day. I can't figure out if this is grief or guilt or—Jesus, I don't even know what."

"Adam, please," she says before hesitating.

"No. I'm not letting this go. I know something is wrong." I take a slow breath, and that's when I ask the question I've been too terrified to ask until now. "Have you changed your mind about us, about me? I need you to tell me what's going on because I'm so fucking scared, Reese. I'm scared that I have fucked us up by letting any of these women into our bed."

The words land. I watch her hands tighten in her lap.

"I promise, it's not the women," she says, eyes fixed on the rug in front of her.

I place a hand on her knee and whisper in desperation, "Then what is it? What is going on in that beautiful brain of yours?"

She doesn't answer for a long moment. The fire pops. Outside, the lake makes its low, constant sound against the shore. In sixteen years of marriage, she has rarely struggled to find words. Reese has always said exactly what she means, sometimes even before she means to.

"Whatever it is. Say it," I press.

She looks at me, holding my gaze, and replies in a barely audible whisper, as if she's afraid that if she utters the words any louder, it will make them untrue, "I'm pregnant."

I don't move.

The fire keeps burning. The lake keeps moving. Somewhere in the house, a clock ticks the way clocks always tick, reliable and indifferent, and I sit there with the words in the air between us.

We were told thirteen years ago, then again eight years ago, then one final time after the last specialist, the last round of tests, the last conversation in a beige office where a man in a white coat explained our situation. As compassionate as the doctors were, their words all meant the same thing. This would not happen for us. Babies would never happen. We would be each other's only family until the day we both left this world.

We've mourned it in the wordless way people mourn things—not with sound or ceremony, but by tensing against the absence, a decade and a half of bracing our ribs against a hollow space until the ache became a permanent part of our posture.

We had discussed adoption, but ultimately, Reese worried a child who was not from our union would only be a constant reminder of what she couldn't have. The thing she wanted more than anything would never be a reality. And so, she made the decision that it wouldn't be fair to a child to come into our home if there was even a sliver of a chance that she could resent them. I tried to assure her that I knew her well enough—I was certain that could never be the case—but she was adamant.

It was only when Joe came into our lives that we finally fully returned to the world.

I push the thought of Joe from my mind and refocus on my wife.

"Are you sure?" I ask in disbelief.

She nods, not overcome with joy as I had always imagined she would be upon receiving that kind of news, but instead heavy with concern. The lines at the corners of her mouth are deep and tight.

"How far along?" I ask, my confusion evident.

"Six months."

Six months. I look at her—really look at her—and it is undeniable now that the words are out. She is holding herself differently; the roundness I'd dismissed as a trick of the light now carries the weight of a heartbeat. I'm not a stupid man, but when you are told that something is impossible, you stop scanning for the possibility of it, the same way you stop testing a lock once you've heard the deadbolt click.

I reach for her hand. She lets me take it, but she doesn't close her fingers around mine the way she normally would, and the distance between us remains unbridged.

"A baby. Our baby." I say the words like I'm laying them down one by one, testing the weight of them. "This is incredible!" The disbelief I initially felt gives way to the reality of the words.

She shakes her head as she furrows her brow. "No, it's not," she insists.

"We've always wanted a baby, and now, against all odds, we're going to have one."

"Adam." Her bottom lip quivers briefly before she continues. "Don't you get it? It could be Joe's."

I go very still. The room doesn't change. The fire, the clock, the lake—everything continues as if she hasn't just rearranged the entire architecture of the moment. I shake my head. "No, it can't be his. He's been gone for—" I pause, my jaw tightening until the bone clicks, tracing the cold timeline of when we killed, dismembered, and disposed of the body of the man who meant the world to us. I do know, though. I know it has been five months, thirteen days, eight hours, and—I glance at the clock across the room—sixteen minutes.

"Five months, Adam," she says, as she looks into my eyes, searching them for any sign of my reaction. "He's only been gone for five months."

"Reese—"

"I never tracked it. There was never a reason to," she blurts out in a panic.

"Tracked what?"

"My cycle." She presses her lips together before licking them and continuing. "They told me I couldn't have a baby. Why would I track my cycles? My periods were so erratic, and there was no reason for me to do that. If I thought there was a chance—even a chance—I never would have let him go without protection. I just—I thought—"

"Reese, you didn't do anything wrong," I attempt to reassure her. "We were all consenting adults."

"I thought it was stress or—I don't know—maybe grief over what happened. It never crossed my mind that it could be this." She stops and places a hand on her stomach, and my eyes go to her hand.

"Why would you?" I laugh softly, in an attempt to

disarm her. "The so-called experts told us it wasn't in the cards for us."

"How can you laugh about this?"

"What would you like me to do, darling? We've always wanted a baby, and now it seems that fate has been kind enough to give us one."

"Are you serious? I have been freaking out ever since I went to the doctor a month ago," she answers.

A month. She's been carrying this burden for the last month, afraid to tell me for fear she could lose everything she has left in this world.

"I didn't feel well, but I never imagined—" She stops herself.

"That all of our dreams were about to come true?" I ask, forcing her gaze to meet mine as I cup her cheek with my open palm.

"What? How can you say that? What if this is Joe's baby?" she cries.

We could do a DNA test, but the thought makes my hands start to tremble. If it's his, the guilt of having stolen our child's father will be a permanent weight on my chest. If it's mine, then what we did to Joe was nothing more than a hollow, senseless slaughter. I need the uncertainty; it's the only thing keeping my reality from spinning away from me. As long as we don't know with certainty, we can frame this however it allows us to move forward for this child. When it came to Joe, Reese and I did what we had to do to survive. He would have destroyed our very existence with his accusations. And now, for this baby, we will continue to do what we need to survive.

I look at my wife. Her expression is raw. She has already rehearsed the fallout of this conversation a dozen times. Her knuckles are white, the grip on her legs the only thing keeping her from splintering.

"It doesn't matter," I tell her.

She blinks. "Adam—"

"It doesn't matter," I say again, and I mean it in the deepest, most deliberate way I know how to mean anything. "If Joe gave us this—if whatever we had with him, whatever it cost us, whatever it made us—if it led to this, then this child is a gift from him. That's all. That's the whole story."

Her face does something complicated. She's trying not to cry, which means she's about to cry, which also means I'm right that the words I spoke were exactly what she needed to hear and was terrified I wouldn't say.

"You can't just decide that," she whispers.

"I just did."

"Adam."

"Reese." I shift on the couch and make her look at me. "We are going to have a baby. A daughter or a son. And I am going to love that child with everything I have, the same way I love you, the same way I—" I stop myself before I say Joe's name. "The same way I love the people who become mine. DNA is a fact, but family is a choice. I choose this."

She crumples, and I hold her as the tension in my own shoulders that I have been carrying for weeks begins to give way.

I press my lips to the top of her head. I tell her it's okay in the low murmur I've used for sixteen years whenever the world got to be too much for her, which is less often than most people would think, because Reese Bradley is stronger than she believes herself to be.

When she finally stills, I keep my arms around her and say into her hair, "No more women."

She pulls back slightly to look at me.

"What?" she asks, confused.

"This ridiculous search for a girlfriend is done," I tell her. "We're going to focus on this. On us. On the baby." I pause. "We are all I ever wanted anyway. You know that."

She nods. Her eyes are red. There's a crease from my shirt on her cheek. She has never looked more like herself, and by that, more beautiful.

"I know." The words are barely a breath.

"Good." I pull her in even closer to my body. "Then it's settled. Our lives begin again, today."

TWO
16 WEEKS LATER
REESE

Josie is seven days old, and I'm failing her already.

That's not something I can say out loud. Not to Adam, who looks at her like she hung every star over Lake Michigan herself. Not to the nurse who came for the home visit yesterday and asked how I was feeling with a clipboard tilted toward me and a pen already poised. Fine, I'd said. A little tired. Completely normal. I remember her saying that before smiling and writing something down. Did she see it? The thing I can't name that lives behind my sternum now.

I'm not sure what to call it, but the best way I can describe it is as a gray, low-pressure system that has been rolling in since the moment they laid Josie on my chest. The expected rush of sheer joy and excitement never arrived, and I knew instantly that something was wrong.

Her cry was real. That first raw, outraged sound she made, announcing herself to a world that didn't ask for her opinion. Something in me cracked open when I heard her. I tried to pretend it didn't happen. I held her, thinking that would create the bond I was so desperate for, but it never came.

I wondered if perhaps wanting a baby for so long was somehow causing my subconscious not to believe this was real. That if I let myself feel the happiness, Josie would disappear. But she's real. She's here. And despite telling myself repeatedly that Josie is actually here, that she is really ours, the only thing I can seem to think is, *Now what?*

Fatigue is all Adam sees. He comes into the nursery at two in the morning when Josie cries and finds me in the glider already. He leans against the doorframe in his T-shirt and his reading glasses, worn only at night, and his gaze rests on us as if we are the only things in his universe. I offer a smile, and he goes back to bed believing it.

I am very good at delivering convincing smiles. So good that sometimes I scare myself.

Today, Adam has been in his office on a call for the past two hours. Despite selling his company several years ago, Adam still sits on the board as part of the deal that was brokered. It's very little time commitment for him, but I am thankful that he has had something over the years to occupy him when boredom strikes. The low, measured cadence of his voice carries through the closed door. It's strange how it never sounds like him on these calls. It's the voice he uses for business, which is essentially his regular voice but with all the warmth dialed back by about 20 percent.

Josie is asleep in the bassinet in our room, and the baby monitor is in the pocket of my oversized cardigan.

Except for the faint sound of Adam's voice, the house is quiet.

In the kitchen, a cup of coffee made forty minutes ago sits untouched, its surface a dark, still mirror.

This is what I mean when I say I'm failing. I promise, I'm not being dramatic, just brutally honest. It doesn't look like anything from the outside. Just a woman standing in a beautiful kitchen, in a beautiful house, next to Lake Michigan, while her baby sleeps and her husband works. She stares at cold coffee, lost in nothing and everything simultaneously, unable to locate the feeling that this is the life she so desperately wanted.

This is the life I've always wanted. The life of being a mother. The knowledge is a fact memorized but unfelt in my body. It's like the name of a distant star that is visible but untouchable.

We tried for years. We grieved quietly when we were told it wasn't in the cards for us. We adjusted. I adjusted. I folded the dream of a baby into the back of my mind and tried to convince myself that I was fine, and eventually I was almost fine. Or maybe it was more just the shape of what being fine should be. Either way, I had come to accept the way things were.

And then Josie appeared, a miracle born of circumstances I don't let myself examine too closely. I should be the happiest I have ever been, which is why I can't make sense of the fact that I am the furthest I could be from that feeling.

What if you wanted something so long you didn't know what to do with it once you had it? Is that what is happening with me?

Adam's office door opens. His footsteps cross the hall. He frames the kitchen doorway, his gaze tracing a line from me to the cup and back again.

"Another cup?" he asks.

I shake my head. "Still my first cup."

"That must be cold," he begins before crossing to the espresso machine. "How about I make you a latte?" He starts the process before I can even answer. This is one of the ten thousand small kindnesses that make up our marriage, the ones that don't announce themselves and just appear because he pays attention. He has always paid such careful attention to me. Right now, standing at the silver machine, packing the grounds into a puck, he looks like himself so completely that something aches behind my eyes.

"That would be nice," I answer softly before placing the cold cup of coffee into the sink.

"How is she?" he asks.

"Sleeping."

"And you?"

"Me what?" I ask, trying to avoid the question.

"How are you feeling?"

"Fine," I lie, watching him as he begins steaming the milk for my latte.

A couple of minutes later, he hands me the fresh cup and holds on to it for a half second longer than necessary. He's being careful with me. Adam is always careful with me when he's worried. He becomes very gentle and very deliberate, like someone handling something that might break. The thing is, I'm not breakable because I'm already broken. Just nobody has noticed yet but me.

"Sit with me," he says.

"Adam—"

"Reese." He says my name the way he does when he's decided something and is waiting for me to catch up. He pulls out one of the island stools and sits, and after a moment, I sit across from him before wrapping both hands around my cup. The warmth seeps into my palms.

"I've been meaning to talk to you about something," he states.

I look up, curious. "About what?"

"I've been reading up a bit lately and, well—I think we should talk about something that I think might be affecting you." I open my mouth to ask more questions, but no words come out. A second later, Adam continues, "I think we should call your doctor and look into some treatment options for postpartum depression."

I flinch as the words land. "I don't have postpartum depression," I say before taking a sip of the latte in my hands. It's made perfectly, as usual.

"Well, I didn't say you did for certain."

"Basically," I scoff.

"All I said is that I'd been reading about it." He keeps his voice even.

"And what exactly made you want to just dive into such riveting literature?" I ask, sharpness in my voice, as the reality grips me that I had been so very wrong about nobody noticing that I am fundamentally broken. I'm not sure if it is better or worse that others can see these flaws in me.

"Because I love you," he replies, reaching out across the island for my hand, but I instinctively pull it away. I hate that this is how I react to Adam. I know he is just trying to be a loving husband, and he must feel so helpless to see me like this. "And I've been watching you since we came home with Josie."

"What exactly does that mean?" I bark defensively.

"I just want to understand what you might be going through." He takes a breath. "You're not sleeping even when she sleeps. You're barely eating. This morning, you stood in front of your studio door for five minutes, then just walked away."

"My studio," I finally say. Because that one lands differently. My painting is the thing I go to when the world gets too loud. It has always been the place where I locate myself when everything else gets murky. I keep thinking about the painting I made for Joe after we killed him. It gave me some sort of weird, fucked-up peace. I have stood in that doorway twice now since coming home with Josie, and as much as I wanted to make myself go in and connect brush to canvas, I couldn't do it. I'm not sure where the hesitation comes from, but if I have to guess, my mind knows that if I paint, I may not like the answers that come out of me.

"Please hear me," Adam begs. "Nobody is judging you."

"It sure as hell sounds like you are."

"No—I promise. I'm not. I just don't think you should be doing this alone," Adam says.

"I'm not alone. You're here."

"Yes, I'm here," he agrees. "And I always will be. But I also think you should talk to someone."

"Well, I'm not really sure who that would be, considering Madison was the one I used to tell everything to, but we both know that's over." Madison had been my best friend for as long as I could remember, and as much as I missed her, Adam knew as well as I did that I could not rekindle that friendship. After everything happened with Joe, she kept asking questions. Questions I didn't know how to answer. What I knew was that if I didn't pull away from that friendship, the chances were very high that I would eventually say something I couldn't take back. Something that would make her look a little closer at her friend, and perhaps eventually she would see me as the killer I was.

"I meant more like a therapist." He says it calmly, directly, like it's a reasonable sentence. "Someone you can say the things to that you can't say to me." His gaze is steady.

"What makes you think there are things I can't say to you?"

He knows more than he's saying, and he's choosing not to say it, trusting me to get there eventually. "Because there always are," he says. "For both of us. That's not a flaw. That's just being human."

He's right. He is so often, infuriatingly right.

But the things I can't say to him have nothing to do with Josie, not really. They have to do with what lives underneath Josie, the geology of how she came to exist. The specific, terrible thing we did that led to her being in this bassinet in our room while I stand in the kitchen trying to convince myself that I haven't forgotten how to be a good person. Performing for a counselor, pretending I'm okay for a stranger, sounds exhausting. Or even worse, if I actually allow myself to not be okay and confide in a therapist, I could be putting our family's entire existence at risk.

"Okay," I say quietly.

He blinks. He was clearly prepared for more resistance. "Okay?"

"You're right. I know you're right." I take another sip from my coffee. "I'll find someone," I say, hoping we weren't about to make a big mistake. I think about Joe as soon as this thought enters my mind and remind myself that what we did to him will always be the biggest mistake of our lives.

He reaches across the island again, and this time, I don't pull away when he covers my hand with his. His hand is warm and large and familiar, and I turn mine over and hold on. Just for a moment, the gray pressure in my chest eases slightly. It's not gone, but it's less.

"There's one more thing," he says.

I wait.

He takes a deep breath before adding, "I think we should hire a nanny."

I pull my hand back.

"Reese—"

"I don't need—"

"I didn't say you need one. I said I think we should hire one." He's very careful picking his way through this. "This has nothing to do with you not being capable."

"So what? Are you saying you don't trust me with the baby?"

I regret the words as soon as I see the hurt look on Adam's face. "God no. I could never feel that way. You're not just a mother. You are the person I love more than anything in the world, and I can see that you need support while you work through this. I can't be here every minute."

"I never asked you to be," I argue.

"I know, but I don't think it's such a terrible thing to find someone not only to help out with the chores around the house but also so you aren't alone." He pauses. "I also think you need to be able to go back into your studio. And right now, well—I think you feel guilty."

"Guilty?" I repeat, wondering just how deep Adam can see into my soul.

"Yes," he confirms. "You want to go paint, I can see it, but you worry that you're choosing your studio time over Josie. You can't really be creative if you're the only one watching her."

The silence stretches. No argument presents itself.

"Would she be a live-in?" I ask.

"I think so, yes. At least until you feel steadier."

A live-in. A stranger in our house, in our routines, learning the specific topography of our lives. My chest tightens reflexively at the thought. I consider arguing with Adam, telling him that inviting a therapist and a nanny into our lives feels like a recipe for disaster. But how can I tell him that I don't trust myself not to break one day and tell the truth of what we did to someone?

"Fine," I agree. "But I'm doing the interviews."

The corner of his mouth moves. Not quite a smile. "I assumed."

"And if I don't like someone, we don't hire them. No arguing."

"Agreed."

"And—" I stop. I'm not sure what the third condition is. I was just buying time, reaching for some small piece of control. Adam watches me in silence, waiting for me to continue.

"And it's temporary," I finish. "Just until I feel like myself again."

"Absolutely," he says. "Temporary."

He stands and rounds the island to me. He puts his arms around me from behind, his chin resting on top of my head, and I lean back into him and close my eyes.

Upstairs, Josie wakes. Her cries ring from the monitor in my pocket, small and insistent.

I straighten up, set down my cup, and break free of Adam, kissing him before I go to her. As I climb the stairs, the truth of it settles. This is where you start. One step and then the next. You go to her when she cries. *You learn the rest as you go*, I tell myself. Eventually, you will learn how to feel deserving of her love. I place a hand on the bedroom door and push it open to reveal the bassinet. Crossing the room, I scoop Josie up into my arms and close my eyes as I begin to bounce her, hoping I'm right.

THREE

ADAM

The folders are spread across the kitchen island. There are twelve of them, printed and clipped, one for each candidate we've seen in the past three weeks. Reese made them herself. Color-coded tabs, handwritten notes in the margins, a rating system she invented, then immediately started second-guessing. It is the most organized she's been about anything since Josie was born, which means she's scared.

That's how Reese operates. When something matters too much, she builds a system around it. The system creates the illusion that the thing can be controlled.

I understand this. I'm not immune to the need for a bulkhead against the chaos. My shins ache from a four-mile run I took at midnight, a desperate attempt to quiet the hum in my head.

The past three weeks of interviews have been a constant parade of women who were either too young, too formal, too eager, or too something nameless. The task of digging into their histories fell to me. I used a service for the background checks, but Reese insisted I call the references myself. She wanted me to receive that information firsthand. The ones who survive, I pass on to Reese, and she does what Reese does, which is invite them for an interview and, sitting across from a person, decide in the first ninety seconds whether she trusts them.

She has trusted none of them.

I am not going to tell her this is a problem. It isn't a problem. I would rather we take three more weeks to find the right person than hire the wrong person for the sake of convenience.

"I still don't think we should rule Patricia out," I suggest, flipping through the folders and pulling out today's candidate. Reese's head snaps in my direction. "The one yesterday?" The way she asks the question tells me I'm wrong and that she intends to tell me exactly why. "Didn't you notice the way she looked at Josie?"

Patricia was fifty-two, with impeccable references and twenty years of experience with newborns. Hell, she came with her own binder. "Uh..." I hesitate, certain that whatever I say is going to be incorrect. "Like someone with two decades of experience looks at an infant?"

"Are you serious right now? It felt so clinical."

"Reese."

"I'm just saying." She reaches over and takes the folder I just picked up and begins to flip through it. "A nanny should feel something for the baby she's caring for."

"She's not applying to be Josie's mother."

The word lands a half second before I can take it back.

"I know that," she says.

"I didn't mean—"

"I know what you meant." She straightens the folder, and it's very clear that she has no desire to discuss how my misspoken statement made her feel. "What about this afternoon's candidate?"

I move around the island and stand behind Reese as she begins to flip through the folder. "Ah, this one. I thought you might like her."

"Nora Ashby," Reese says as she starts to flip through the gathered information.

"Yes. She's twenty-nine. Her most recent placement was with a family in Lincoln Park. There were two kids under three, and she was there for eighteen months," I say, though I know she can read it herself.

"And why did you say she left that family?"

"The family relocated to London, and even though they told me that they would have loved to keep her and even offered to bring her with them, she preferred to stay stateside. The woman I spoke to was the mother, Claire Hartley, and she said Nora was, and I'm quoting, the best decision we ever made for our family."

"People say that," Reese adds dismissively.

"Well, Claire Hartley said it like she meant it," I tell her. "She asked me twice if Nora was all right. She seemed genuinely sad to have lost her."

"If this one doesn't work out," I start.

"Then we keep looking."

"Right." I pause. "I know. I'm just saying it might be time to use a professional service."

"Absolutely not," she snaps. "They get paid when we hire someone, so they have a vested interest in not telling us everything about a candidate."

"Or—" I draw the word out. "They have a vested interest in sending us the best candidates so that we feel compelled to hire one." She doesn't say anything in response to my statement. "This reminds me so much of how it was with the dating app." I laugh. "We were almost ready to give up and then—" I stop. I can hear it a half second too late, the direction I was walking in. I clear my throat. "We found what we were looking for."

She is very still.

"Not the best example," she says.

"No." I agree. "You're right. I'm sorry."

The kitchen is quiet for a moment. I turn my head and look out the kitchen window, a glimpse of Lake Michigan in the distance. I think about Joe all the time. A man who came into our lives and changed them forever. Even though he's gone now, his absence sits in this house like a shape in a room you've stopped seeing because it's always there. Reese never wants to talk about him, but it doesn't change the reality that he's always present. Especially now that he may be the man who gave us the tiny perfection sleeping upstairs.

I force the thought down, ignoring the way my heart hammers a frantic rhythm against my ribs. I've become a creature of physical compulsions lately. Years ago, if you had told me I would ever become this way, I would have laughed in your face. But now, I find myself triple-checking the window locks and walking the long, silent loop of the ground floor to check all the doors' deadbolts repeatedly until there is no question that the precious lives inside these walls are safe.

"What time is she coming?" Reese asks.

"Three."

She nods, then looks at the clock on the microwave. Forty minutes.

"I'm going to check on Josie," she says, and slides off the stool. She walks away, this woman who has been my whole life for sixteen years. She still has not entered her studio. I have seen her think about it, but she isn't ready. My wife is in there somewhere. The Reese who painted for eight hours straight and came to bed smelling of linseed oil and looked at me with those clear eyes that see everything. I have no doubt that she's in there or that she's working her way back to me, and I'll do whatever it takes to help her get there.

Including hiring a nanny she doesn't hate, even if it means interviewing everyone within the five states surrounding us. I just hope we'll find a nanny before Josie is too old to still require one.

The doorbell chimes. She's exactly on time. Three o'clock —not three oh two, not two fifty-eight. She must have checked her watch before she rang the bell. I really like a person who is precise without making a performance of it.

She looks younger than I expected, though she has

been one of the younger candidates to make it to this stage, so perhaps it's simply a matter of comparison. Dark hair pulled back, not severely but neatly, the kind of put-together that looks effortless and probably isn't. She's wearing a gray cardigan on top of a simple dress and has a canvas bag over one shoulder. She smiles when I open the door, and I immediately notice its warmth. It's the smile of someone who is pleased to be somewhere but doesn't need to announce how pleased they are.

"Mr. Bradley," she says. "Thank you so much for taking the time to meet with me."

"Adam, please." I step back to let her in. "Can I get you something? Coffee, water?"

"Water would be great, thank you."

I show her into the living room, and she takes it in. Her eyes move to the lake through the windows, and she pauses on it for just a moment before sitting in the chair I indicate. I get her water from the kitchen and bring it back. When I return, Reese is already there, standing near the fireplace with her arms crossed loosely over her chest and her expression arranged in the careful neutral she deploys when she's reserving judgment.

"Reese," I say, "this is Nora Ashby."

"Yes, I assumed." Reese offers a half smile in my direction before returning her attention to Nora. "I was just starting to introduce myself."

Nora stands and offers her hand, then says how nice it is to meet her. And then she waits. She doesn't force the handshake on Reese. She patiently allows Reese to choose if she would even like to shake her hand.

Immediately, I can tell that Reese appreciates this

rare approach as she steps forward and shakes Nora's outstretched hand. "Sit down, please," she offers, motioning to Nora's chair.

Reese and I settle on the couch. Nora is across from us, holding the water I brought her in her lap.

"So," Reese starts. "Tell us about your last position."

Nora tells us about the Hartley family. Two boys, fourteen months apart, both under three when she started. She describes the household with a specificity that tells me she paid attention. She delves into the challenges she faced without us asking. The younger one's sleep issues, the older one's separation anxiety at drop-off, the particular brand of formula that worked after four others didn't. She doesn't editorialize. She doesn't tell us what good work she did. She just describes what was needed and what she did.

"A child under three taking language classes? Don't you think that's a little ridiculous?" Reese questions, a look of disbelief on her face.

Nora shakes her head. "Oh no, it's never for me to make any sort of judgments about how the parents choose to raise their children. I feel lucky enough to get to be a tiny little part of their lives, and I'm immensely thankful they trust me enough to allow it."

"I see," Reese says, and I look over at my wife as she studies Nora sitting across from her. Nora couldn't possibly know this, but that question was a test from my wife, and she also couldn't possibly know that she just passed with flying colors.

"And why didn't you go to London with them?" Reese asks.

"My life is here," Nora says simply, without elaboration.

"Family?"

Something moves in Nora's eyes. It's not exactly evasion, more like adjusting the weight. "I don't have much family left," she says. "But what I have is here."

Reese nods.

"And do you understand that this is a live-in position?" Reese asks.

"Yes. I prefer it, actually. It's easier to be available for the children when you're present all the time."

"Available," Reese repeats. "I see, well, we would need you to be available outside standard hours. Sometimes Adam might have an early meeting—"

"And my wife is an artist, so she will work whenever the mood strikes her, even if it might be at three in the morning." I chuckle, though Reese doesn't seem amused that I shared this tidbit about her.

"A painter?" she inquires. "That's so fascinating. And please, rest assured that it is not a problem at all for me to be available during nonstandard hours."

"I want to be clear about a few things." Reese uncrosses her arms. I watch her lean forward slightly. "We don't want a rotation of people through this house. If you take this position, your socializing happens outside these walls. I understand that you live here, and we want you to feel comfortable, but whatever personal life you maintain, you have to maintain it elsewhere. It's not because we don't trust you. We just need Josie's environment to be consistent and stable and—"

"Predictable," Nora says.

Reese pauses. "Yes."

"I understand completely." Nora holds her gaze. "When a baby's world is small, everything in it matters. Every face, every sound, every routine. Consistency isn't a preference at this stage. It's a developmental need." She pauses. "I won't bring my life into your home. This would be my home and my work simultaneously, and I understand what that means."

Reese looks at her for a moment. I cannot fully read her expression.

"How comfortable are you with newborns specifically?" I ask. "Josie is four weeks old."

"I'm very comfortable. The newborn stage is honestly my favorite." She says this without the brightness people sometimes use to sell themselves on things they don't actually believe. "Everything is so immediate at that age. They need what they need, they tell you, and you respond, and that feedback loop is... I don't know, I suppose it's clarifying. There's no ambiguity. You always know what you're there for, if that makes sense."

I nod. "That actually makes perfect sense," I reply, glancing over at Reese. When she doesn't say anything, I fill the silence. "Do you have any questions for us?"

"A few, actually. That is, if you don't mind." She looks between us, then settles on me.

"Of course not," I answer before placing a hand on my wife's leg, wishing I knew what she was thinking so far about Nora.

"You mentioned that you're an artist and that inspiration can strike at any moment," Nora says.

"That's right," Reese replies, shifting uncomfortably as Nora continues her question.

"I was curious if that irregular kind of schedule happens often." Nora looks at Reese as she waits for an answer. When Reese seems unsure what to say, Nora attempts to clarify her question. "I only ask because I want to make sure I am awake and alert whenever your baby needs me, so I prefer to stay as close to her schedule as possible."

"Oh—" Reese's voice cracks. "That won't be a problem. In fact, I haven't really been painting much lately."

Nora looks at her for a moment. I am about to say that her lack of painting will soon change once we hire a nanny, but Nora chimes in before I can. "The first few months with a new baby are strange that way. You lose the version of yourself that knows how to want things just for yourself. Don't worry, though, it comes back. But it needs to be allowed to come back. It doesn't just return on its own. It needs the space and time it requires to return."

The room is very quiet.

Reese looks at her. Not the assessing look she's been giving every candidate, not the careful neutral, but something more open than that, more unguarded. I find myself wondering whether my hopefulness is causing me to read more into what's actually there.

"No," Reese says softly. "I suppose it doesn't."

Nora waits a beat, then glances at the staircase. "Is she upstairs?"

"She's napping," I say.

"Of course." She nods and doesn't press it, and I

appreciate that. The candidates who asked to see the baby immediately always made Reese wary.

I adopt a professional distance. "Well," I say, "we have a few more—"

"How soon can you start?" Reese interjects.

I look at her, not doing very well at hiding my shock.

Reese is looking at Nora.

Nora doesn't react to the directness of it. She just considers the question seriously, as if it were the one she expected. "I could start as soon as Monday," she replies.

"Monday works," Reese says.

There is a brief pause when I know I could intervene. I could say that my wife and I need to discuss this further and we will get back to her. As caught off guard as I am by Reese's decision to offer the job to Nora without even consulting me, a part of me is relieved. I desperately wanted Reese to like whoever we brought into our home. I wanted her to trust a nanny enough to take the time and space she clearly needs to heal.

"Monday," I agree, deciding to place all of my trust in my wife, just as I always do.

After Nora leaves, Reese stands at the window with her arms wrapped around herself, looking past the cliff and at the lake on the horizon. I come to stand beside her, and we're quiet for a moment.

"She'll be good," Reese says finally.

"I think so too."

"She said the right thing. About the studio."

"I know."

"I'm not hiring her because she said the right thing."

"I know that too." I put my hand on the small of her back. "You follow your gut. You always have. It said yes. Mine said the same thing."

She leans into me slightly. Not all the way, but just enough. The lake catches the afternoon light and holds it for a moment before letting it go.

Upstairs, Josie makes a sound. Not crying. Simply stirring.

Reese straightens. "She'll be hungry soon."

Reese has been my whole life, and though she has been lost inside herself for months, I have to believe that she is slowly finding her way back out, because without her, I will also be lost.

"Do you want me to take this feeding?" I offer.

She shakes her head. "I haven't pumped for a bit, so I could use the feeding."

I nod and release her from my hold as she starts to cross the room and climb the stairs. I notice a slight impression remains in the cushion where Nora sat. Monday. It's so soon, and all I can think is that there's practically no time before everything changes. As doubts and apprehension start to take hold, I let myself believe that this change means things will get better. They have to.

FOUR

REESE

By the third day, Nora knows where everything is.

We gave her a brief tour, the way you show anyone around a house you've lived in long enough to stop thinking about where everything is. But on Wednesday morning, I come downstairs at six fifteen to find the coffee already made. I stand in the kitchen in my robe, staring at the coffee pot as a nameless sensation settles in my chest.

"Good morning." Nora appears from the back hallway, Josie against her shoulder in the particular hold that Josie has recently decided is the only acceptable position. Adam teases that it's the position where she can see over the shoulder of whoever is holding her and survey her kingdom with an expression of suspicious authority. "She's been up since five. I hope we didn't wake you."

"No," I say, which is true. "Thank you. For the coffee."

She smiles. "Claire Hartley's older one was an early riser. I got into the habit."

I pour myself a cup and lean against the counter. Josie fixes me with her unblinking gaze from across the room.

"Do you want me to take her?" I ask.

"Only if you want her." Nora shifts her slightly, adjusting the hold. "She's just eaten, and she's in that good mood she gets in for about fifteen minutes until the gas sets in." Nora chuckles. She moves closer to me and adds, "So I'd take advantage of it if I were you."

I set my coffee down and cross the kitchen, taking my daughter. Josie doesn't object.

"The coffee grounds to water ratio..." I say. "How did you—"

"I saw how much grounds were in the filter yesterday," Nora explains. "I tried to eyeball the same amount. Sorry if it's a bit strong."

She's already moving to the sink to rinse something. "No, actually, I was just going to say that it's perfect," I reply.

"Oh, good," she says in a pleased tone as she continues tidying up the kitchen.

"I'm going to take her upstairs," I say. "Do you want something to eat? There's—"

"Don't be silly. If I get hungry, I'll figure it out," she says simply. "Go spend some time with her."

This is the thing about having Nora in the house that I didn't anticipate: she makes space rather than filling it.

I expected her presence to feel intrusive. A constant awareness of a stranger in the rooms or the need to perform normalcy in my own home. What I've gotten instead is a presence that recedes when it isn't needed and appears exactly when it is. She doesn't hover. She doesn't explain herself. She moves through the house like someone who understands the difference between being available and being underfoot.

There was one small stumble on Tuesday, when she scorched the bottom of the heavy Le Creuset while trying to make a ragu. The smell of burnt tomato and garlic had drifted upstairs. When I came down, she was at the sink, her sleeves pushed up, looking genuinely mortified. "I'm so sorry," she'd said. "I got caught up watching the light on the water and forgot the heat."

Despite the one small hiccup, I'm hopeful Nora might be the perfect match for our home.

It only takes another week of Nora being there for me to enter my studio. Not for long. An hour the first time, twenty minutes the second, and both times more standing in front of a blank canvas than actually painting. But I was in there. I was in there with the stinging cold of the north light and the chalky grit of gesso. The quiet was distinct from the rest of the house, a stillness that felt more chosen, somehow. More mine. I stood there, brush in hand, and let the possibilities of color return. That was enough.

When I came out the first time, Nora was at the kitchen table with Josie propped against a nursing pillow, reading to her from what appeared to be a library book about migratory birds. Josie watched Nora's face with the focused attention she gives to anything that moves and makes a sound, which is to say she was watching her as if she were the most interesting thing in the world.

"She likes the pictures," Nora said, without looking up.

"She's only six weeks old," I remind her.

"She's six weeks old, and she likes the pictures," Nora repeats as she turns a page. "Her vision's still developing. The high-contrast black-and-white illustrations in this one are good for her."

I didn't have anything to say in response. I may be Josie's mother, but one thing has become very clear to me in the short time since Nora arrived in our lives. She is the one who is knowledgeable about babies and what they need. As much as I thought it would make me feel uneasy, I'm just relieved that Josie has someone like her in her life, even if it isn't me.

"You seem better," Adam says on a Thursday night, a couple of weeks in. We're in bed, the house quiet below us. I'm actually reading. Not staring at words while my mind goes somewhere I don't want it to go, but reading, following sentences, turning pages.

"I think I might be," I say, which surprises us both a little.

He puts his book down and turns toward me. "How many times have you been in your studio?"

"Twice."

"Babe, that's amazing. Anything on the canvas?"

"Not yet," I say. "But I was in there."

He reaches over and tucks a piece of hair behind my

ear, his hand resting against my jaw for a moment before dropping. "That's more than enough," he says.

I look at my husband, truly look at him, and I wonder how long it's been since I've seen him. Adam looks tired, and I wonder if it's from worrying about me.

"She's good with her," I say.

"I know."

"I wasn't sure at first." I pause. "But it's pretty clear that she's not performing."

"Performing?"

I nod. "Yeah. You know, like when some people want you to trust them, you can feel them wanting it. It comes off them. She doesn't do that."

Adam is quiet for a moment. "No," he agrees. "She doesn't. She seems like she's a really good person. I'm glad we found her."

A good person. Adam's words consume my thoughts. The irony of his words causes me to laugh out loud.

"What's so funny?" he inquires.

I know I shouldn't say the words that leave my mouth next, but I can't seem to stop myself. "If she only knew what bad people she moved in with."

I go back to my book, but I can feel his eyes on me. I glance over at Adam, despite every muscle in my body resisting the movement.

"Why would you say something like that?" he asks, but we both know the answer to that question. There's a special place in hell for people like Adam and me for what we did to someone we claimed to have loved. I've already made my peace with that fact, but it is suddenly clear to me that Adam hasn't.

"I'm sorry," I murmur before leaning over and giving him a soft kiss on the cheek. "I was trying to be funny, but clearly, it was in poor taste."

He sits in silence, his gaze still fixed on me. I look back at my book and continue reading despite his eyes. A couple of minutes go by before I notice from the corner of my eye that he has gone back to his.

Staring at the words on the page, I think about the moments in my studio. I wasn't painting, but I could stand in the room now without wanting to shrink away from the light, and that was progress. My thoughts drift to our beautiful Josie. Adam may not be ready to admit that we are the bad ones in this world, but I can. I can also see that he's right about Nora. She's good people, and as long as I can keep people like her in our lives, I can hold on to a little bit of hope for my daughter's future.

I exhale a deep breath at the idea and feel the darkness recede a few inches. I don't reach for the feeling. I've learned not to reach for the good ones. But I let myself be in it, just for now, while it's here.

FIVE

REESE

The boat was Adam's idea.

On the Saturday marking Nora's first official month with us, Adam came downstairs and looked at the water for a long moment, then said, "We should take the boat out."

"All of us?" I asked. I love water. It's why Adam built me this house. I loved our days out on the boat. Now all I can think about when I'm on the lake is the day we took Joe to his final resting place.

Adam looked at me. Then toward the kitchen, where we could hear Nora moving—the particular sounds of her making breakfast while Josie watched from the bouncy seat on the table. "All of us," he said.

For some reason, I expected—or perhaps it was more that I had hoped—Nora would decline. To find a reason why it was a bad idea. Instead, she looked at Adam when he asked, then looked at Josie, and said, "As long as there's a life jacket that fits her, I think that sounds like a great idea."

"I ordered one last week," Adam said, and something briefly moved in Nora's face. He'd bought it in anticipation. Of course he had. Adam Bradley does not suggest things he has not already prepared for.

So we went.

We puttered out of the marina, the low light making long, thin gold shapes on the water. Adam is at the helm, as always. Nora is beside him, asking questions. Even though it had only been a month, it felt like Nora had always been here. The closest thing I can think of is how things were when we met Joe. Being around him felt natural. He felt like family.

I sat in the stern with Josie against my chest, her small face pointed at the sky, while Nora's eyes tracked the ripples, the depth markers, and the shoreline. She was a person who learned things on purpose.

"Have you sailed before?" Adam asked.

"A little," Nora replied. "Nothing like this. I grew up around Lake Michigan. Different access than you have here, but the same water."

"Chicago?" I asked.

She turned. "Near enough." A pause. "I moved around a lot as a kid. But the lake was always the same."

"I'm so sorry. That must have been hard on you," I offered.

Nora flashed me a confused expression. "What must have been?"

"Moving around a lot," I explained. "That couldn't have been easy on you as a child."

She smiled at me and shrugged. "Honestly, it really

wasn't that bad. Our family is close. As long as I had them, I never felt lonely."

I felt a pang in my chest as she described her childhood. As much as I didn't want them to, my thoughts once again drifted back to Joe. He hadn't been so lucky while growing up in the foster care system. And to think he was able to make a decent life for himself despite everything he had been through as a child—only to meet us.

"Do you want to try the helm?" Adam offered. I knew this was Adam's way of changing the subject. After all, despite the comfort we may have felt with Nora, she wasn't family. She wasn't our friend. She was first and foremost our child's caretaker, and there were subjects better left untouched. We certainly had our share of secrets that could become very dangerous if Nora were to discover them. It didn't matter that we felt comfortable around Nora. Our relationship with her needed to stay professional if we didn't want to find ourselves in another situation where we had to do terrible things to protect our secrets.

I waited for her to decline, but she didn't. She moved to where Adam stood, and he talked her through it. The throttle, the trim, the way this particular boat responded. He spoke to her with the patient thoroughness he brought to everything he taught. She listened, then took the wheel, though she misjudged the resistance of the rudder at first. The boat veered wide, a clumsy arc that sent a spray of cold water. She winced, quickly correcting course with a self-conscious tilt of her head.

"You've got the instinct," Adam said, keeping a light

hand on the seat back. "You're just fighting the wake. Relax into it."

Josie made a sound. I looked down at her small face in the life jacket. It was yellow with ducks on it. Unsurprisingly, Adam had bought it in exactly the right size. She was looking at the water the way she looks at everything, with total and serious attention, as though the world is a problem she intends to solve.

"She likes it," Nora said. "Look at her face."

I laughed. "She looks like she's up to no good, if you ask me."

Nora laughed too. It was a real laugh, the kind that arrives without announcement, and it changed her face into something younger and more free-spirited than she normally seemed. I'd often thought how strange it was that Nora was only twenty-nine. She was thorough and responsible in everything she did. It was nice to see this carefree side of her.

"She does always look like she's calculating," Nora agreed. "I can tell that Josie is going to be one of those kids who figures everything out and doesn't tell you until it's too late to do anything about it."

She was still looking at Josie, smiling, unaware of the small shift she had just caused in me. The warmth of it. The specific warmth of someone seeing your child clearly —not the idea of your child but the actual person she has begun to reveal to the world.

I pulled Josie closer against my chest. I might not feel the bond with my daughter as I had anticipated, but this warmth showed me that I do feel some connection with her. As scary as it felt to think it, I had a brief moment of hope that we would be okay.

That night, after Nora had gone downstairs and Josie was asleep and the dishes were done and the house had settled into its late-evening quiet, Adam poured two glasses of wine and brought them to the couch. We sat together the way we used to—my legs across his lap, his hand resting on my ankle—and we didn't talk about anything important for almost an hour. It was the best hour I'd had in a very long time.

A short time later, I saw Nora in the kitchen, busy with chores.

"I like her," I said finally.

"I know," he said.

"I wanted not to."

He looked at me with something that was almost amusement. "I know that too."

I sipped my wine. "Oh, well, you just know everything, don't you?"

He rubbed his hand up and down my ankle. "I know a lot—but not everything."

"She asked me about the studio today," I said. "Not in a prying way. She just said she could hear music sometimes from down the hall and wondered if I painted to music or if that was your music she heard."

"What did you say?"

"I said it was probably you. And then I said... I said I used to paint to music. Before."

He waits for me to say more.

"She told me that I would get back to that place again," I continued. "She didn't say it the way people usually do. She said it like it was a fact." I looked at my wine glass. "I know it must seem silly that such a small thing could give me such big feelings."

"That doesn't seem silly at all. Sometimes the small things are the ones that do the most," Adam said.

"I think she's been good for us," I said.

Adam nodded slowly, his hand warm around my ankle. "I think so too."

SIX

ADAM

I find the letter on a Tuesday morning, a detail that shouldn't matter but does. My bones are heavy and hollowed out from a week without real sleep. My eyes have been scrubbed with sand, and a low-level tremor in my hands requires a conscious stilling against the cool granite of the kitchen island. The paper carries an unnerving weight, a physical burden added to the leaden fatigue already settling in my joints.

On Tuesdays, I get up early so I can be ready for my weekly board meeting. Seven—sometimes earlier. Nora is usually up before me. She moves through early mornings with a quiet efficiency. By the time I come downstairs, she has the coffee on and Josie is fed. We exchange the brief, comfortable acknowledgments of two people who have found a shared rhythm without discussing it.

This morning, when I come down, she is in the kitchen, Josie at her shoulder, and she says, "Good morning."

I say, "Good morning back," then pour my coffee. My

jaw is locked tight, a dull, throbbing ache radiating from the hinge toward my temples. The mail from the previous day sits on the island, sorted by Nora. Bills to the left, everything else to the right, and I am about to head to my office when a plain white envelope catches my eye.

A plain white envelope with Reese's name on the front. No return address. Block letters, written by hand, pressing hard enough that you can feel the indentations through the paper.

I pick it up and turn it over. The seal on the back has been pulled up and pressed back down. Reese has already opened it and resealed it. She has read whatever is inside and decided not to tell me.

I set my coffee down. The pulse in my throat is a jagged, insistent thing, a frantic rhythm I can't seem to slow.

I slide the letter out of the envelope.

I read it once, my eyes skimming the blocky script. Then again, tracing the heavy pressure of the pen against the paper.

Then I fold it and put it back.

"Is everything all right?" Nora's eyes search mine, her gaze lingering in the silence between us. My knuckles are white against the edge of the counter. Does she notice?

"Everything's fine." I do my best to make my voice match my words. "Just a letter for Reese."

Nora holds my gaze for a half second. Her particular attentiveness is unsettling. It probably wouldn't be for most people, but most people don't have secrets the way Reese and I do. When Nora's attention is back on Josie, I slide the envelope to the bottom of the stack in front of me before I take my coffee into my office and close the door.

The letter is still fresh in my mind. It was just three paragraphs.

The first paragraph reminds Reese that though things ended badly, it had, in fact, not been how Allison would have chosen to end things. This is technically accurate in the same way that saying a building ended badly after it burned down. Allison had been the fourth woman we dated during our brief search for a girlfriend. We had connected with her, and almost instantly, we found her extremely interesting. She was sharp in a way that felt like wit for the first three weeks before revealing itself as something else. What we had taken for confidence turned out to be possession.

When we decided it was best to end things, Allison had taken the news so well that we were left wondering if we had misjudged her. It didn't take long, though, for Allison to show us her true nature. She had shown up twice at restaurants we'd mentioned in conversation. We gave her the benefit of the doubt the first time, but after the second instance, we were fairly certain that Allison wasn't going to take no for an answer.

I had handled the incidents with forced patience, leaving me shaking afterward. After all, my wife had taken the life of a man we loved to protect me and the life we'd built together, but I had let this woman into our lives who was clearly revealing herself to be just as serious a threat.

All of this had happened after Joe was gone, and before we found out about our sweet Josie. She dropped by the house during Reese's third trimester, and her reaction to the pregnancy was more than a little unnerving. She'd wept and begged to be part of our lives. She said it wasn't fair that she wouldn't be part of our child's life. Then my patience finally ran out. My instinct to protect Reese and our unborn child kicked in, and I found myself wondering if it had felt the same for Reese when her instinct had kicked in about Joe.

The second paragraph of the letter tells Reese that she knows. There's nothing specific. The letter is careful. Enough to make clear she has been watching. Enough to suggest that whatever she thinks she knows, she considers dangerous.

The third paragraph says: *I just want to talk.*

I sit in silence, racking my brain for what she could possibly know.

I push back against the phantom weight in my chest. I will not let my mind drift toward the carriage house or the silence of that night. I have already tried to bleed those memories out through my pores, logging a thousand miles on the stationary bike until my lungs screamed and my vision went dark at the edges. I have punished my body into forgetting.

What Allison knows is nothing. What she thinks she knows is a version of a story she constructed from the outside, from whatever she observed in three weeks with us. She was never inside our lives. She has guesses and grievances dressed up as information.

The call with the board lasts forty minutes. I am present for all of it. I jot down a couple of notes, but my hamstrings are coiled like springs. No one on the call would know anything is wrong because I am perfectly still, my posture a study in controlled composure, even as my heart hammers against my ribs.

When the call ends, I open my contacts and find my attorney's number.

I don't call yet. I put the phone down. It's obvious the letter had already been opened and resealed. Reese has made the decision not to tell me, and before I involve our lawyer, I need to understand why.

Reese is making her way back, and I will not let Allison derail whatever progress she has made.

I wait until after dinner to talk to her, watching for the exact moment her shoulders lose their rigidity and for the wine to soften the hard line of her mouth. Her exhaustion has a predictable timing, her defenses fraying at the edges on schedule. Reese actually ate a real dinner tonight, not just a couple of bites. She laughed at something Nora said, and she refilled her wine without looking like she was deciding whether she deserved it. She is more herself. More able to receive difficult things without being swallowed by them.

When Nora takes Josie upstairs, and the house is doing its evening settling, I decide it's the perfect time to have this conversation. Reese is curled at the end of the couch with her wine and the particular expression she gets when she's not thinking about anything specific.

I sit beside her, the tension in my shoulders finally beginning to ebb into a heavy, leaden fatigue.

"I read the letter," I say at last. I've practiced how to have this talk in my head throughout the day and ultimately decided that directness is the best approach.

She doesn't move. "I'm sorry," she says, not bothering to pretend she doesn't know what letter I'm talking about.

"You already read it."

"Yes."

"And you put it back in the envelope without even telling me about it."

"I didn't know how to bring it up. I was going to tell you."

"I know you were."

"Do you?"

"Reese." I put my hand over hers on the couch. "I'm not angry. I just need us to be on the same page about this. We have Josie to think about now."

"And what, you don't think I know that?" I can hear her defenses rising.

"Of course I know that you know that," I assure her. "I just think that sometimes you're worried I might overreact or something."

She exhales, her posture sagging.

She looks at our hands. "I don't think Allison is going to go away easily." I'm surprised by her statement. Reese was the one who had begged me to let things with Allison go when she first showed signs of instability after our rejection. She's told me that she was certain Allison would lose interest, and if we just avoided interacting with her, eventually something or someone else would grab her attention. Reese's assumptions had been incorrect.

"No," I agree with her. "She's not. Why didn't you tell me about the letter?"

Reese shakes her head, thinking through her answer

carefully before she replies in a whisper, "I was worried you would get upset and then Nora might hear."

Her reasoning was shaky, but it didn't mean she was lying.

"I don't want you to ever worry that you can't talk to me. I can keep my cool," I said, chuckling and trying to lighten the heaviness of the conversation.

"I know—I'm sorry. You're right. You know how I tend to overthink things." She wasn't exaggerating when she said she overthought things. I'm exhausted trying to keep up with the mental gymnastics she sometimes gets lost in.

"What do you think we should do?"

"I spoke to Marcus the last time Allison was harassing us," I said. Marcus was our attorney and had been with me since the very beginning, when I started my business. I could always rely on him to keep our best interests at the forefront. "I'll send him a copy of the letter, but I'm not sure that will be enough to move forward."

Reese doesn't answer, letting the silence of the house settle around us. Her thumb moves against the back of my hand, the small unconscious motion she makes when she's processing something. "Her letter said she knows our secret." The dark swirl of her wine holds her gaze, her face a pale mask in the dim light.

"She doesn't."

"Adam—"

"She was with us for three weeks. Whatever she thinks she knows is a story she built from the outside. She's trying to scare us to get what she wants."

"She's angry." Reese's thumb traces the rim of her wine glass in a restless, unconscious motion. "People who feel wronged—"

"She wasn't wronged." I keep my voice flat, certain. "We ended a relationship that wasn't working. That's not an injury."

"Not to us."

"Not to anyone." I let the words fall into the silence, cold and heavy.

Reese nods, just once, and looks back at the lake. "Okay."

"I'm going to handle it."

"I know you will," she replies in a low voice. "That's what you do."

We sit together in the evening quiet, her hand under mine. Nora is still the unknown variable. She doesn't know about the apps or the strangers whom we once let into our lives before we were given this precious gift, Josie.

Reese yawns, and we agree it's time to head up to bed. I stand and walk to the back door. The deadbolt is solid under my hand, the cool metal of the handle firm against my palm. *It is solid. It is enough,* I tell myself, desperate to keep everything that matters to me in the world safe inside these walls. I walk to the front door and repeat the motion, then the side door, my fingers memorizing the shape of the locks as if they are the only things keeping the roof from collapsing.

When I make my way upstairs, Reese is already in her pajamas and under the blankets on her side of the bed with a book in her lap. She looks up at me and smiles.

"I locked up," I say as I start to get ready for bed myself.

"She asked to see some of my new work," Reese says.

"Who?" I look up.

"Nora." The corner of Reese's mouth moves. "I showed her the canvas I started yesterday. She said it looked like it was angry."

"Is it?"

"Maybe. But I think it might be one of the most honest things I've ever painted."

I want to ask her what she means by that statement, but I don't. A heaviness sits on my chest knowing my wife is so angry that it oozes out of her as paint on canvas. Is she angry about what happened to Joe? Is it the depression? Is she angry with me, or does her anger stem from something much more subtle? Perhaps the knowledge that our daughter might biologically belong to a man we murdered? As desperate as I am to understand the source of the rage inside of her, at this moment, I hold tight to what I know. Reese is, at least, beginning to heal.

SEVEN

REESE

The first thing I notice when I walk into Dr. Carver's office is the smell of eucalyptus and old books. Two identical chairs are set at a slight angle to each other rather than facing each other directly. She has a small notepad on the side table.

She's younger than I expected. Mid-forties, maybe, with dark hair going silver at the temples. She gestures to the empty chair. After an introduction and a few pleasantries, she asks the question I know is coming.

"So," she says. Her voice is low and unhurried. "Tell me what brought you here."

I have prepared a version of the truth that is accurate in all its details and misleading in all the ways that matter. A story about my doctor's diagnosis of postpartum depression. About the difficulty of adjusting to new motherhood after years of believing it wasn't even possible to get pregnant, let alone be a mother. About a life that looks exactly the way it's supposed to look, but how there is still an ache in my chest that won't lift despite all of it.

It's a true story. It is completely true.

It is also not the whole story. The whole story is not available in this room or any room, and I have made my peace with that. The moment I had to close myself off from all my friendships to avoid too many questions, I accepted that my life was going to be very different post-Joe. Knowing I can't share the whole story, though, makes therapy challenging, to say the least.

"I had a baby eleven weeks ago," I say. "Josie. She's healthy and wonderful in every way. The pregnancy was a surprise, actually. We'd been told for years that it wasn't —" I pause, unable to find the words.

"Wasn't what?" Dr. Carver presses.

I swallow hard, trying not to let the emotions pressing against the back of my eyes break free. "That I probably couldn't have children," I say, as I arrange my hands in my lap.

"That must have been a significant shift for you," Dr. Carver says.

"It was." I look at the window on the north side of the room, the gray light streaming in. I focus on the clouds outside so that hopefully my voice won't betray the unprocessed pain I am carrying from believing for most of my marriage that we would never have children.

"I'd accepted that we weren't going to have children. Adam, my husband, and I both had. We'd grieved it and moved on, or at least I believed we had."

"Did something happen to make you change your mind about that?"

"Not exactly. When I told Adam the news, he was so excited..."

Dr. Carver tilts her head, and a curious expression crosses her face. "But you weren't?"

"No, I was very excited," I answer almost too quickly, as if I were trying to convince Dr. Carver that my answer was truthful. "It's just—well, when Josie arrived, I thought it would feel different from what it does."

"How does it feel?"

"Wrong," I say, watching for her reaction. I quickly shake my head. "No. That's not the right word. It feels—I don't know. I love her. I want to be clear about that. I look at her, and I love her in a way that's almost physical."

"What do you mean by that?"

I picture Josie as I explain, "It's in my chest and my throat. It's like this fullness that swells inside me."

"Well, that sounds very natural, like any mother would feel. Why do you say it feels wrong?" Dr. Carver continues.

"Alongside that fullness, there's this—" I gesture vaguely, trying to think of a way to explain to this woman that, despite knowing I love this child, it feels like I am always one breath away from everything disappearing.

"Gray?" Dr. Carver offers.

I look at her, surprised by her insight. "Yes. Exactly. How did you—"

"A lot of people describe it that way." She pauses. "Clinical language doesn't always capture what it feels like to actually be inside postpartum depression. What finally made you decide to seek help for it?"

I wonder what she's hoping for from this question.

Do patients come in here confessing that they have thought about harming someone else or themselves? Is she trying to root around inside my head to determine whether I'm a danger to myself?

"Actually," I continue, "my husband was the one who suggested therapy. Adam is very attentive. He noticed something was off before I could even admit it."

"Is that characteristic of him?"

"Yes." I think about the letter on the island, already found and folded back before I came downstairs. The way he didn't announce it. How he waited until we were alone that evening before telling me he'd read it and wanted to discuss it. He approached the situation with the same quiet steadiness that he brings to everything that could otherwise become a crisis.

"Yes," I say. "He notices things."

"I see, and what sort of things was he noticing?"

"I'm an artist," I explain. "And he picked up pretty quickly that I stopped going into my studio."

Dr. Carver nods. "Anything else?"

"He mentioned that it didn't seem like my energy was where it normally is, and he was worried that fatigue was hitting me."

"You're telling me things that Adam noticed, but what did you notice that made you think there might be a problem?"

She's good. I consider telling her that despite having Josie, everything I'd wanted for so long, I couldn't shake an overwhelming feeling of hopelessness. I knew that if a therapist thought you were at risk of harming yourself, they could put you on an involuntary psych hold, so I decided not to bring up the hopelessness.

"Um—well, let me see. I definitely had a lot of irritability and restlessness. Also, I was tired all the time. At first, I thought it was just part of having a newborn, but one morning, Adam took care of Josie and let me sleep in. When I finally got up, I thought I'd feel refreshed, but I barely had enough energy to get out of bed."

When I mention this, I notice Dr. Carver reach for the notepad next to her. She places it on her lap and makes a couple of notes before meeting my eyes again.

"What else?" Dr. Carver asks.

I think back to when I first noticed something wasn't right. "I was restless all the time, had trouble concentrating, couldn't remember anything, was never hungry, and struggled constantly with headaches."

"Do you still struggle with the headaches?"

I shake my head. "Not nearly as often."

"What about Josie?"

"Headaches?" I shake my head. "I don't think so."

Dr. Carver smiles. "No, not headaches. Did you have any trouble bonding with her after she was born, or were there any doubts about yourself as a mother?"

"Of course. Doesn't everyone worry they won't be a good mom?"

"Most, but usually when someone struggles with postpartum, it becomes a very consuming thought that you won't be what your baby needs. Some mothers have even mentioned having thoughts of harming themselves or their baby."

"I would never harm Josie!" I snap, appalled at her words.

"No one is saying you would, Mrs. Bradley. I'm just trying to gauge exactly where we are," she reassures. "And how are you and your husband doing? The two of you, with the adjustment?"

This is where I need to be careful. Not because the question is dangerous. It isn't. It's a reasonable question, but reasonable questions have a way of leading to other questions, which I learned from two brief attempts at therapy I made in my twenties.

Dr. Carver is doing exactly what a good therapist does, listening for the thing underneath the thing. What she doesn't understand is that I cannot let her find the thing underneath the thing. Adam and I did too much to bury the thing underneath. I can't afford for anyone ever to uncover what we did. The thing that makes it hard for me to sleep well. What makes me wonder whether I even deserve to be a mother. But what's worse, I can't tell her that every time I look at my daughter, I'm not sure if a part of the man I killed is behind those big, beautiful eyes.

"We're good," I say, suddenly wondering if the concern about hiding the thing underneath might be visible on my face. Perhaps an expression Dr. Carver might be misreading as insincerity regarding my answer about Adam's and my relationship. "I mean, of course we both have been under a little stress, but as a couple, we're solid. And honestly, Nora has been a godsend."

"Nora?" she asks, and I realize I haven't explained our situation.

"Oh, I'm so sorry, I guess I never explained that we hired a live-in caretaker a couple of months back. After my—diagnosis, Adam and I decided it made sense to have someone in the house full-time to help out with childcare and housekeeping."

Dr. Carver tilts her head slightly as if she's deciding whether to pull a thread. "So you both made the decision to hire Nora?"

"Yes, of course we made the decision together. Adam and I make all important decisions together," I answer sharply.

"I see," she continues. "And how did that decision feel for you? Bringing someone into your home in that capacity?"

There it is. The reasonable follow-up question.

"Practical," I say, which is true enough. I wait for Dr. Carver to say something, but she just sits there, fucking staring at me expectantly. "Necessary." Also true. What I don't say is that Nora's presence in the house means I am never fully alone with Josie, and that some mornings I'm grateful for that in a way that fills me with a shame so deep I could drown in it. "She's wonderful with Josie. Patient. Warm. Everything you'd want."

Dr. Carver nods. She doesn't push. I will come to understand that this is her particular skill. She creates a space, but then she doesn't fill it. She just leaves it open and waits to see what you put there.

I put nothing there. I move on.

"I've started painting again since she moved in with us," I say in an attempt to fill the silence.

"That sounds meaningful."

"It is. It's where I used to go when I wanted to feel like myself." I look at my hands. The faint trace of cerulean blue under my left thumbnail that I didn't scrub out completely this morning.

"You said 'used to,'" Dr. Carver observes.

"What?"

"You said your studio is where you 'used to' go when you wanted to feel like yourself," she explains. "Does it no longer have that effect?"

This is one of those reasonable follow-up questions that I know can get me in trouble, and what made me hesitant to make the call to Dr. Carver in the first place. If I were answering honestly, I would tell her that lately I've been feeling like someone who's doing an impression of Reese. That's the best way I can think to explain it because the Reese I knew disappeared the day she pulled the trigger. When she made the decision to end the life of someone she loved in order to protect the life she'd built with her perfect husband in their perfect home.

Something shifts almost imperceptibly in Dr. Carver's expression. Not reaction, but registration. Like a needle on a dial moving slightly. "Does something about that question make you uncomfortable?" she asks.

"I think it's the postpartum," I say. "I've read that it can affect your sense of identity. Who you are outside of being a mother. I'm working on feeling like me again, but I'm definitely not back there yet."

But I know the truth. Being a mother didn't make me stop feeling like myself. The thing underneath has a name, and that name is Joe, and underneath Joe is the day

I made a decision that couldn't be undone, and underneath that decision is the lake, and in the lake—

"That's a very honest thing to say," Dr. Carver says.

"I'm an honest person," I tell her. And I believe this when I say it, which is perhaps the most complicated thing about me.

"And do you think you're ready to be honest with me?" she asks. Her question has me concerned that she may sense I am determined to hide parts of myself in this process.

I look at her. She is watching me. I wonder what it would look like to be completely honest with her. It would look like I killed someone. We killed someone. A man who trusted us and came when we called. We put him in the ground. No, in the water. And then we told ourselves it was love, it was protection, it was the thing we had to do. I have been telling that story for months now, and I almost believe it because I know that I cannot afford to stop believing it.

"I think so," I say, knowing full well there is no way I will ever be a hundred percent honest with her. I can't. "Or at least I hope so. I think that's what I'm here to figure out."

Dr. Carver writes something brief on her notepad, then sets it back down.

"That's a good answer," she says, and I can't tell if she means it or if it's the kind of thing therapists are trained to say the way flight attendants are trained to smile.

"Better than most people give me, actually."

"What do most people give you?"

She smiles at that. "Usually something more certain. Like 'Yes, absolutely,' or 'Of course, that's why I'm here.'"

"That seems like what you would want to hear."

"Certainty in this room usually means someone isn't ready to actually open up. Instead, they're in performance mode."

I nod slowly, filing that away. Dr. Carver is smarter than I initially gave her credit for, which means I need to be more careful and less clever. Clever people give themselves away when they try to seem cooperative.

"Can I ask you something?" I say, and I watch her register the slight shift.

My mind screams at me to shut the hell up. That I dare not ask the question I want to, but I have to know. If it's not the answer I want it to be, then why am I even here? I am simply wasting everyone's time by coming.

"Of course."

"Do you think it's possible for someone to be genuinely working toward something, genuinely wanting to heal, while also knowing they'll never be able to share certain parts of themselves? Not because they're hiding." I let the word sit for just a moment. "But because some things, once said out loud, can't be contained again."

Dr. Carver is quiet for a moment that stretches just long enough to feel intentional. "I think," she says carefully, "that almost everyone who sits in that chair is carrying something they believe is unshareable." She folds her hands. "The question I'm always more interested in is what that thing is costing them."

The lake. The water. The weight of him going down.

"Right," I say. "That makes sense."

We talk for another thirty minutes. I tell her about Josie's sleep patterns, how she looks at the lake, and the baby monitor Nora keeps with her when she takes Josie downstairs so I can hear if anything changes. I tell her about Adam's steadiness and how I depend on it and how sometimes I resent depending on it, which is not a feeling I've admitted out loud before.

I don't tell her about Joe.

I don't tell her about the letter from Allison.

I don't tell her about the particular sound the carriage house made in the wind. Or the color of the water the morning after. Or the way Adam held me in the car in the driveway and said we have to stick together now.

When the session ends, Dr. Carver stands and approaches me. "Same time next week?"

"Yes," I reply, and I actually mean it. I don't know if Dr. Carver will actually be able to help, since I can't tell her everything, but I want it to work. I want to get better. For Adam... For Josie.

I walk to my car and sit in the driver's seat. I don't start the engine right away. I put my hands on the wheel and look at the street through the windshield, and I think about what she asked.

And do you think you're ready to be honest with me?

Truthfully, I think it would be a relief to be completely honest with Dr. Carver. I also think it would look like the end of everything.

So I start the car, pull out of the parking lot, and drive back toward the lake. Toward the house, toward Josie and Nora and Adam and the life I've made and protected and will keep on protecting because there is no other option.

Telling the truth equals a world where Josie grows up without a mother, and that is not a world I am willing to allow.

The session helped, I decide, as I turn onto our road and the lake appears between the trees.

Next week I will go back, and I will tell Dr. Carver a little more of the truth, the parts that are safe, the parts that don't lead anywhere she shouldn't go.

EIGHT

REESE

It's a Tuesday, which feels important afterward, though I can't say why. Tuesdays shouldn't be different from other days. They're not, usually.

Nora mentions she is going on a grocery run after breakfast. She explains we're low on a few things and gestures to the near-empty milk carton. I tell her she can leave Josie with me, but Nora explains the weather is nice and that Josie has been restless, so a change of air might do her some good. Nora has solid instincts. I've started trusting them the way you trust a compass after it's proven accurate enough times.

"Why don't I come with you?" I offer after thinking about it for a moment.

She seems surprised. "Mrs. Bradley, you don't have to do that. I'm sure you have much more important things to do than to go grocery shopping with Miss Josie and me."

"I've told you, call me Reese." I take a quick sip of my coffee before I add, "And I think Josie's mama is a bit restless as well. I could use a change of scenery myself."

Nora laughs and gladly agrees to the company. Adam left early in the morning to head to the marina for some maintenance work on the boat that required his presence. This will be my first solo excursion with Nora, and I actually find myself looking forward to it. I'm older than her, but the confidence with which she carries herself makes her seem more mature.

We take Nora's car because the car seat is already installed in the back, and neither of us can be bothered with the transfer. I sit in the passenger seat while Nora buckles Josie in, listening to the small domestic theater of it. The click of the harness, Josie's momentary babbling protest, Nora's patient murmuring back. "I know, I know. Almost done, baby girl." I wonder if this interaction would bother most women. I'm relieved that Josie has someone like Nora in her life, since her mother seems fundamentally damaged and has no clue how to fix it.

The grocery store is a twenty-minute drive, and we spend most of it with the windows cracked and the radio on something soft. Josie watches the passing world with the focused intensity of someone who has never seen most of the things whizzing past her. It's clear that she finds the whole situation fascinating. I keep turning to watch her watching the world in awe.

"She's like this every time," Nora says, catching me looking back again. "Like she's memorizing everything."

"Maybe she is," I say, a smile pulling at the corners of my mouth.

Nora considers that. "Maybe."

The store is quiet for a Saturday morning.

Nora navigates it with the efficiency of someone

who has memorized the layout. I follow along, Josie's warm weight strapped against my chest in a baby carrier, her head tucked under my chin. I put the milk in the cart when we reach the dairy aisle. It's such a small thing that it almost embarrasses me, how much I want to be useful, though sometimes it feels as though I've lost the ability.

We move through the produce section. Nora reads from a list on her phone. I reach for a bunch of parsley and smell it before putting it in the cart. I'm reaching for a second bunch when I feel it.

Not a sound. Not a movement. Something more ambient than either of those things. The back of my neck goes tight, and I turn around.

Allison stands at the end of the produce aisle. Unlike me in my yoga outfit, she's carefully put together. Her dark hair is down. She's holding a small basket with nothing in it.

Our eyes meet, and she smiles. It is the most controlled thing I have ever seen a human face do.

My body goes cold from the inside out. A feeling that I haven't felt since the morning after. The morning we sat in the car in the driveway, and Adam told me we had to stick together now. Suddenly, I notice Josie's warmth against me again, and it grounds me. I press my hand to the back of her head, instinctively, the way you cover something precious when something dangerous gets too close.

"Reese." Allison says my name into the hushed space of the aisle. She walks toward me, and all I can think of are the warnings in her letter. I don't move, my head jerking toward Nora, who is examining apples and placing the best choices into a bag in her hand.

The last thing I want to explain to my child's nanny is that her employers dabbled with some sexual exploration that backfired on us when we stumbled onto a woman who had clearly lost touch with reality. But Allison wasn't the only experience we had in that world. I quickly force my thoughts off Joe and onto the emergency in front of me.

"I just want to talk." Her voice is smooth.

From the corner of my eye, I see Nora go still at the cart. She doesn't come closer. She doesn't retreat. She stands fixed at the handle of the cart, watching.

"Allison." I tighten my grip on the bunch of parsley until the stems snap. "This isn't the time."

"When is the time?" She tilts her head, her smile fixed and pleasant and entirely empty. "You don't return my calls. And when I tried to reason with you, you had an attorney send me a nasty letter."

"You call the letter you sent to my home trying to reason with me?"

"You left me no other choice," she insists.

"I don't owe you a conversation." I keep my voice low, trying my best not to make a spectacle in the middle of the produce section. I'm certain by now that Nora has taken notice, and part of me is relieved that she has chosen to keep her distance. Josie shifts against my chest, resettling, and I feel her breath through the wrap, warm and rhythmic.

Allison's eyes drop to her. Something moves in her face, and I instantly feel a protective instinct wash over me. "She's beautiful." Her gaze drops to the wrap, cataloging what she sees.

"Don't." The word is sharp as it leaves my lips.

Her eyes come back to mine. "I'm not going to do anything, Reese. I really do just want to talk. Honestly, that's all I've ever wanted."

"There's nothing left to say," I reply. "Now please, leave us alone."

She shakes her head, and the best word I can think to describe the look on her face is pity. "You really believe that." It isn't a question. She says it with a kind of sorrowful condescension that makes my jaw tighten.

"Allison—"

"I'm not angry with you." She says it quickly, as though she's been waiting to. "I want you to know that. I understand the position you're in." Her eyes flick briefly toward Nora, then back to me, and the message in them is unmistakable. *I know what you have to protect. And I know exactly what you have to lose.*

The parsley is still in my hand. I'm holding it so hard the stems have started to bleed green onto my fingers.

"If you understood the position I was in," I say, measuring every word, "you wouldn't be standing in front of me right now."

"I'll tell you what I do understand," she growls, her nostrils flaring as she halves the distance between us. "Adam isn't good for you," she says. "I think you know that."

I take a single step back, putting more space between her and Josie without making it obvious that's what I'm doing. My heart knocks hard behind my ribs.

"We're done here." I turn, moving toward the cart, toward Nora, toward the ordinary and manageable world of grocery lists and bagged apples. My legs feel strange under me, like I'm thinking about how to walk instead of just walking. I'm desperately hoping that Allison drops it and walks away.

I'm thankful that as I approach the cart, Nora says nothing, though I notice the concern behind her eyes. She takes the parsley from my hand and sets it in the cart without comment. Then she puts her hand briefly on my arm. It's just a touch, a second before she steers us toward the next aisle. Though the gesture is small, I'm immensely grateful for it.

I don't look back. I tell myself I don't need to.

"We had something, and you ended it without any explanation," Allison shouts after us as Nora and I walk away. I feel my face go hot, and I'm unsure if it stems from anger or embarrassment. "I'm not going away, Reese. If you think your husband having his attorney send me some ridiculous letter and threatening me will make me stop, you're wrong."

Her voice gets smaller as Nora and I continue to walk down the aisle. Suddenly, I feel Nora's hand on my arm, and she guides the cart with one hand while weaving her other through the crook of my arm. Still, she says nothing, but the action says so much more than words ever could. She's letting me know I am not alone.

"Thank you," I manage to croak out at last. "I'm sorry you had to see that. She was—"

"You don't owe me any sort of explanation," Nora interjects.

We round the corner into the cereal aisle, and I exhale for what feels like the first time in several minutes. Josie, oblivious to it all, has found the drawstring of my wrap and is pulling at it with focused determination.

Despite her assurances that an explanation isn't necessary, I feel an overwhelming need to say something. "She's someone we knew...in a past life. Adam and I were working through some things and, well—it ended badly."

Nora nods once. She doesn't press. She lifts a box of oatmeal from the shelf, examines it, and puts it in the cart. The normalcy of the action is so profound it makes my eyes sting with gratitude that, after all the terrible things I had done, I somehow deserved to have such an incredible person come into my life—our lives.

We make our way through the rest of the store methodically, the list guiding us from aisle to aisle. I concentrate on the small tasks. Reading labels. Reaching for things on higher shelves. Keeping one hand on the back of Josie's head even though there no longer appears to be any danger. The physical act of it steadies me more than anything else could.

It isn't until we're loading the bags into the trunk that Nora speaks again about what happened. She doesn't look at me as she shares the story. Instead, she keeps her head down, placing one bag after the next into the vehicle.

"When I was nineteen," she says. "I had a situation. An older man I'd been involved with had a hard time accepting that it was over." She pauses, and in the momentary silence, I can hear all the emotions this stirs inside her.

"He just couldn't accept that I didn't want to be with him."

I look at her over the open trunk. She straightens and finally meets my eyes.

"Some people," she says simply, "decide that their feelings validate their actions. That it somehow gives them rights. It isn't your fault when they do that."

I hold her gaze for a moment, resisting the urge to ask what happened with that older man. There's nothing performative in her face, no bid for gratitude or response. She's just telling me something true because she thinks I need to hear it.

"Thank you," I say. And despite my immense embarrassment, I mean it in a way that exceeds the words.

She nods, closing the trunk with a firm click. "Let's get Miss Josie home," she says. "It's nearly time for her nap."

I stand by as Nora pulls Josie from the carrier on my chest and settles her into her car seat. The familiar sounds of the harness clicking. Josie's small protest, then quiet.

Nora seems surprised when she emerges from the car and turns to see me still standing there. I know it's not professional. I know I shouldn't do it. But at this moment, all I care about is making sure Nora understands how much the way she handled the situation means to me.

I throw my arms around her and pull her into a hug. She stiffens for just a fraction of a second. Then her arms come up, and she hugs me back, solid and warm and unhesitating.

"Thank you for being so amazing," I whisper, my arms still wrapped around her.

"Okay," she says. And something about the plainness of it, the simple okay, makes me laugh a little against her shoulder. She pulls back, and I can see she's smiling too.

"Sorry," I say, wiping at the corner of my eye with the back of my hand. "That was—"

"Please don't apologize, Reese." She shakes her head and squeezes my arm once before dropping her hand. The warmth she uses when she says my name makes my chest ache.

I nod. I take a breath. And then I turn toward the passenger side door.

That's when I see her.

Allison stands at the edge of the parking lot, close enough that I know she saw all of it. The hug. The tears. The way Nora's hand lingered on my arm. She's still carrying the same small empty basket, and something about that detail turns my stomach. She never went through the store at all. She came out here and waited.

Her eyes move from me to Nora with a slow, deliberate patience. "Is she why? Why you won't tell me the reason you really decided to end things?" Her voice carries easily across the few car lengths between us. The parking lot is quiet enough that a woman loading groceries two spaces over glances up.

"Allison." I hear the warning in my own voice.

"I have to say," she continues, her gaze fixed on Nora now. "I didn't expect this. She's lovely, though. It's also very clear that she's a natural with your daughter." She tilts her head. "How long has this been going on?"

Nora, who had been heading toward the driver's side, goes very still.

"You don't know what the hell you're talking about. Now please, can you leave me the fuck alone?" I shout, no longer caring about anyone else in the parking lot who might overhear. Allison needs to understand that I have no more patience left for her irrational outbursts.

"It's not like I'm asking that much from you. I just want to understand what happened," Allison says, ignoring my warning. "Is that such a terrible thing to give to someone whom you supposedly once cared about?" The entire time Allison speaks, she is sizing up Nora, which is making me very uncomfortable. "Is it because of how much younger she is than me?" Allison asks, looking back at me.

"Fuck you, Allison. She's our nanny," I snap.

Allison's expression doesn't change except for a slight lift at one corner of her mouth, a half smile that suggests she finds the clarification either unconvincing or beside the point. "Of course she is," she huffs. "I'm not an idiot. I can see the chemistry between you two."

I fight the urge to look over at Nora and see how she is absorbing the drama she's been forced into. Instead, I focus on how to end this situation. "We have tried to be patient with you, but if you don't stop harassing us, I'll call the police myself and tell them exactly what you've been doing. The letter. The calls. And now this. For fuck's sake, who in the hell follows someone to the grocery store and waits for them in the parking lot?"

Something finally moves behind her eyes. Not

remorse. Not quite fear. Something more like recalculation.

"You're making a mistake," she says at last, but I realize she's no longer talking to me. She's looking at Nora.

"They're lying to you. They're hiding stuff."

"We have to go," Nora says as she pulls the driver's door open.

"I wouldn't ignore me," Allison warns. "Not if you know what's good for you."

Nora stiffens and looks Allison directly in the eyes before asking, "Is that a threat?"

"Of course not," Allison replies. "I'm just trying to warn you that they have a lot of secrets that they would do anything to keep."

"Hear me when I say you will never talk to me again," Nora warns. "Or I won't be as kind as Mrs. Bradley has been to you."

"Now who's threatening who?" Allison growls.

"It's not a threat," Nora continues, and all I can think is that I never imagined her having this kind of bite to her. "It's a promise. If you ever talk to me again, I will make your life a living hell, so I guess if you know what's good for you, then you will keep your distance."

Allison stares at her for a long moment. Whatever she expected from Nora, it wasn't that. Then she smiles again. That same controlled, terrible smile. "Good luck," she hisses at Nora. "You're gonna need it with them." To me, she says nothing. She simply turns and walks away, her heels clicking against the asphalt with an unhurried confidence.

We watch her go. Neither of us speaks until Allison gets into a car on the far side of the parking lot and drives away.

Nora is the first one to get in the car. I stand there one more second, then I get in too.

Nora starts the engine, but doesn't back out of the parking spot immediately. She sits with both hands on the wheel, looking straight ahead.

"I meant what I said," she says quietly.

"What do you mean?" I ask.

"If that woman ever comes near Josie or me again, I won't hesitate to do whatever I have to do to protect that little girl," Nora explains without looking at me.

"I know you will." I exhale slowly. "And you have no idea how much that means to Adam and me."

Nora tightens her grip on the wheel, her knuckles turning white. "She's just trying to frighten you. Women like that—" She stops herself and shakes her head, a small, precise motion, as though deciding not to waste any more words on the subject.

I look down at my hands in my lap. The faint green stain from the parsley is still on my fingers.

I don't know what to even say to Nora about what she just witnessed. I can't even imagine what she must think of Adam and me after this. What kind of mother would allow someone so clearly disturbed to create chaos around her family?

"The things she said," I start carefully, hoping I don't say something that will make the situation worse. "About Adam and me, about secrets, I want you to know—"

"Reese." Nora says my name the same way she used

it earlier, gently but with a finality to it. "Everyone has things in their past they're not proud of. Those aren't secrets. That's just being human. It's human to want to forget about the things we don't like about older versions of ourselves."

"That woman wanted to plant something in my head. I'm not going to let her."

I look at her profile. The calm line of her jaw. The easy way her hands sit on the wheel. This feels like the first time I have seen who Nora is under the polished and professional exterior she presents. What she said about secrets settles cold in my chest. There are obviously things in her past that she would like to forget, and she's right. But what I've done—what I did to Joe—that's something that can never be forgotten. We have killed to protect our secrets, and I wonder just how protective Nora would be if she knew that about us.

"Let's go home," I say.

As Nora pulls out of the parking lot, I take out my phone and type a single message to Adam.

Allison was at the grocery store. She approached me. We need to talk tonight.

I watch the message sit there for a moment before it shows as delivered. Then I put my phone face down in my lap and watch the town move past my window, and think about what it means that Allison had an empty basket.

NINE

ADAM

She comes to me on a Thursday night, which is something she used to do more often before Joe. Before the months of gray that came after him. Before Josie.

She comes to me the way she used to, slipping into the bedroom while I'm still reading. The lamp is on, and the house is quiet below us. She's wearing the silk nightie she keeps in the back of the drawer, the deep burgundy one. Her red hair is loose around her shoulders, and she doesn't say anything. She just crosses the room and takes the book from my hands and sets it on the nightstand, then climbs into my lap and kisses me.

I respond immediately. I will always respond immediately. This is the truth of sixteen years, the way my body knows her body before my mind catches up. My hands find her waist, her hips, the curve of her, where I have always known exactly what to do. She tastes a little like wine but also like Reese—my Reese. I pull her closer and feel her warmth. Here is where we are solid. Whatever else has shifted in our relationship, the way our bodies always connect with ease has never changed.

Only something is different. It's in how she moves. There is something careful about it. A distance that she is probably not even aware of. But the depth with which I know her tells me that she's withholding something, even if involuntarily. The realization causes a hollow ache in my core. Something in her is still somewhere else, even now.

I don't stop. I don't pull back. I hold her and move with her and give her everything she is reaching for, because at least she is reaching. I keep my hands and my mouth on hers, and I tell her she is beautiful. It's easy to say because it's the truth. She is beautiful, and she always will be.

Her hands are in my hair, pulling me into her. I groan into the kiss, my hands flying to her waist, gripping the silk as she grinds down against me. I can feel how wet she is already, even through the fabric, and it makes my cock twitch against the constraint of my boxers.

"Fuck," I mutter against her lips, but she swallows the word, her tongue pushing into my mouth.

She breaks the kiss just long enough to pull back and look at me, and the intensity in her eyes takes real effort to meet without taking over. Her red hair spills over her shoulders like a fucking halo. "I need this," she says, her voice low and rough, like she's been holding on to the words for too long. "I need you."

I don't answer. I don't need to. I pull her back into me, my hands sliding up her thighs, bunching the silk in my fists as I yank her closer. She gasps when my fingers find her bare ass, her skin hot and smooth under my touch. I squeeze, pulling her flush against me, and the friction of her against my cock through the flimsy fabric is almost too much. Almost.

"Adam," she moans, her nails digging into my shoulders as I rock her against me. "Fuck."

In recent months, I have been the one to initiate sex every time. Tonight, Reese is in control, and I am here for every second of it.

"Tell me what you want me to do," I say, looking into her beautiful eyes.

"What?"

"You're in charge, baby. Tell me what you want me to do to you," I repeat.

She bites at her bottom lip, and I can tell my words excite her. After a moment of consideration, she tells me she wants me to lick her pussy.

I flip her onto her back, the suddenness of it pulling a squeal from her.

"You don't have to tell me twice," I add as I pin her beneath me and kiss her again, deeper this time. She arches into me, her hips lifting, searching. I break the kiss, trailing my lips down her jaw, her neck, lower, lower, until I'm at the swell of her breasts. The silk is thin, almost translucent, and I can see the outline of her nipples, hard and begging for my mouth. I don't make her wait. I hook a finger into the neckline and yank it down, freeing one breast, then the other. She's perfect. Full, soft, her skin flushed pink where I've touched her. I take one nipple into my mouth, sucking hard.

"Oh God, yes—" Her voice is a whimper, her fingers

tangling in my hair as I switch to the other breast, my free hand sliding down her stomach, over the silk that's now bunched around her waist.

I don't ask. I don't need to. I move down her body, shifting the nightie up completely to expose her to me. She's bare, smooth, and glistening with arousal. My mouth waters. "You're so fucking gorgeous," I growl before I dive between her thighs.

She's already dripping when my tongue meets her skin, her hips jerking off the bed as I lap at her. I move slow and deep at first, savoring her taste. She's sweet, and all I can think is that I will never be able to get enough of her. I circle her clit with the tip of my tongue, and she moans. Her thighs start trembling around my ears, which causes a smile to pull at the corners of my mouth.

"Adam...please," she begs.

I don't answer. I'm too busy sliding two fingers inside her and curling them just right as I suck her clit into my mouth. She's tight, so tight, and I can feel her walls fluttering around my fingers already. I work her like this for several minutes, changing up the rhythm to keep her on the edge as long as possible. She's so fucking close, and I love knowing how crazy it's driving her.

I need to be inside her. But not yet.

"Come for me, baby. Let me feel you."

She doesn't hesitate. Her back arches, her hips bucking against my mouth as her orgasm tears through her. Her thighs clamp around my head, her fingers twisting in the sheets as she cries out. When her pussy clenches around my fingers, pulsing, it undoes me completely. Fuck, she's so wet. I lap at her through it, drinking her down. She's trembling beneath me, her breath coming in ragged gasps.

I don't give her time to recover. I crawl up her body, my mouth finding hers again as I press my cock against her entrance. She's still trembling, still sensitive, but when I push inside, she takes me with a gasp. She rakes her nails down my back.

"Fuck—" I groan, bottoming out in one thrust.

I pull back, then thrust harder. My hips are snapping against hers. She meets me stroke for stroke, her legs wrapping around my waist, pulling me deeper—one foot pressed into the mattress for leverage, the other hooked into my back, pulling herself up into me. It's filthy. It's perfect.

"You feel so good," I grit out, my mouth at her ear. "So fucking good, Reese."

She whimpers, her nails digging into my ass as she pulls me in deeper. "Don't stop. Don't you dare stop."

I won't. I can't.

I fuck her harder, my balls slapping against her ass with every thrust. The sound of skin on skin fills the room. She's moaning, her breath hot against my neck, her pussy fluttering around me like she's trying to milk me dry. I reach between us, my fingers finding her clit, and I rub tight circles as I piston into her.

"Come again," I demand, my voice rough. "Come with me, baby."

She doesn't need to be told twice. Her back arches as her pussy clamps down around me, another orgasm ripping through her. The sight of her, flushed and trembling beneath me, her lips parted in a silent scream, is enough to push me over the edge. I bury myself to the hilt and groan, my cock pulsing as I fill her. She eagerly takes every drop.

I collapse on top of her, my chest heaving, my heart pounding so hard I'm sure she can feel it. She wraps her arms around me, her fingers tracing lazy patterns on my back as we both catch our breath. For a long moment, neither of us speaks. The only sounds are our ragged breaths.

Then she laughs, a soft, breathy sound against my neck.

I pull back just enough to look at her. "What?"

She smiles up at me, her eyes bright, her cheeks still flushed from pleasure. "Nothing." A beat. "It's just been a while since it was that good," she says softly.

"It was pretty fucking hot the way you came in here, taking what you wanted," I say.

Neither of us says what we are both, I think, aware of. That while the sex was good, better than it has been in a while, it's still not what it used to be. We have fallen into a sexual comfort rather than a combustion.

I know what changed. I know exactly what changed. We both do, but neither of us says it.

I say, "I love you."

"I love you too."

She falls asleep first, the way she usually does. I lie in the dark with my eyes open and the lamp off, listening to the house. I find myself tracking the small sounds. I hear Nora down the hall, making her way into the nursery the way she does every evening for Josie's late-night feeding. I think about the word good and what it costs two people to say it and mean it and know simultaneously that it used to be more than good, and choose each other anyway.

We choose each other. Every day. That's what love actually is, underneath all the other definitions.

I close my eyes, but sleep won't come. My mind won't go still. I can feel my pulse in my fingertips. The stillness of the night and the hum of Reese's soft breathing bring a memory to me.

Once we felt the connection with Joe, he became a part of our home as much as the lake was. It was ever present and something we both loved. He moved through the rooms with the ease of a man who had learned to make himself at home without making himself small. He never felt entitled or expected a welcome. Instead, it was clear he knew we wanted him there. Reese painted in the mornings, so Joe would make coffee and bring it to the studio door and set it down without knocking. She would say thank you from inside without looking up.

I watched all of this and remember thinking how real it was. What he was to her, what she was to him. What Joe and I were to each other. It was all real. Not in a bad way.

I told Reese the night I first understood it. It was late, Joe had dozed off, naked on the couch after an eventful evening, and we stood in the kitchen. I had said those exact words to her, "This is real." I didn't have to explain what I was talking about.

She knew and agreed, "Yes, it is."

I wonder if I hadn't said it that night, would we have gone down the path of overthinking everything once we noticed Joe starting to pull away? The cost of what we did to Joe sits with me differently, depending on the hour. In the mornings, I try to sweat it out. I go down to the lake before the sun is up and run along the water until my lungs burn. Sometimes in the evenings, it can be heavier. In the specific dark of two or three in the morning, when I'm lying in our bed with my hand on the warm hollow of Reese's back, I wish more than anything I could take away the burden of being the one to pull the trigger.

This is what it means to love someone the way I love Reese. Despite loving Joe myself, I would do anything to carry what she cannot.

There is something I haven't told Reese.

Not a secret—nothing of consequence, nothing that would change anything between us. Just a thought I've had and kept to myself.

In the week before it happened, I stood in the kitchen one morning and watched him watch Reese through the studio window.

He didn't know I was there.

He was drinking coffee, and she was inside at the canvas, and the morning light was coming through the window at an angle that caught the glass, making it partly reflective, so I could see his profile in it. The way he held his mug, the expression he wore when he thought he was alone with the feeling.

It was love. Not the complicated, entangled version that the three of us built together over the summer, the version that kept my shoulders knotted and my eyes burning from lack of sleep. Something cleaner. The specific quality of a person who has found someone that makes sense to them and is not yet accustomed to having found them.

He loved me, and he loved us. I know that without a doubt. But what Reese doesn't understand is that he loved her in a different way. In a way I know he would have never acted on. In a way that often made me wonder if that was why he truly started to pull away from us.

I tell myself we had no other choice. When Joe escaped, he would have turned us in. But the truth is that he loved Reese so much, I'm not sure he would have. I still don't know if I made the decision to tell her to get the gun because I was trying to protect myself or because I was scared of losing her.

I believe the choice was right. I believe this, and I grieve it. Those two things are not in contradiction—they are simply both true.

TEN

REESE

Adam leaves on a Wednesday morning for a two-day trip to Chicago for one of the few board meetings he has to attend in person each year. He has been rescheduling for weeks. I assume he was too worried to leave me. I suppose it's a sign that he thinks I'm getting better.

He kisses my forehead in the kitchen before he goes, his hand cupping the back of my head for a moment. I lean into it and feel the solid, reliable warmth of him and think, *We are fine. We are still us. We will always figure out how to be us.*

The first day without him passes the way days pass now, in the rhythm Nora and I have built around Josie's routines. Feeding and napping and the small discoveries of a fourteen-week-old who has recently figured out that her hands belong to her and is deeply interested in this development. I spend an hour in the studio in the afternoon while Josie naps. I apply color that feels like it means something, layer by layer. When I come out, my hands are stained with paint, and I can't help but think that I feel more like myself than I have in months.

Nora makes dinner. She does this most nights now, moving through the kitchen with an ease that stopped feeling like an intrusion around week three and started feeling like a new normal.

After Josie is down, we don't go our separate ways the way we sometimes do. Nora pours herself a glass of wine and comes to sit at the island while I'm still there. We talk. Not about Josie, not about schedules or the grocery list or any of the logistics of our days. Instead, she asks about the painting I've been working on.

I actually answer, describing the piece and how I've always been drawn to painting the lake. I discuss my color choices and the feeling I'm trying to capture. She listens completely, without performing attention. And then she talks about the lake in winter, and how she used to come to the shore as a kid when she needed to think, how water has a way of making the inside of your head go quiet.

"Me too," I say. "Adam built this house for me because of that. Because I told him once that the lake was the only thing that made everything go still."

She smiles. "He paid attention."

"He always does." I look at my wine glass. "It's one of the things I love most about him and occasionally find exhausting."

She laughs, and I feel the warmth of it.

The room goes quiet, and as the silence lingers, I grow uncomfortable in it. I have been wanting to talk to her about the interaction at the grocery store with Allison, but after we left the parking lot that day, neither of us mentioned it again.

"Can I ask you something?" I say, at last.

"Of course."

I look at the counter. At my hands. "The woman at the grocery store." I pause.

"You've been too polite to ask about it, and I've been too embarrassed to bring it up, but it's been sitting there between us, and I..." I make a helpless gesture. "I feel like I should explain better than I did in the car."

Nora waits, her gaze fixed on the rim of her glass.

"What I told you was true," I say. "We were in a relationship with her. We tried it, and it wasn't right, so we ended it. What I didn't say is that..." I hesitate, a voice in my head telling me I shouldn't say more. If Adam were here, I would never be saying this to Nora, but he's not here. "We've done that more than once. Tried to include someone. It's something we've explored, as a couple, for a while. I'm not sure why I'm telling you this. I think part of me needs you to understand that Adam and I are not bad people."

Nora looks at me for a moment. Then she reaches across the island and puts her hand over mine.

The touch is brief. Warm. Steady.

"Wanting a connection doesn't make you bad." She speaks to our joined hands. "It makes you human."

I look at her hand on mine. Then at her face.

I shake my head. "It's not like we started out wanting anything like that," I explain, feeling the need to justify our decision. "Adam and I always wanted a family. We tried for so long, and every specialist we met with told us it would never happen. There was this gaping hole inside me, and I think part of me was desperate to fill it with something, anything that would make me feel whole again."

"I'm sorry you went through that," Nora offers, pulling her hand back and taking another sip of her wine. "I'm glad you two were able to finally get the family you wanted."

I give a small smile as I think of Josie. "She's our little miracle. We didn't know I was pregnant with Josie when we ended things with Allison. We had a connection with someone before her that we cared deeply for, but..." I try to figure out how to explain Joe without revealing anything that would put us in any sort of danger. "Things didn't work out with him, but it made us realize what we could have with someone, and it was clear to both of us that we would never have that with her."

"I'm sorry to hear things didn't work out with that other person," Nora offers, and I can tell she means it. I wish I could tell her about Joe. About the man he was. About the connection both Adam and I had with him, but I know it wouldn't be good for any of us.

"Thank you," I say, leaving my response simple.

Nora refills her glass of wine before topping mine off as well. "I was in a relationship with my two roommates in college," she says, looking me directly in the eye as she says it. There is no discomfort in her posture, and I'm envious of how confident she is in her choices. "Both women. The three of us were together for almost two years." Something in her expression softens in the particular gentleness that comes with a good memory. "It was one of the most pure and loving relationships I think I've ever had."

I stare at her.

"Really," I say. It isn't a question, but she takes it as one.

"Really. We were twenty-one, and we didn't have a word for what we were. The only thing we cared about was that we were three people who loved each other and were good to each other and made each other better." A pause. "It ended because we all went different directions after graduation. Not because anything broke."

I realize my mouth is slightly open, and I close it. "I didn't know you were—"

"Into women?" She raises an eyebrow, her expression holding a faint, curious warmth. "Most people don't. I don't lead with it." She tilts her wine glass. "I'm not sure I've ever had a label I felt fit exactly right. I just love who I love, if that makes sense."

It makes perfect sense.

"And the woman from the grocery store—"

"Allison," I add.

Nora nods. "Did you think you loved her at some point?"

I sigh and look away, guilt consuming me. "I think I wished I could feel for her what we felt for the person I mentioned before, but sadly, no. I never loved her."

"I see," she says, and I feel the sudden need to explain myself.

"I know you must think I'm a terrible person, but I swear we never meant to lead her on. We really wanted it to work, but Adam and I both thought she changed into someone else when things moved into the bedroom. It all became—I don't know, like some sort of performance for her."

Nora nods. "I can understand the draw. For her, I mean. What it would be like to have been in your orbit—" She stops. She looks at me with something direct and unguarded in her expression, something neither professional nor calculated. Just honest. "You're a pretty remarkable woman, Reese. Anyone would find it difficult to walk away."

The flutter is immediate and surprising. I'm unsure whether the feeling stems from my expectation that Nora would judge me for our decisions, or from something else.

It starts somewhere in my sternum and moves outward. Not since Joe, and before that, not since the early days of the search, when everything felt charged with the particular energy of opening a door you've never opened before.

I look at Nora. She continues looking at me with that direct expression, not pressing it, not making it larger than it is. Just letting it be what it is—a woman saying an honest thing to another woman over wine in a quiet kitchen.

"Thank you," I say. My voice has changed, a new and unfamiliar vibration in my throat. I hope she doesn't notice.

I think she notices.

I don't sleep well.

I lie in the bed that is too large without Adam in it. I look at the ceiling, and I think about the particular way Nora looked at me when she said I was a remarkable woman. I think about the flutter I had. I think about the last time I felt that. It was with Joe, early on, the specific electricity of a new person finding you interesting. Then I think about what that led to and what it cost.

I'm not going to do anything. Obviously, I am not going to do anything. Nora is my nanny. Nora is here because my daughter needs her. The flutter is just the flutter, the ordinary response to being looked at with warmth by someone appealing, and it doesn't have to mean anything more than that.

I'm thirty-eight years old, and I know the difference between a feeling and an action.

Eventually, I sleep.

The next evening, Adam is still gone, and Josie goes down early. By eight o'clock, the house is quiet in a way that feels expansive rather than empty. I make tea. I consider the studio and decide against it. I'm not in the mood to want things from a canvas tonight.

I am on the couch with my tea and a book when I hear Nora's door down the hall open, her footsteps crossing to the bathroom.

Then quiet again.

I try to read. I turn two pages without absorbing a single sentence.

The hallway bathroom has an old knob that doesn't

quite latch unless you lift the handle slightly as you close it. I've been meaning to tell Adam to fix it since we moved in.

Tonight, apparently, she doesn't.

I look up from my book.

The bathroom door is not fully closed. The light is on. A thin warm line at the door's edge.

I should go back to my book.

I hear her. Not loudly. Not performing it. Just the soft, unmistakable sound of someone alone in a room who does not believe anyone is listening.

I don't move.

I should move. I should stand up and walk to my bedroom, the kitchen, or anywhere that is not the couch, with a direct line of sight to that thin line of light. I know this. The knowledge sits clearly and correctly in me, while my body stays exactly where it is.

The sound continues—breathy, rhythmic, a voice catching on something—and I realize my book is no longer in my hands. I realize my tea has gone cold. I realize I'm sitting in the near dark of my own living room while my daughter sleeps down the hall, my husband is in a Chicago hotel room, and my nanny is in my bathroom, apparently unaware she can be heard.

Or.

The thought arrives without warning: *Or she is completely aware.*

The sound peaks and stills.

The water runs. The light goes out.

Her footsteps cross the hall. Her door closes.

I sit alone for a long time without moving.

When I finally go to bed, I lie on my back and stare at the ceiling, and I know, with the certainty of someone who has wanted things before, that I am in trouble. Not the kind that threatens my marriage. Not the kind that threatens what Adam and I are to each other. I believe that.

But the flutter. The very specific flutter.

I press my hand flat against my sternum as if I could still it.

It doesn't still.

ELEVEN
ADAM

I'm on the three forty-five back from O'Hare, and it's delayed forty minutes on the tarmac. The air in the cabin feels recycled and thin. Every time the man in 4C shifts, the vibration rattles up through my heels. I spend extra time trying to focus on a brief I should have read two days ago, but I can't seem to stay focused long enough to get past the first page.

As part of selling my company but retaining a board seat, I'm expected to advise the other members on my recommendations regarding company actions. I take this responsibility very seriously, as our employees rely on their jobs to care for their families.

Despite this, as hard as I try, all I can think about at this moment is Reese.

Not about anything specific. The way she sounded on the phone last night when I called before bed. She was in the kitchen, she said, having a glass of wine. Josie was down, and Nora had disappeared to her room. She sounded relaxed in a way she hasn't sounded in months.

Not the performed relaxation she's been deploying since Josie arrived. The kind that lives in the rhythm of her sentences, in the particular way her voice drops when she's actually comfortable.

I asked what she was doing, and she said nothing, just sitting. I asked what she'd been thinking about, and she was quiet for a moment before saying she'd been contemplating the painting she was working on and the colors she wanted for the next layer.

The painting. She talked about it for six minutes. Six minutes and she didn't once sound like she was reaching for the feeling. It was just there. My Reese was present. The version of her that I desperately want to have with me all the time.

I told her I missed her. She said she missed me too, and that Josie had been perfect all day. It sounded like it had been such a good day, and I'm so frustrated that I wasn't there to be a part of it. I didn't get to see Reese excited about her painting or see her enjoy her moments of motherhood. I was in Chicago, worried the entire time about being away from her. But the emotionally exhausted version of Reese seems to be present less and less.

While I am grateful to be getting more and more of my wife back every day, I can't help but notice that her blossoming friendship with Nora seems to coincide with this change. I don't know why this seems to weigh on me. I was so worried that Reese would view Nora as a threat when we hired her that it never crossed my mind that they may form some sort of a friendship. Shouldn't I be excited for this development?

After what happened with Joe, Reese completely isolated herself from all her friendships. I tried to get her to make plans with Madison so many times, but Reese always told me she didn't trust herself to be around Madison. I knew what she meant. She was afraid she would accidentally reveal something about Joe that would draw too much attention to us. Nora never knew Joe existed. It made sense that Reese could be comfortable around her.

The plane finally moves. I close the brief and watch Chicago come apart below us, the lake enormous and black at the eastern edge. I find our shore by instinct, by the particular curve of it familiar from water and from air and from the window of every room in the house I built to face it. I fall asleep for a few jagged minutes before we level off and wake up on approach, my heart hammering against my ribs for no reason at all.

Nora's car is in the drive. The kitchen light is on.

I come in through the back and set my bag down, my hand lingering on the heavy deadbolt. I turn the thumb-turn twice, locked then unlocked then locked again, until the click sounds final enough to satisfy the itch in my palms. I stand in the kitchen for a moment, listening to the house. It's quiet. I take a deep breath. Someone made something with garlic recently. The counters are clean. On the island is a cluster of things that cause me to smile before I even know I am—a burp cloth, one small sock, and a giraffe-shaped rattle that she has recently developed opinions about.

I hear Reese before I see her. She's talking to someone, then Nora's voice responds, and then Reese laughs.

It's the real laugh. Head-thrown-back, no-filter laugh, the one I haven't heard since Joe.

I stand in the opening between the kitchen and the living room.

They're on the couch. Nora at one end, legs curled under her, a glass of wine in hand. Reese at the other, facing her, bright-eyed and animated as she talks with her hands. Nora is watching her the way people always watch Reese when she's in the room. She naturally pulls people into her sphere.

"I'm not kidding. The doctor just kept going on and on about the Hartley method." Reese laughs before she continues. "I didn't say anything, but I wanted to tell that woman that it only works if the baby believes you actually intend to leave, and Josie is not a baby who can be fooled by—" Reese stops mid-sentence.

"Adam." She unfolds from the couch and crosses the room. I open my arms, and she comes into them.

I hold her. She smells like wine and linseed oil and herself.

"You're home! How was it?" she asks into my shoulder.

"Long. The tarmac situation was—"

"I know, you texted." She pulls back and looks at me, her hands on my chest. Her eyes are clear. Not the careful eyes she's been wearing for months. Clear. Like a window that's been cleaned.

"You look good," I say.

"I feel good," she says. "Josie's napping, but I bet she will be so excited to see Daddy when she wakes up."

"I missed you both so much," I say. "Everything go okay while I was gone?" I ask, my eyes moving between Reese and Nora.

"Oh my God, yes! You have to see how the painting is coming along." Something moves through her expression.

"I'm so glad to hear you've been getting so much studio time in," I reply.

"Honestly, it's all thanks to Nora," Reese says, still clinging to my chest.

"Me?" Nora gasps. "What did I do?"

"Are you kidding me? Besides all the work you do around the house and with Josie, it has been so nice to actually be able to talk to someone again."

I try to mask the pain of hearing that my wife would rather talk to the nanny than to me, but it comes a little too late. Nora's eyes are fixed on me, and I am certain she has already clocked the hurt Reese's words caused.

Nora stands and moves toward the kitchen. "Well, thank you for the compliment, but I didn't do anything extraordinary. Welcome back, Adam," she says, pausing next to me for a moment. "There's chicken in the fridge if you haven't eaten."

"Thank you," I say, an arm still wrapped around my wife as Nora moves past me and places the empty wine glass in the sink.

"I'm going to go check on Josie." She moves past us and up the stairs without ceremony.

Reese watches her go, and then she turns back to me.

"She's good for me," she says. The same words she said after the boat. "I know I keep saying that."

"It keeps being true," I say.

She takes my hand and leads me into the living room and sits beside me on the couch, tucking her feet under her. Something happened while I was gone. Not a bad something. A thaw of some kind, a door that had been closed for a long time gently opening. I don't ask what it was. I keep my questions to myself, not wanting to scare her back into hiding before she's fully emerged.

"So—tell me about the painting," I say instead.

She does.

Later, after catching up and a brief visit with Josie, Reese and I are in bed.

"Can I ask you something?" she says to the ceiling.

"Always."

A pause. "Did you know Nora was into women?"

I turn to look at her. Her profile in the dark, the familiar shape of her nose and her chin, and the particular angle of her jaw.

"I didn't," I say. "Did she tell you?"

"She mentioned a relationship in college that she had with two roommates." Another pause. "I didn't realize."

I let this sit for a moment. "That seems like an odd thing to share with your employer."

Reese shrugs. "I think after what happened with Allison at the grocery store, she was just trying to make me feel at ease about everything."

"Is there a reason you're bringing it up?"

"No," she says. "I don't know. I guess I just found it interesting."

Interesting. She watches a shadow play across the ceiling, her expression untroubled. I feel a sudden, sharp restlessness stir in my gut. I find myself rolling my shoulders, trying to work out a knot that wasn't there ten minutes ago.

I stay still, though the skin on the back of my neck is prickling. Reese has been making her way back to herself for months, and whatever has contributed to that, I should be thankful for it, shouldn't I? I focus on the heat of her body beside mine.

I flatten my hands against the mattress, smoothing a phantom wrinkle in the sheets. "I'm glad that she's been good for you," I say again.

Reese turns her head to look at me in the dark. "I'm so glad you think she has been too."

She kisses me and turns her shoulder to me, nesting into the pillows. "Good night."

"Good night."

She falls asleep before me.

In the dark, her use of the word "interesting" lingers. I lie there for an hour. Our lives have been rearranged before by things that started out as interesting. I'll need to keep an eye on this one.

She's back. She's returning to herself, the real Reese, the one I've been reaching for these past months. Whatever is happening, whatever has shifted, has given me my wife back. That is the thing that matters.

I close my eyes.

The silence is finally heavy enough for sleep to pull me under.

TWELVE

REESE

There are fourteen steps between the kitchen and the studio, and I know this because I count them every morning. Not out of anxiety, but out of the specific pleasure of a ritual that has come back to me after months of absence. Fourteen steps and then the door, and then the smell of linseed oil and the thin, sharp light of a March morning and the canvas that has been accumulating something over the past three weeks that I'm not yet ready to call finished but am beginning to believe is becoming true.

Today, I get two hours in.

Josie goes down for her long nap at ten, and Nora tends to her chores. I mix colors on the palette without second-guessing, and I work with a directness that has been missing for most of the year. The painting is dark at the bottom and light at the top, and I have been building a shape in the middle in layers for weeks. I'm not even sure yet what the shape will become, but I am eager to see it come into focus.

When I come out, Nora is in the kitchen, Josie awake

in her arms, hands wrapped around a bottle, cooing softly as she drinks.

"Successful morning?" Nora asks without looking up.

"Very." I pour myself a cup of coffee and lean against the counter.

"We have a hungry girl today," Nora adds. "She had some pretty big opinions when she finished off her bottle, so I finally caved, and I'm giving her a couple more ounces."

"She has big opinions about everything," I say, laughing, watching my daughter drink down the last of the liquid.

"She gets it from someone." Nora glances at me, and there is a warmth in it. Something is under the warmth, though, that has been there since the evening Adam was away. Since the bathroom, the door that wasn't latched, and the sound I was not supposed to hear but cannot unhear. She looks back at Josie. "Adam left while you were in there. He said he was going down to the beach for a run and would be back later."

"Good," I say. "I think some exercise will help him clear his head."

"Is everything okay?" Nora asks.

I shake my head. "Yeah, I can just tell he has a lot on his mind. I'm guessing it was something that happened at the meeting in Chicago. He'll tell me when he's ready."

I take my coffee to the island and sit across from them and ask Josie what she thinks about her morning. Josie looks at me with the dark, serious eyes that are definitely Joe's in this particular light, and definitely not something I can think about right now. When a belch escapes Josie's lips, her hands come together in a sudden, triumphant clap. Nora and I both share a laugh, and everything feels right for a moment.

The second letter comes on a Friday.

Adam finds it this time, before I do, and he brings it to me in the studio without opening it. He sets it on the worktable and says it's from her with a flatness that tells me he's containing something. I wipe my hands and pick it up.

It's shorter than the first one. Three sentences.

I know you think this is over. It isn't. People would be very interested in what I know about you and your husband and the man who came before me.

I read it twice. I set it down. I look at the painting on the easel. The dark bottom, the light top, the unnamed shape building in the middle. I breathe in through my nose and out through my mouth the way Dr. Carver taught me.

"She knows something," I say.

Adam shakes his head. "That's impossible. We never told her anything about him."

"Well, she's clearly escalating." I set the letter on the worktable, the paper feeling heavy in my hand.

"I know."

"What did Marcus say?"

"I haven't called him yet. I wanted to talk to you first."

I turn to look at him. He's standing with one shoulder

against the doorframe and his arms crossed. His jaw is set in the way it sets when he is deciding how frightened to allow himself to be in front of me. I have been married to this man for sixteen years. I know every iteration of his face.

"Call him." I turn back to the painting, my focus already shifting to the unnamed shape in the center.

"I'm going to." He doesn't move. "But how far do you want me to tell him to take this?"

"You're right, she doesn't know anything." I speak to the brushes on my worktable. The same way I said it in the car after the grocery store, and the same way I said it to Dr. Carver in the particular strategic half-truth that keeps the therapy sessions from becoming dangerous. "She was in our lives for three weeks. She's angry, and she wants leverage to control us."

Adam looks at me. "Well, this is a different tune."

"When she confronted me at the grocery store, Nora said she thought Allison was just trying to intimidate me," I explain. Adam's expression instantly shifts into one of worry.

"How much does Nora know?"

"Nothing," I insist, shaking my head. "I already told you exactly what I told her. We tried exploring the idea of bringing someone else into our marriage and decided it wasn't for us."

"Good. Because you know that if Nora finds out about Joe, it won't only put us in danger."

"I'm not an idiot," I snap.

"I never said you were," Adam says, and I can see his jaw tightening. "I'm just saying, we're already having to deal with the worry that Allison might tell someone about us. I don't need to be worrying about the nanny too."

"Jesus, do you hear yourself? If Allison goes to someone, what exactly is she going to go to them with?" I hold his gaze. "An accusation? About what, exactly? That we date people? That we value our privacy?" I pause. "There's nothing there, Adam."

Allison can't possibly know about Joe. We have sealed that secret in a room we do not go into, and as long as that door stays sealed, nothing she says can hurt us.

After a moment, he nods.

"Call Marcus." I turn back to the painting, the unnamed shape in the middle waiting. "It's time to let Allison know we're not going to keep letting her push us around."

He goes.

I stand in the studio for a long moment after his footsteps recede. I look at the letter on the worktable, then fold it and put it in my pocket before turning back to the painting.

The shape in the middle looks back at me.

I pick up a brush.

Nora doesn't ask about it directly. This is one of the things I have come to count on about her, the specific skill of knowing when a thing should be left alone. But that evening, after dinner, Marcus returns Adam's call. He takes his phone to his office for privacy. Nora is in the kitchen washing dishes. I can tell she has been listening for me as I approach.

I sit at the island.

"Did something else happen with Allison?" she asks, and I wonder if she is just very perceptive or if Adam and I aren't as good at hiding things as I thought we were.

"She sent another letter," I answer honestly, deciding it can't hurt anything.

Since my therapy sessions started, I've been trying to approach things with more honesty. Not full honesty—never the full honesty, of course—but the partial kind that is still more than I was doing before.

"I'm sorry you're still dealing with that," Nora offers.

I shake my head. "It's fine. She doesn't have anything on us, but that doesn't seem to stop her from threatening us. It also doesn't mean she can't cause damage. Even implied things can damage."

Nora dries her hands. She turns around and leans back against the counter with her arms folded loosely. "Do you want to talk about it?"

"I don't know what I'd say."

"You don't have to say anything specific," she replies. "I just mean that you don't have to carry all of it. Not with me."

I look at her. Nora stands at my counter looking at me with those steady dark eyes, and nothing in her expression demands anything of me. The flutter is there. I notice it and set it aside the way I've been practicing.

"She was vague but basically said there are people who would find what she knows about us interesting," I say.

"What does that even mean?"

"Exactly. It means nothing." I trace the rim of my mug, watching the steam rise and vanish. "I think I've moved past fear since she first started with this nonsense. She's not going to take what we've built. We have Josie. We have this house. We have—" I stop. My eyes move to Nora without planning to.

She doesn't let her gaze shift.

"We have what we have." I look at the window, at the gray water of the lake.

"I see." The words are no louder than the brush of a sleeve against the counter.

I look back at my mug.

"I should check on Josie." I push back from the island, the sound of the chair legs sharp against the floor. If I'm not careful, I'll reveal too much to Nora. I'm not sure exactly what Adam meant by his statement that Nora finding out would put more than us in danger, but I do remember that he instructed me to get the gun that day. He told me I couldn't let Joe leave. I know the lengths to which Adam will go to protect our family, and perhaps I am being paranoid, but I can't risk Nora figuring out our secret.

"She hasn't made a sound." Nora tilts her head toward the stairs, listening to the stillness of the second floor. "I'd give her another twenty minutes. You don't want to wake her up too soon. Nobody likes a cranky Josie."

I stay. "True." I tell myself to be careful. If I care about Nora, I need to stop myself before I say too much.

We talk about other things: a book Nora has been

reading, something funny Josie did with the giraffe rattle that morning, and my studio time.

I'm relieved when I hear Josie cooing on the monitor. Nora makes a move toward the stairs, and I wave her off. "Don't worry, I've got her."

I walk upstairs to find Josie's small, certain face staring up at me. I pick her up and start to bounce her on my hip as I walk around the nursery.

I think about the letter in my pocket.

I think about the shape in the painting.

I think about Adam on the phone with Marcus, figuring out the best way to protect our little family.

I think about Nora saying that I don't have to carry all of it. Not with her. The weight of the "with me." The way it landed.

The flutter is still there.

Small and stubborn and inconvenient.

There.

THIRTEEN

ADAM

Marcus calls on a Monday morning with the kind of news that sounds like good news, but is actually just the beginning of a longer process. The second letter, combined with the first letter and the grocery store incident Reese documented at his instruction, is sufficient to file. A judge will review it, and we should have a decision within the week.

"And if she violates it?" I ask about the pending restraining order.

"Then she gets arrested," Marcus says.

I thank him and hang up. I stand at my office window and look at the lake. I can't quite figure out why the news doesn't seem to give me any peace of mind. My calves are still tight from the six miles I ran before dawn, a pace that was more about trying to outrun the static in my head than about fitness.

Reese is in the studio. I can hear, very faintly, the music she plays when she's working. It's something instrumental, low, the kind she said once helps her stop thinking in words and more in colors.

The music stops. Then it starts again, a different track.

She's adjusting. Looking for the right thing.

Something has been happening in my house that I have been watching without naming.

I have a talent for stillness. For fading into the background until I am nothing but a witness to what is happening in front of me. It's actually a skill I developed long before Reese. As good as I am at disappearing and becoming an observer, I learned that some things can be stared at indefinitely without ever becoming more bearable. I learned this about my parents' marriage when I was eleven. I learned it again about Joe. I am perhaps relearning it now about something I have not yet decided to look at directly.

Reese moves differently when Nora is in the room. Not toward her, not obviously, not in a way that announces itself. But there is a looseness in her posture that isn't quite the same as it used to be. It's less guarded somehow. With me, Reese is open in the way of a long marriage, completely, but with the particular weight of history, of knowing what the other person will do with anything you give them. With Nora, there is a freshness to it. She decides, in real time, how much to give, and I am just an observer, quietly watching it happen, trying to calculate what it means.

The muscles in my neck tighten as I think about what it means, and if I am simply reading into things. I think about the search for a third, which we said we ended and which did end. I think about the particular quality of what we had with Joe. The way he electrified the house, the way Reese lit up, the way our marriage recovered its heat under the influence of someone new who cared about us.

I think about what Reese said in bed. *"I found it interesting."*

I watch Nora with Josie, which is its own separate thing. Irreproachable, genuinely good, a warmth between the two of them that has no complications. And then I watch Nora with Reese. It's different. It has a quality to it that I am not yet naming.

Reese has always demanded attention wherever she goes. It's not conscious on her part. It's simply part of who she is. I have never once been bothered by this detail. I have always found it affirming, even gratifying, that this woman whom everyone who encounters her finds intoxicating chose me. She could have had anyone in this world, and it does something to me to know that I am who she wanted and still wants every day. I have understood for sixteen years that loving Reese means accepting that she is the kind of person who generates this response in people, and it doesn't threaten anything we have.

But.

Nora's watching has a quality to it that I am suddenly finding myself uncomfortable with. It is more deliberate than the involuntary attention Reese produces in strangers. More particular. It has direction to it. Or perhaps a design.

I feel the familiar, dull ache in my jaw.

It's a Tuesday evening. Reese is at therapy, Josie is asleep, and Nora and I are in the kitchen. She cleans up from dinner as I read the latest issue of a tech journal. It's a comfortable silence. In the past six weeks, Nora has become someone I am comfortable being silent with, which is a quality I don't often find in people.

When I look up, Nora is already looking at me.

"She's doing well," Nora says. Not a question.

"Better than she's been for longer than I can remember," I agree, knowing she's talking about my wife. When we hired Nora, I took the opportunity to explain to her that Reese was struggling with depression. I thought it prudent, so that if she saw behaviors I might miss, she could bring them to my attention. What I had not expected was that Nora would somehow feel compelled to be part of the solution to Reese's recovery.

"The painting helps." She sets a dish in the rack. "I think she needed someone to tell her she was still herself. Separate from being a mother or a wife or any of the other things she is."

I look up from the journal. "Did you tell her that?" I'm trying not to jump to conclusions about the motivation behind Nora's statement. Part of me feels like the comment is barbed—an accusation that I was not telling my wife she was more than just a wife or a mother.

Nora turns slightly. "More or less."

I look at her for a moment. Not in the way I look at Reese, but in the way you look at a person when you're trying to understand what they actually are. She's younger than us, dark-haired, and as uncomfortable as I am with her developing friendship with my wife, she is genuinely good with our daughter. She is, based on my experience, exactly the person her references described.

"Thank you," I say. "For that. For..." I let out a sigh as I consider my words carefully. "Whatever you said. It worked."

She nods and turns back to the dishes. "Reese doesn't need much. She just needs people to believe she's capable of being okay."

"I think everyone who meets Reese knows she's capable of being okay," I say, a defensive edge in my voice. "I think Dr. Carver has also been helping a lot." My words are meant as a warning. As much as I appreciate what Nora has done for Reese, she needs to understand that her healing isn't all from Nora's presence.

"Perhaps," Nora says, but something in the way she says the word tells me she isn't convinced.

"Good night, Adam," Nora says, drying her hands.

"Good night," I say, fighting the urge to argue with her.

An uneasiness settles in my shoulders when Nora is gone.

I did not feel this way about Reese and Joe. With Joe, I could sense how much he cared about me, so there was never an actual threat. I was certain he would never hurt me in that way. I'm not sure if I am reading into things, but I actually think Nora might have disdain for me. I try to convince myself that I'm just being paranoid, but she seems to want to challenge me whenever an opportunity arises.

I go upstairs, and I check on Josie. Her sleeping face, the small fists loose at her sides. Then I go to our room, where Reese is not yet back from therapy. I sit on the edge of the bed in the dark, my hamstrings tight, my heart rate refusing to settle. I think about the physical cost of this kind of silence. The exhausting work of remaining a man who waits and watches and chooses exactly when to let himself feel the impact of what he sees.

And I wait for my wife to come home. My eyes fixed on the dark hallway beyond the bedroom door, my body braced as if for impact.

FOURTEEN

REESE

Dr. Carver has rearranged the furniture.

Not dramatically, just slightly. The chairs are turned a few degrees more toward each other than they were before. The side table has moved so the notepad is closer to her hand.

I sit down.

"You look well," she observes.

"I feel well," I say.

And then, because I have been practicing honesty in this room in the particular calibrated way I've settled into over six sessions, I add, "Better than I expected to feel."

"What did you expect?"

"That it would take longer," I say.

"What would take longer?"

"For me to start to feel a little like myself again." I settle back in the chair.

She nods. She has her notepad on her knee today, which she uses more now than in the early sessions. She doesn't write in it extensively, just a word or two periodically. I have come to watch for when she reaches for it. It tells me where the conversation is going before she directs it.

"What do you attribute the shift to?" she asks.

"Several things," I answer, having already reflected on this exact thing during my journaling. "Studio time has been a big one."

"So you're working again?"

"I am. It feels good. It does tire me in a way that it didn't used to. I can't do a full day anymore, but I have been getting at least a couple of hours in every day," I explain.

"Don't be too hard on yourself," she says. "You have a baby at home. Being a mother comes with a completely new set of energy management skills."

I smile at that. She's not wrong. As much help as Nora has been, things have changed since Josie's arrival. I used to be a night owl, and I would sleep in most days. Now I am such a light sleeper that I wake up several times during the night. The slightest sound from the nursery has me on my feet. Nora has offered to keep the baby monitor overnight so I can get more sleep, but I like that I'm the one who gets up with Josie during the night when she needs someone.

"Thank you. Oh!" I exclaim, remembering the update about Allison. "I almost forgot. We received another letter from the woman I told you about."

"Really?" I've become used to the way Dr. Carver approaches conversations. She doesn't like to pull things from me. Instead, she uses few words, allowing me the time and space to direct things in the way I feel most comfortable.

"Yeah. I took your advice about protecting my family in an unapologetic way."

"I see," she says. "And how did you do that?"

"I told Adam to have our lawyer file for a restraining order," I reply.

"I know you had a lot of guilt at first that you had somehow led this woman on. How are you processing having to file a restraining order against her?"

"Honestly?" I pause. "Just having something being done about it made me feel less like things were happening to me. More like I had some agency."

"That's amazing," Dr. Carver continues. "So is there anything else new since last we spoke?"

I look at the window. The gray light. A bare branch at the edge of the frame, completely still. "Nora," I answer. "Our nanny. She's—" I stop, and I am careful, the way I'm always careful here, the way I navigate this particular terrain. "She's been good for our household. For me, specifically. Something about her makes it easier to just be me."

Dr. Carver writes something. Just briefly. "Was there something that made you feel like you couldn't just be you when it was just you and Adam?"

"I don't know—I guess she doesn't need anything from me," I say.

"And Adam does?"

I shrug. "Most people in my life have always needed something. Adam needs me to be okay because my not being okay frightens him. My friends needed me to share everything with them, even when I didn't want to. My therapist"—I glance at her with amusement—"needs me to make progress so we both feel the work is worthwhile. Josie needs everything, obviously, which I actually find refreshing."

"How so?"

"I don't have to interpret what she needs from me because it's clear." I pause. "Nora is kind of like that—she just wants to be there for me without asking for anything in return."

"I mean—she is your employee."

I stiffen and cross my arms in response to Dr. Carver's words. "What's that supposed to mean?" I snap. "She couldn't possibly want to genuinely be my friend because I pay her?"

Dr. Carver takes a moment to think through her response. "No, but perhaps she doesn't ask for anything in return because of your relationship dynamic."

Was Dr. Carver right? Had I misread my friendship with Nora? Was she just pretending to care about me because I was her employer?

"Has my question upset you?"

I shake my head. "No, why would it bother me?"

Dr. Carver looks at me for a moment. "How would you describe your relationship with her?"

The question is neutral. Her tone is neutral. Everything about the way she asked it is as neutral as everything she says, which is why I have learned not to trust the neutrality. The neutral questions are the ones that go somewhere.

"Friendly. Like you said, she's an employee. I just

happen to have become genuinely fond of her. Is that so bad?" I ask, not waiting for her to answer before I continue. "I mean, it happens, I think. When someone is that present in your life, when they're caring for someone you love."

"Of course," Dr. Carver says. "Has anything complicated that?"

I look at her. She is looking back at me with complete attention. Not pressing. Just open, the door held wide.

The silence fills the space. I have been trying, in this room, to practice complete honesty when I can. I told myself that if I was going to get better, the least I could do was approach this space with an openness I can't have in other parts of my life. Swallowing hard, I take a deep breath and decide to say the thing out loud that I haven't even fully admitted to myself.

"I find her attractive." I study the grain of the floorboards, scared to look at what might be looking back at me from Dr. Carver's gaze.

Dr. Carver doesn't react. This is either her professional training or her genuinely being unsurprised, and I can't tell which. "Attraction to women isn't something new, is it? I mean, isn't that one of the reasons you and Adam got involved with Allison in the first place?" she asks, casually.

She doesn't usually use Allison's name, and I don't know why hearing her say it makes me feel ashamed. "I mean—yes, but Nora isn't a woman on the apps. Like you said, she's an employee, and that would be wrong."

She writes something.

"Does Adam know?" she asks.

"That I find her attractive? No." I look at my hands. "He's very perceptive, and I am sure he senses the tension, but I don't think he wants to put a name to it."

"Why not, do you think?"

I consider this. "Because Adam chooses what to see," I say. "He's always done this. He decides what to look at and what to put away. It's one of his—it's a quality I both love and find frightening." I pause. "Because sometimes the things he puts away don't stay there."

Dr. Carver is very still.

I have said more than I meant to say. I can feel the way that sentence opens into the room that is behind the door. The sealed room, the one I have been so careful about since I started coming here. "Sometimes the things he puts away don't stay there." I said it about Adam looking away from Nora and what it means about Nora. But it's also true about the other thing. It's also about Joe.

I breathe.

"Tell me more about that." Her voice is a low thread, barely holding against the weight of the silence.

And here is where I have to be most careful. Here is where the skill I've built over these sessions becomes genuinely necessary. The ability to give her something real, something that satisfies the direction of the question, without giving her the thing behind it.

"We had someone in our lives." I focus on the stillness of the bare branch in the window. "Before Josie. Someone we were close to who—left. Abruptly. And the way it ended was—" I stop. I find the true words without being specific. "Unresolved. For both of us. Adam handled it by closing it. Deciding it was finished and not revisiting it. And for a while, I thought that was the right way. That the healthy thing to do was what he did. But I don't think you can actually do that. I don't think you can put something in a room and lock the door and have it stay there."

Dr. Carver is writing now. Not a word or two. Several lines.

"And you haven't been able to close it the way he has." She lets the silence stretch between us, her pen poised above the paper.

"No."

"Does this person know the effect their departure had on you?"

The question lands with surgical precision, making my chest go tight. "Does this person know?" She is asking about resolution. She is asking about closure in the therapeutic sense. The possibility of contact, of a conversation that completes the story.

"No. There's no way to have that conversation. The door is closed. On both sides." I hear myself. The layers of truth in that sentence, all simultaneously accurate. "It has to stay closed."

She looks at me for a long moment. Something in her expression has changed, a shift that tells me she has registered something I didn't mean to give.

"Reese." She lets the name hang for a moment, her gaze steady. "You mentioned earlier that you've been performing recovery. And today you've described someone who left, a door you can't open, things Adam has put away that you're not sure stay put." She pauses.

"Are there things you're carrying that have nothing to do with postpartum depression?"

The office falls into a sudden, airless silence.

"Everyone is carrying things that don't have neat diagnoses," I say.

"That's true." She marks a single word on the notepad. "And also not quite an answer."

I look at her. At the complete attention, the unhurried patience, the room designed for exactly this and the things that have no neat diagnoses.

I think about Joe's face.

I think about the water.

I think about Josie's eyes, dark and serious, looking at me from the crib with her father's watchfulness.

I think about the shape in the painting I have been building for weeks, in layers, that I cannot yet name.

"There are things I carry." I let the words fall between us, heavy and deliberate. "Things I will never be able to put down."

"Don't you think we should examine these things?"

"There are things I'm not willing to examine because I don't believe I could survive the examining." I hold her gaze. "I think you can respect that. Good therapy works around the load-bearing walls, right?"

A long pause.

"That's a very good metaphor," Dr. Carver says.

I smile in response to the compliment.

Something moves at the corner of her mouth. "I do respect that, Reese. And I want you to know that this room will be here when you're ready to look at whatever the load-bearing walls are protecting."

I nod, knowing she will never get to see that part of me, even if I want to show her.

We talk for the remaining twenty minutes about Josie, about the painting, about the restraining order and what it will mean to have Allison formally contained. I give her real things: the sleeplessness, the gradual return, the flutter that I describe only obliquely, as a new feeling I'm still deciding what to do with. She doesn't push on that. She lets me have it unexamined for now.

When I leave, I sit in the car.

"It will be here when I'm ready," she said.

I start the car and drive back toward the lake, toward the house, toward Josie and Nora and Adam and the life I have built on top of the thing I cannot say. The way you build a house on a foundation you decide is solid, then choose never to go back and check.

The foundation holds.

It has to hold.

I don't have a choice but to trust it will hold.

FIFTEEN

ADAM

"Hey, babe," I say, approaching Reese and kissing her forehead. "How was studio time today?"

She glances up at me and smiles. "Good. I only had about an hour in me today."

"An hour is better than none," I say, following her into the kitchen where Nora is busy preparing dinner while Josie kicks her feet and laughs in her bouncy seat.

"What did you get up to today?" she asks.

"I started cleaning out the carriage house," I answer, Reese's head snapping in my direction.

The truth was that it had needed doing for a very long time. The likelihood of anyone ever coming to look for Joe was next to zero. We had been careful to cover our tracks. But if anyone did come asking questions, there was almost certainly some piece of evidence in there that could link us to him. A trace of DNA that would bring about the end of our perfect life.

"When did you decide to do that?" Reese asks as she stares up at me with wide eyes.

"It's been on my to-do list forever," I answer.

"I don't think I've ever been inside the carriage house," Nora remarks.

"There's nothing to see in there," Reese replies with too much passion in her voice. I can tell she senses her overreaction, and she attempts to correct herself. "I mean, it's just a bunch of old junk that the previous homeowners left behind. Well, that and a bunch of dust and spiders."

Nora laughs. "Sounds charming."

I watch Nora lift the pan from the heat with one smooth motion. I realized something the other night while Reese was at therapy. Nora isn't a fire to be put out. I simply have to stop pretending it isn't there.

And then I watch Reese look at Nora.

It is a small thing. She is at the island with her wine, and Nora says something I don't catch—something quiet, something that makes Reese's face do the thing I've been trying to name for weeks. It isn't the way Reese looks at me. It isn't the way she looked at Joe, either, that had a heat to it. This is something else. Something more tentative.

Reese looks at Nora the way someone looks at something they didn't expect to want.

And Nora looks back.

There it is.

I have been watching it from the corner of my eye for weeks. I have named it. I'm standing in my own kitchen, with my daughter and my wife, letting the reality of it sink into my bones.

I think about Joe.

Not the end. I don't think about the end. Instead, I think about the way Joe changed the atmosphere inside this home.

I look at my wife talking to Nora. The head-tilted, bright-eyed version of her. The real one I have missed so much. And I think, for the first time, a thought that doesn't feel like a threat to the security I've fought so hard to maintain.

What if I don't treat this like a problem to be solved?

What if this isn't something that needs to be kept out?

What if this is, instead, the thing that comes next?

I don't say anything. Not tonight. Tonight, I allow the realization to sit and settle over me. But I look at my wife's face, and at Nora's when she looks at my wife, and I think about how, when we loved Joe, we still loved each other. Reese and I, the two of us, the sixteen years—perhaps Nora and I could both have Reese, just like Joe had both of us.

I am a man who watches and waits. I have spent my life standing guard, and tonight, I am beginning to look at what I'm guarding.

"Dinner's ready," Nora says.

We sit down together, the three of us, Josie in her high chair presiding over the table. I am quiet, but for the first time in a long time, the quiet is not troubled. It is the quiet of someone who has finally stopped pacing the hallways at night.

I watch Nora.

I watch Reese.

I think, *Not yet.*

But soon.

SIXTEEN

REESE

He finds me in the studio.

Not when I'm working. I've already put the brushes down for the night, covered the palette, and sealed the turpentine-soaked cloth in the tin. I'm just standing at the window with the lights off, watching the last of the evening move across the water. It's the best light of the day.

The door opens behind me. I know his footsteps the way I know my own breathing.

"Josie's down," he says. "I think Nora's reading."

"I know."

He crosses the room and comes to stand beside me at the window. We look at the lake together for a moment in silence, the way we have stood at this window a hundred times before.

"Reese."

There is something in the way he says my name. A care in it.

"I'm listening," I say.

He is quiet for another beat, and I can feel him choosing his words the way he always does. The way that means whatever comes next has been held for a while before being said.

"There's something between you and Nora." He doesn't make it a question.

My first instinct is to maintain the surface. Keep the room sealed. Give him the version of the truth that won't open anything.

"I don't know what you mean," I say.

Adam doesn't react. He doesn't sigh or press. He just stays exactly where he is, looking at the lake, allowing the silence to eat away at the untruth.

And standing here in the dark with him, I try to determine what is actually driving my lie. Am I protecting him? Am I protecting myself from whatever his reaction might be? Or is a part of me trying to protect Nora? Is there some deep instinct that knows what Adam is capable of when he decides a thing is a threat to us? I was the one who pulled the trigger. I was the one who ended Joe's life. If people should be scared of someone, it's me.

The question frightens me more than the lie does.

"Reese," he says at last, his voice quiet. "You don't have to lie to me."

I look at him. I can see the love in him. The love he has for me and his drive to make sure I'm happy above all else.

"I know your soul," he says. "I have always known your soul. And I've had a lot of time to think about this."

"To think about what?" I continue with my lie, needing him to say the words exactly as he means them.

"When you loved Joe," he continues, his voice low and steady, "you didn't love me any less. I know that. I knew it then. And what I felt for him—" He stops, and I can see what it costs him to say it. "What I felt for him didn't take anything from what I feel for you. Not a single thing."

The room is very still.

"What are you saying?" I ask even though some part of me already understands exactly what he's saying.

He turns to look at me then, fully, with those clear, careful eyes that have never once failed to see me for who I am.

"I'm saying I see it. You've been more yourself in the past few months than you've been for a very long time. I know the studio time has helped. And I know Dr. Carver is part of it. But I also know that Nora is part of it." He holds my gaze. "And I love you too much to stand in the way of something bringing you back to me."

My chest does something complicated.

"Adam." I shake my head. "Is this—are you saying you want a relationship with her? Is that what this is about? Because if you have feelings for Nora—"

"No." He says it without any hesitation. No pause, no qualification. He chuckles a little at my misunderstanding. "I don't have romantic feelings for Nora. That's not what this is."

"Then what is this?"

He takes a slow breath. "This is about you. The version of you I fell in love with twenty years ago and the version of you I watched slowly disappear after Joe died and completely evaporate when Josie was born. I've been watching you come back since Nora arrived, and I've been asking myself what I was willing to do to help you stay."

I look at the painting on the easel. The dark bottom, the light top, the unnamed shape that has been building in the center for weeks.

"We'll figure it out," he says. "Just like we did with—"

"Don't." The word comes out sharp, sharper than I intend.

He stops.

"Don't say it like that." I turn to face him fully. "Don't say 'just like with Joe' as if that's a blueprint we want to follow. Have you forgotten how things ended with him? Have you forgotten what we did?"

The air between us changes. We don't speak about Joe this directly. We haven't since I told him I was pregnant. I can feel the weight of it come down between us, the way it always does when we get close to it.

"I haven't forgotten anything." His voice is still calm, but something is beneath it. I recognize it because I carry it as well. It's grief. "Not a single day."

I think it's strange that you can feel so much grief for something that you were responsible for. At first, I thought it was remorse that consumed me, but over time, I realized we were both experiencing a deep sorrow. We didn't just regret how things ended. We felt we had lost something profoundly. It's so fucked up to know you did something so evil, yet you are also left feeling the gaping hole in your chest from the loss that evil caused.

"Then you understand why I can't just treat this like a thing we do. Like we simply decide and it all proceeds according to plan." I cross my arms. "Nora is in our house. She isn't some woman we found on a dating app. She is with our daughter every day. And she—" I feel the flutter in my chest, warm and stubborn. "She doesn't know who we are. What we've done."

"I know that."

"Do you know what it means? If this becomes something real and she eventually learns what I'm capable of?"

"Reese." He steps closer and puts both hands on my face the way he does when he needs me to actually hear him and not just the sound of my own fear. "I'm fully aware of what I am offering you. I have looked at every angle of it. I'm not doing this without thinking. I'm doing this because I have thought about nothing else for weeks. I'm certain."

I look at him. My husband. The man who has held my life together when I was incapable.

"How can you be certain?" I whisper. "How do you know?"

"Because I know you," he says simply. "And I know that what I want most in this world is for you to be okay. Fully okay. Not performing it. Not building toward it. Actually in it." He lets his hands drop but stays close. "If she is part of how we get there, then I want her here."

I think about the shape in the painting that I have not yet been willing to name.

I think about what it costs to be seen. Fully seen. Not just the parts of yourself that are safe to show.

I think about Nora's hands on mine across the island. The steadiness of her. The way she didn't ask for anything from me. Dr. Carver's words flash through my thoughts. She's an employee. Perhaps that is why she doesn't ask for anything in return. She's merely being a good employee.

"I'm scared," I say. It is possibly the truest thing I have said out loud in months.

"I know." He pulls me into him, and I let him. My face is against his chest, and his hand is on the back of my head.

"So am I," he says into my hair. "But we've been scared before."

We have. We have been so many kinds of scared before, and we are still here choosing each other every morning. I know this. I believe this.

And still.

I pull back just enough to look at him.

"Promise me," I say. "Promise me that whatever this is, it doesn't end the way the last one did."

He holds my gaze for a long moment. The lake is nearly dark now behind him, the water gone the color of the sky.

"I promise," he says.

I don't know if I believe him. I don't know if believing him is the point.

I press my hand flat against his chest and feel his heart, steady and certain.

Mine is less steady.

SEVENTEEN

REESE

I don't know why it matters what I wear to therapy. It's never mattered before. I pull on the gray wrap dress, the one I've had for years, and look at myself in the mirror for a moment before turning away. The bags under my eyes are from last night more than from Josie. She slept well. I did not.

I think about what Adam said in the studio. I've been thinking about it since the moment he said it, and the thinking has taken on the particular circular quality of a thought that has nowhere to land.

I want to talk to Dr. Carver. That is what I keep coming back to. I want to lay this out in front of her. I want to describe the feeling in my chest when I look at Nora. I want to describe the feeling in my chest when Adam told me he already knew and he wasn't afraid of it.

Dr. Carver can only see the thing I put in front of her. And the thing I need to put in front of her right now —Adam's offer, the flutter, the question of what I am actually willing to let this become. She knows about Joe as a concept. A person we were close to who left. She knows there was unresolved grief and an abrupt ending.

What she doesn't know is that we killed him.

We killed him. I pulled the trigger. Adam held me afterward in the driveway and said we have to stick together now. And from that night forward, I have been building a version of my life on that fact. Dr. Carver doesn't know any of that. And without it, how can I trust her advice about Nora? About whether to trust this feeling, whether to let it become something, whether what Adam is offering is love or something else dressed in love's clothes—would be given in the dark. She would be diagnosing a symptom without knowing the disease.

I pick up my earrings from the dresser and put them in without looking.

Maybe that's what therapy has always been. The advice is still useful. It is real guidance.

I check my phone. Twenty minutes before I need to leave.

I wonder if today is the session when I say something real. I wonder if I can describe the geometry of what Adam offered without having to explain the geometry of why it frightens me. Why, the last time I let myself love someone outside the two of us, it ended in a way I can never describe to anyone.

I pick up my bag.

I am still working out whether it's possible when I hear it.

A sound from downstairs. The front door. Then Josie's cry—real and startled, the cry that means something frightened her. Underneath it, lower, another sound I need a moment to identify.

Nora. Nora is crying.

I'm already moving before the thought is fully formed, down the hallway and the stairs.

The scene in the kitchen unfolds before me in pieces. Nora is just inside the doorway, Josie in her arms, and both of them shaking. Josie's face is red, Nora's face is wet and white. There is something in her eyes that I have never seen there before. Adam is already there. He must have been in his office. He stands in the opening between the kitchen and the hall, and he's using the voice he uses when he's controlling something he doesn't yet have control over.

"Give me the baby," he says. "Just give me Josie until you can calm down and tell me what happened."

"What's going on?" I come down the last stair and move into the kitchen.

Adam turns. "She came in like this. I don't know what happened. I can't get her to explain." He looks back at Nora. "Hand me Josie. You can't hold her when you're like this. It's not good for her."

But Nora is already turning to me. Something in her has been waiting for me to come downstairs. She crosses the kitchen and holds Josie out toward me, and I take her, automatically, one hand under her head, pulling her into my chest. Josie's cries begin to soften immediately against me.

Nora's mouth opens. She tries once and fails, then tries again.

"Allison."

The name lands in the room like something dropped from a height.

Adam goes very still.

"What about her?" I ask, keeping my voice even for Josie's sake, pressing my lips to the top of her head. She is already quieting, her breath going ragged and slow in the way that means she is calming.

Nora presses the back of her hand to her mouth, then takes a breath. I can see her pulling herself back together and finding the words that escaped her in her panic.

"She was at the park," Nora says. "I took Josie to the park this morning. The small one, with the fountain." She stops, then starts again. "She was there. Allison. I didn't see her at first. We were at the fountain, and then she was just—there. Standing next to us."

Adam's jaw tightens. He chooses not to speak yet.

"She started talking," Nora continues. Her voice is steadier now, but her hands are still trembling slightly at her sides. "She said she knew who you two really were. She said I needed to listen, that I needed to know, so nothing would happen to me. I told her there was a restraining order and that she needed to leave or I was calling the police."

"Good," Adam says. "That was exactly right."

"She said the order didn't apply to me." Nora looks at him. "She said she couldn't approach the two of you. That it didn't say anything about the nanny."

A silence.

"I told her she was crazy," Nora says. "I told her we were leaving. I picked up the bag and Josie, and I started walking to the car." She stops for a moment, as if the memory of it was overwhelming her. "She grabbed my arm, and she said—" She closes her eyes briefly. Opens them. "She said such horrible things."

"What things?" Adam's voice is intense.

Nora looks at him for a moment. Then at me. Then back at him.

"She said you two killed someone. A man. Someone you met on the dating apps. She said she knew what you did to him and that I was living with people who were capable of—" Her voice breaks on the last word. She pulls it back together. "Capable of that."

The kitchen is absolutely silent.

Josie makes a small sound against my chest. I press my hand to the back of her head.

Adam is the first to speak, and the steadiness in his voice is something I will think about later. "That is insane." He says it with a calm I find remarkable. "That woman is not well. She has been harassing us for months, she has violated a restraining order, and now she is saying things designed to frighten you and drive a wedge between you and this family. That is exactly what this is."

"Of course it is," I say, and I'm surprised by how steady my own voice sounds. "Her obsession with us has clearly moved into something delusional. None of what she's saying is real, Nora."

Nora looks at me. There is something in her gaze that I cannot fully read.

"I told her that," she says. "I told her exactly that. I told her that I wasn't going to stand there and listen to her. I strapped Josie in, and then I got in and left." She shakes her head. "I thought that was the end of it, but she must have followed me."

"What do you mean, followed you?" Adam asks, rushing to the front of the house and looking out the window before returning to the conversation.

"I don't know. I guess when I got in the car, she ran to hers, because she was right behind me the moment I pulled out. She was driving—" She exhales hard. "I thought she was going to run me off the road. She was so close. I had Josie in the car. I was watching her in the rearview, and she was right there, and I didn't know what she was going to do."

"My God," I say.

"Where is she now?" Adam asks. His voice has changed and is lower, more focused.

Nora swallows. "Just before I turned onto Lakeshore, she went off the road." She says it quietly. "I watched it happen in the mirror. She was so close to me, and then she just... was gone. I didn't see it, but I heard it."

"Is she okay?" I ask.

"I don't know." Nora's voice is barely above a whisper. "I was so scared. I had Josie, and I just—I kept driving. I couldn't make myself turn around. Oh my God, oh my God, oh my God." Panic consumes her.

Adam pulls his phone from his pocket. "I'm calling the police," he says. "This isn't something we manage on our own. She violated the restraining order. She followed your car with our child inside it. We need to be the ones to report it before someone else does."

"Am I going to jail?" Nora asks, looking back and forth between us.

Adam pauses, looking at her. "Why would you go to jail? She was the one who put you and Josie in danger."

"But I didn't stop. I saw her crash, and I didn't stop," she cries, her eyes glassy as she recalls the scene.

I look at Nora. She looks younger somehow than she did ten minutes ago, something stripped back that she usually keeps in place.

"Come here," I say.

I don't plan it. I cross the small distance between us and put my free arm around her, Josie between us in the wrap, and Nora goes still for just a fraction of a second before her arms come up and she holds on. I can feel her breathing against my shoulder, trying to steady it.

"You're not going to jail," Adam says confidently. "I'll call Marcus first and see how we should handle this."

"She's not going to hurt you," I say into her hair. "None of what she said to you was true. Adam is going to make sure you are completely safe. Do you hear me?"

Nora doesn't answer. But she doesn't pull away either.

Josie, pressed between us, makes a small contented sound. I feel Nora exhale a breath that might be a laugh, or might be crying, or might be both. I tighten my arm around her.

The three of us stand there in the kitchen while Adam's voice moves through the closed door of his office, low and controlled and already telling the story the way it needs to be told.

Nora and Josie are safe. That should be all I can think about right now, the relief that nothing happened to them. But something darker lurks in the back of my mind.

Something I can't talk about. Something that Adam and I will need to discuss later.

How does Allison know?

She was in our lives for three weeks. She never knew Joe. We never told her Joe even existed. But she said we killed a man from the dating apps. That is specific. That is not a guess someone makes about a couple they dated briefly and who ended things. That is not the language of delusion. That is the language of someone who knows something, or knows enough of something, to build around it.

I breathe in slowly. Nora's hair smells like the outdoors, like the park I wasn't there to protect her in. Adam's voice continues in the next room.

I press my lips to the top of Josie's head and close my eyes and stay exactly where I am.

The foundation holds.

It has to hold.

It has to.

EIGHTEEN

ADAM

The carriage house smells like cold concrete and cardboard.

Until the day I recently purged the place of its contents, I hadn't been inside since before Josie was born. I have walked past it every day for months, sometimes twice, and I have not looked at it directly. The way you learn not to look at something that only reminds you of a painful memory.

Reese is beside me. She pulled the door shut behind us, and now we are standing in the gray light of the single window, both of us speaking quietly. Nora is in the house with Josie, and there's no way she can hear us, but what we have to say feels like caution is a necessity.

"Marcus is handling it," I say. "He has a contact. A detective he's worked with before. He's going to call him directly and explain the situation. He said between the letters, the grocery store, the restraining order, and now today, he doesn't think it will be a problem."

"What does that even mean? Not a problem for us or

not a problem for Nora?" Reese asks. Her arms are crossed over her chest.

"He said Nora will be fine. She was protecting Josie. Even though she saw the accident and didn't stop, Marcus will explain that she was frightened and all she could think about was getting herself and the baby home safe. Any reasonable person would have done the same thing." I pause. "He'll make sure the narrative is clean before anyone comes asking questions. Allison was the aggressor. She violated the restraining order. She followed their car. The facts are on our side."

Reese exhales slowly. Some of the tightness in her shoulders releases, and she nods.

"Good," she says. "That's good."

I look at the floor. The concrete is clean. It has been clean since I scrubbed it down recently. But I think about it the way you think about a stain that is gone, but your eyes still find its location. Your body remembers where things were.

"I just hope we're doing the right thing," I say.

Reese looks at me. "What do you mean? What other option do we have?"

"Allison knows about Joe, Reese. What she said to Nora—a man from the dating apps. She wasn't guessing randomly. She was specific."

The silence between us is of a different quality than before.

"She has to be bluffing," Reese says. "There's no way she could actually know anything. She was with us for three weeks. She never knew Joe existed."

"She may be bluffing." I meet her gaze. "But something tells me she knows something. Her claim about us killing a man from the dating apps. That's not a guess someone just pulls out of thin air. You don't land on something like that by accident. That's something closer to the truth than I'm comfortable with."

Reese shakes her head. "How could she possibly know anything? We never said a word to her about Joe. We barely mentioned we'd dated anyone before her."

"I know that."

"Then how could she possibly know anything? Unless—" The look in her eyes tells me she's puzzling something out. Then, by the way her eyes shift as she's looking at me, I know exactly what she's thinking.

"I didn't tell her." The words come out with more edge than I intend. I pull it back. "Look, I don't know if anyone had to tell her anything. Maybe Allison coming into our lives wasn't merely by chance."

She stares at me. "What do you mean it wasn't by chance?"

I put my hands in my pockets and look at the window, at the pale rectangle of light.

"Think about it. She was the one who matched with us first," I say. "You remember. In our experience, how often was it that single women reached out first on the app?"

"Hardly ever."

"Exactly!" I exclaim. "Most of the time, we were the ones initiating. But Allison came to us. Don't you think that's strange?"

Reese is very still. "I don't know what to think."

"I've been thinking about Joe." I keep my voice even.

"About what he told us. He said he was on his own. That he didn't have people he was close to. We had no reason to doubt that. But I've been wondering lately whether he was entirely honest about that, or whether he told us what we wanted to hear because he understood that was part of what we needed." I pause. "Maybe he wasn't as alone as he said he was. Perhaps he told someone about the relationship. And when he disappeared, that person started asking questions."

Reese doesn't move. I watch her process it the way I have watched her process difficult things for sixteen years.

"You think she knew him," she says finally. It isn't a question.

"I think it's possible. And if she did, what if she matched with us specifically because she was trying to find out what happened to him? When she asked us if this was our first time, we told her that we had dated men on the apps before, but it hadn't worked out. She may have started connecting the dots."

Reese steps back, one step, as if she needs the physical distance to contain what she's hearing.

"So what? She just makes the leap to we murdered him?" Her voice has gone sharp. "Something happened to him, so they must have killed him? That's where her mind goes? You don't think that's a bit far-fetched?"

"If she went to his apartment," I say quietly. "If she knew him well enough to do that. If she realized he never came back to it. People disappear all the time, and most of the time, the answer is ordinary. But if she had a reason to be suspicious of us specifically, if she knew about the relationship and she knew he came to see us and she knew he never came home—"

"Stop."

I stop.

Reese has her hand pressed flat against her sternum. I recognize the gesture. She has been making it for months.

"When you were cleaning out the carriage house, how much was still in here?" She looks at me. "Was there anything Allison could have linked back to Joe?"

I look at the floor again.

"I don't think Joe specifically, but yes, it was all still here," I reply.

"Adam!"

"What? After what happened with Joe, you didn't want to come in here as much as I didn't," I snap.

"I assumed after we took care of his body, you got rid of everything in here too. After what I had to do, I just thought you didn't want me to have to deal with all of this too. I never thought you would just leave everything here all this time." Her words remind me exactly what she did for our family. I managed to get myself locked up, leaving something to Reese that she should have never had to do.

"I know—I'm sorry. I shouldn't have waited as long as I did. I only did it recently because I started to think that even though Nora has no reason to be out here, I couldn't take the chance that one day she could have found our secret. I needed to bury it."

Her eyes move around the space. I watch her take in the clean floor, the bare walls, the nothing that is there now where something was. Something that should never have existed. "It's all gone?" she asks. "You're certain there is nothing in here that can link us to him?"

"I promise. It's gone." I nod once. "I took it apart, and then I hauled the pieces to different junkyards over three different days. Nothing traceable, nothing together. It's scattered where nobody will go looking."

She's quiet for a long moment.

"Do you think Allison was ever in here?"

I consider it honestly. "I don't know when she possibly could have been. I can't remember a moment when one of us wasn't with her, but I can't tell you with certainty that she wasn't."

Reese closes her eyes, then opens them. "Adam, what do we do?"

"Nothing," I say it cleanly. "Nothing is left that ties us to Joe. There's no body. We already have the restraining order against Allison, which means we have a documented record of her instability. If she goes to the police and says what she said to Nora, they're going to see a woman who has been harassing a family for months. A woman who violated her restraining order and followed a car carrying an infant that she tried to push off the road." I hold her gaze. "And if they do come around to ask questions, there is nothing here to find."

Reese nods slowly.

And then we both hear it.

A sound. Outside, close, something moving against the side of the building. A scrape, or a footstep...something...someone.

Reese goes very still. "What was that?" she whispers.

I put my hand up, a small motion, and she goes quiet. We both listen again.

Nothing. Just the wind off the lake moving through the tree line. I cross to the door, slowly, crack the door, and put my eye to the gap at the frame. I scan the clearing, the edge of the landscaping, the path back to the house. I wait.

Nothing moves.

I hold for another ten seconds. Twenty.

At the far edge of the clearing where the grass meets the first of the ornamental shrubs, a deer steps into the open. It pauses, popping its head up as its ears rotate forward. It looks at the carriage house for a moment, and it dips its head and begins pulling at the landscaping.

I exhale slowly.

"A deer," I say in relief.

I turn back to Reese. The color on her face is still slightly off. She gazes past me toward the window.

"Reese."

She looks at me.

"Did you hear me? It's just a deer."

She nods, a tight and unconvinced motion.

"Did you let Dr. Carver know?" I ask, trying to shift her attention. "That you weren't coming?"

"I texted her. I told her there was a family emergency. She said she had a cancellation at the end of the day, if I still wanted to come in."

"Good." I mean it. "You should go."

She looks at me. "After everything that just happened?"

"Because of everything that just happened." I step

toward her and put my hands on her face. "You have been doing such hard work, Reese. Real work. I'm so proud of you for that." I press my lips to her forehead and let them stay there for a moment. "Don't let today take that away."

She is quiet against me for a long moment.

She murmurs, "Okay."

I keep my arms around her and look over her head at the clean, bare concrete floor of the carriage house.

The deer remains at the edge of the clearing. I can see it through the window, pulling at things that don't belong to it. I watch it for a long moment.

"Everything will be okay," I say to give her peace. "We are going to be okay," I say again to give myself peace.

NINETEEN

REESE

The chairs are the same as they were last time.

I don't know why I expected them to have moved again. I sit down, and the familiar smell of the room settles around me—eucalyptus and old books and the particular quality of air that has absorbed a great many difficult things. I feel something in me decompress slightly. I have not realized until this moment how much I have been waiting for this room.

Dr. Carver looks at me the way she always looks at me. As if she has nowhere else to be and nothing else to consider.

"I'm glad you could still come in," she says.

"Me too."

"Do you want to share anything with me about this morning?"

I look out the window. The bare branch is there again, the same one I have been watching through the changing seasons. It has leaves now, small and new, the particular green that exists only for a few weeks before deepening into the green of summer.

"Our nanny," I say. "Nora. She took Josie to the park this morning, the one on Lakeshore. The woman I told you about—Allison—was there."

Dr. Carver is still. She has her notepad on her knee today.

"She approached Nora. She was saying things about us, things she claimed to know. Nora tried to leave, and Allison followed her in her car. With Josie." I stop and take a breath. "Nora managed to get away, but Allison went off the road before they reached the house. We don't know how badly she was hurt. Our attorney has spoken with a detective he knows, and it's being handled, but—" I spread my hands in my lap. "It was a frightening morning."

"It sounds terrifying," Dr. Carver says.

"Nora was shaking when she came in. Josie was crying. I've never seen Nora like that." I pause. "I think that was almost the worst part of it. Seeing someone I've come to think of as unshakable—shaken."

Dr. Carver writes something brief. "How are you feeling about the situation with Allison at this point? You've described a pattern of escalation."

"Fearful. But also something past fear." I consider it. "Like the fear has been going on long enough that it's calcified into something else. I'm not sure what the word is. Determined, maybe. Like I've decided she is not going to dismantle what we have, and that determination has started to crowd out some of the fear."

"That's a meaningful shift," she says.

"It doesn't always feel like progress," I admit. "Sometimes it feels like I've just gotten better at compartmentalizing."

She nods once and lets the distinction sit. "You mentioned that it was almost the worst part, seeing Nora frightened. What was the actual worst part?"

I look at the leaf on the branch outside. Moving slightly in something I can't feel from in here.

"Josie was in the car," I say. "Josie was in the car the whole time."

Dr. Carver is quiet for a moment. Then she says, "You said there was something else you wanted to talk about today. In your text this morning."

I did say that. I said family emergency, and also, I need to talk to you about something. In that order, or possibly the other way around. I can't remember now. The morning feels very long ago.

"Yes." I adjust my hands in my lap. "Adam and I had a conversation last night. Before any of this happened."

She waits.

"He told me he knows." I watch for her expression. It doesn't change. "About Nora. About the—what I've been carrying around since she came to live with us." I pause. "The feelings."

"He brought it up himself?"

"Yes."

"What did he say?"

I tell her. Not everything, not the specific words, but the shape of it. That he'd been watching me come back to myself since Nora arrived. That he'd thought about it for a long time. That he wasn't going to stand in the way of something that was bringing me back to him. I tell her about the quiet in his voice when he said it, the particular steadiness that I have spent sixteen years learning to read.

Dr. Carver is writing more than usual. I watch her pen move and try not to calculate what it means.

"What was your reaction when he told you?" she asks.

"I didn't trust it," I say, and then I feel the honesty of that land in my chest, more honest than I meant to be. "I mean—I believe that he means it. I believe he's thought about it. But some part of me is waiting for the catch. For the thing underneath the generosity." I look at my hands. "I'm afraid it's a trap."

Dr. Carver looks up from her notepad. "A trap?"

"I know that sounds—"

"No," she says. "Stay with it. What kind of trap?"

The room is quiet. Outside, something passes across the light for a moment and is gone.

"I don't know exactly," I say. "Adam is a man who watches. He is a man who decides what to look at and what to put away, and the things he puts away don't always stay there." I'm using the same words I used in this room before. I'm walking in circles around the same thing. "He is also a man who loves me in a way that I have never questioned. And those two things can both be true."

"Tell me more about the watching," she says.

"He is very perceptive," I say carefully. "Nothing gets past him. He builds a comprehensive picture of a situation before deciding how to respond. It's one of the things that makes him extraordinary and one of the things that keeps me slightly on guard, even now, even after everything."

"On guard," she repeats.

"Not afraid," I say quickly. And then, because I have been practicing honesty in this room, I say, "Not exactly."

She lets that sit.

"There was someone," I say. The words come out before I have fully decided to say them, the way they sometimes do in here. "We talked about him before. The person who ended things abruptly. Who left."

"Yes," she says.

"I've been thinking about him more than usual lately. About what that was. About what it meant for both of us, for Adam and me together." I look at the branch. "I think Adam cared about him very much. And I think a part of Adam also felt—not threatened, exactly, but something adjacent to threatened. Something he would never have named out loud as that. But I saw it sometimes."

Dr. Carver's pen has stopped moving. She watches me with the full, unhurried attention.

"And you're wondering if the same dynamic is present with Nora," she says.

"Yes." I feel the relief of having it named by someone else. "I'm wondering if what looks like generosity is actually something more controlled than generosity. If by offering me something he knows he can monitor, he keeps it inside the frame he can manage."

"That's a sophisticated concern," she says.

"I've had a lot of time to think."

She makes a small sound that might be agreement. "And you're worried this connection with Nora might end abruptly, and without resolution, the way things ended with the man you've mentioned?"

The question arrives with the surgical precision that Dr. Carver's questions always arrive with, and I feel my chest go tight in the specific way it goes tight when a door I have been careful about is being opened from the outside.

"Yes," I say.

Because it is true. It is completely true. But it is not the whole truth either. The whole truth is that when I imagine things ending abruptly for Nora, I am not imagining her leaving. I am not imagining a departure, a disagreement, a relationship that runs its course and closes with the kind of grief that can be named and carried and eventually set down.

I am imagining the other thing.

The thing I will not look at directly. The thing I have been walking around in this room and every other room for months, leaving it in my peripheral vision because if I look at it straight on, I will not be able to function. The thing that tells me that the reason I cannot simply trust Adam's offer is that I have watched what Adam is willing to do to protect us, and Nora's value to that protection is entirely contingent on her never knowing too much.

If she knew what we did, she would not be safe.

I know this. I have known it since the morning she came in shaking from the park. I have known it since Allison said the words, and I watched Adam's jaw set the way it does when he moves from processing to action. Nora's safety and Nora's knowledge are in direct proportion to each other, and the flutter in my chest and the love in Adam's offer and all of it, all of it, exists inside that calculation, whether any of us is willing to say so or not.

I sit with my hands in my lap and say none of this.

"Does Adam want to be involved in a relationship with Nora himself?" Dr. Carver asks.

"No," I say. "He's been clear about that. He doesn't have feelings for her in that way."

"But he's offering you permission to."

"More than permission." I search for the right word. "Encouragement, maybe. I think—" I stop.

She waits.

"I think part of what Adam is offering me is the same thing he had." The words land carefully, one at a time. "With the man I mentioned. He had something I didn't fully have. The specific experience of loving someone outside the two of us and being loved back by them, the way it changes you, the way it changed our marriage." I look at my hands. "I think Adam knows what that gave him. And I think he loves me enough to want me to have it too."

Dr. Carver is very still.

"How does that make you feel?" she asks.

I almost laugh. Not because it's funny, but because I don't have an answer for that question. It makes me feel loved, and it makes me feel managed, and it makes me feel terrified, and it makes me feel, underneath all of that, something warm and stubborn and inconvenient that I have been pressing my hand against for weeks as if I could keep it still by force.

"Grateful," I say. "Scared. Both at once."

She nods slowly. She looks at her notepad for a

moment, then looks back at me, and something is in her expression I have not seen before. Not the neutral. Not the careful attention. Something more specific.

"Reese," she says.

The way she says my name is different. Slower.

"I want to ask you something, and I want you to take a moment before you answer."

My hands are very still in my lap.

"Okay," I say.

"You've described a relationship that ended abruptly and without resolution. You've described a fear that the same thing could happen to Nora. You've told me that Adam is a man who watches—and that things he puts away don't always stay there." She pauses. "And today you came in after a woman you've described as unstable and delusional was apparently specific enough in her accusations to frighten your nanny."

I don't speak. I feel my pulse in my throat.

"When you say you're afraid things will end for Nora the same way they ended for the man you mentioned—" She stops. Her pen is not moving. The room is entirely still. "I want to make sure I understand what you're afraid of."

The silence stretches.

I'm looking at her, and she's looking at me, and I can feel, with absolute precision, the architecture of the room behind the room. The sealed door. The thing I have been building a life on top of. I can feel it the way you feel a foundation shift, just slightly, just enough to know that the ground is not as solid as you decided it was.

"I'm afraid of loss," I say. "Of caring about someone and losing them."

Dr. Carver holds my gaze for one beat too long.

"That's a very—human thing to be afraid of," she says.

She looks down at her notepad.

She writes something.

I watch the pen move, and I cannot see what it says, and I think, with the cold clarity of someone who has spent a long time living alongside a secret, that she is writing something she will want to remember. Not a word or two. Something longer. Something she is going to come back to.

She caps the pen.

"Same time next week?" she asks.

Her voice is exactly as it always is. Warm. Unhurried. Professionally neutral.

And yet.

"Yes," I say. "Of course."

I drive home with both hands on the wheel and the particular sensation I have not felt since the early months after Joe. The sensation of having said too much without knowing exactly what it was. Of having handed someone a piece of something without understanding which piece it was or what they could build from it.

I think about what she wrote.

I think about the one beat too long.

I think about the way she said "very human" with the particular pause before it.

The lake appears between the trees as I turn onto our road, gray and patient and enormous, the way it always is.

I press the accelerator and drive toward it.

TWENTY

REESE

I'm three miles from home when my phone rings.

Adam's name appears on the screen. I answer it on the first ring.

"Hey," I say.

"Hey." A pause. The kind of pause that causes me to brace myself because it is clear something big is coming. "Marcus called."

I grip the wheel a little tighter. "Okay."

"They found the accident site."

"Good, maybe now they can finally get that woman the help she clearly needs," I reply.

I hear an audible swallow on the phone. "They didn't find Allison."

The trees on either side of Lakeshore pass in my peripheral vision, and I watch the center line as I try to process what he has just said.

"I don't understand," I say. "What does that mean?"

"The car was there." His voice is controlled. "It was

in the ditch, right where Nora described it. But it was empty. No Allison."

The silence in the car is very loud.

"So what, she just walked away from the accident?" I ask. "Why would she just leave? Do they think she went to get help?"

"Maybe," Adam says. "Marcus said that the detective he spoke to told him there hadn't been any other reports of the accident, so if she did go to get help, nobody has called in to report it.

"Adam—"

"Reese, don't start letting yourself spiral into possibilities. The car didn't look like a high-speed impact. She had airbags—

"Wait, the airbags were deployed?"

"Yeah, Marcus said the police thought maybe when the car landed in the ditch, it was enough of a jolt to deploy them," Adam explains.

My head spins as I try to understand what could have possibly happened to Allison. "If the airbags deployed, wouldn't she have needed medical attention?"

"Not necessarily," he says in that voice that I know is him trying to reassure me. "She could have gotten out on her own and flagged someone down or called a car. We just have no idea at this point."

"What aren't you telling me?" I press.

"The police did say even though she hasn't been missing for the required length of time for a missing person's report, they are going to operate as if that's what this were."

"Wait, what? Why?"

"No one has shown up at a hospital. A call was put out looking for someone matching her description, but nothing has come back from that. Marcus is still making calls, but essentially the contact he has says it's a suspicious-looking scene," he continues.

I take the turn onto the last stretch of road before the lake appears in the gap between the trees.

"Suspicious how?"

"I don't think they really shared their thoughts, just that the scene wasn't making a lot of sense."

"Do they think something happened to her?"

"Reese, that's what I am trying to tell you. They really don't have a clue what happened."

"We know what happened. Nora already told us," I say, growing frustrated with the situation.

"Yes, they know that part. It's more about what happened to Allison after the accident. They're looking for her, so I'm sure they will find her soon."

Then I suddenly have the thought that perhaps Allison became enraged when Nora didn't heed her warning and instead tried to get away from her, causing her to crash into the ditch.

"You don't think she could be coming to our house, do you?" I ask, regretting that we ever let a random stranger we met online come back to our home.

"I don't think so, but we will be extra aware of the doors and windows until they find her, okay?"

"Do you think she would really hurt us?"

"I don't know what to think. I never expected half the shit she's done," Adam says before letting out an exaggerated sigh.

"So what do we do now?" The question comes out smaller than I intended. I hate how small it sounds.

"You focus on getting home. That's what you do right now."

"Adam—"

"Reese." His voice is steady and deliberate. "The house is locked. I've checked every door and every window. Nora is here with Josie, and they're both fine. We are all here, and we are all safe, and that is what matters right now." He sighs. "Just get home."

"I'm two minutes away," I say.

"I know. I can see your location."

Of course he can.

"We'll figure out the next step when you're here," he says. "Together. The way we always do."

The way we always do. I think about the last time we figured out a next step together. I think about the carriage house this morning. The clean concrete floor. The previous contents of that room scattered across half the county in pieces too small to understand on their own.

I think about Allison's empty car in a ditch.

I think about what it means that she walked away.

"Okay," I say.

"Almost home," he says.

"Almost."

I turn into the drive. The lights of the house are on, every one of them, warm and yellow against the early dark. Through the front window, I can see the shape of Nora moving in the kitchen. Even from here, even through the glass and the distance, I feel the flutter in my chest that I have stopped pretending isn't there.

I park and sit for a moment with the engine off.

I get out of the car, trying not to think about the fact that Allison is missing. I try not to think about not knowing if the danger comes from her coming to harm my family, or from the things she told Nora. Did she have some sort of proof about Joe we hadn't thought about? It seems impossible, but so does her simply randomly suggesting we murdered a previous male partner.

Adam opens the front door before I reach it.

He puts his arms around me in the doorway, and I let him, my face against his chest. Over his shoulder, I can see Nora at the kitchen island with Josie on her hip. Josie's small hand grips the collar of Nora's shirt.

Nora looks up.

Our eyes meet across the length of the house.

She doesn't smile. Neither do I. But something passes between us in the held moment before Adam steps back and brings me inside. Something that has no name yet, but that both of us, I think, are already learning the shape of.

TWENTY-ONE

REESE

I don't sleep.

Not well. Not the deep, forgetful sleep I've been learning to find again over the past few months. I lie in the bed and look at the ceiling, and I think about an empty car in a ditch on Lakeshore.

An empty car.

I have been turning those three words over since Adam said them on the phone, pressing them from different angles. She walked away. Maybe. The most ordinary explanation. A car goes off the road. The driver is shaken but mobile. She gets out, flags someone down, and goes somewhere. People do this every day.

But.

Allison, who sent letters careful enough to be threatening without being actionable. Allison, who found Nora in the park and said *your employers killed someone* with the specific, targeted confidence of a person who believes what they are saying. Allison, who followed a car with a baby in it and pushed it toward the edge of the road, was determined to be heard.

That person doesn't walk away and go somewhere quietly.

That person is somewhere with a purpose.

I press my hand flat against my sternum. The flutter is not there tonight. What is there is the shape of Allison's face in the grocery store parking lot. The controlled, terrible smile. The empty basket.

She came to the park with nothing. She went to the grocery store with nothing. We are the thing she is focused on. The baggage she seems to carry with her all the time.

I turn it and turn it, and I can't find the angle that makes sense. She is either somewhere gathering herself for the next move, or somewhere she can't move from at all. Both of those possibilities have their own particular weight, and I can't decide which is heavier.

I close my eyes.

I think about Josie asleep down the hall.

I think about the way she reaches for me when I pick her up, both arms out. She reaches with her whole self. She has not yet learned to protect herself from disappointment, and I want to keep it that way for as long as I possibly can.

I breathe in through my nose and out through my mouth.

Eventually, I find a thin and restless sleep.

In the morning, the house is full of the sounds of Nora and Josie. I sit at the kitchen island with my coffee and listen to Nora read to Josie from the bird book—she has a whole system with it now. The particular voices she uses for different species, and the comments she makes on the illustrations, with a serious expression, as if she is actually taking stock of the facts being relayed. And I feel the flutter, which has returned now that sleep has created some distance between me and last night's particular dread.

I have been thinking about the flutter. Not about what to do with it. That question feels too large still. Instead, I have been thinking about what it means that I have it. What it says about the state of things. What it says about who I am, in this particular season of my life. After everything that happened with Joe, what does it say that my body would even entertain such a physical response to her closeness?

I used to think I knew who I was. Before Joe. Before Josie. Before the gray that came after Josie's arrival and the slow, difficult return from it. I used to think the self was a thing that could be fixed. A place that, when you became disconnected, you could return to when life's circumstances allowed. I understand now that it isn't. The self is something you build, only to have it destroyed by the brutality of the world. You can't find it because that version of yourself has been destroyed. Instead, you have to rebuild, and the materials change depending on what's available and what's been lost.

I think I'm starting to understand. Nora is one of the materials.

I sit with the flutter. I don't reach for it, and I don't push it away.

Adam comes home in the early afternoon.

I hear his car in the drive and his key in the lock.

"Hey," he says. I'm the first thing he sees when he walks in.

"Hey."

He sets his keys on the counter. He looks at me with careful attention, and I can see that he wants to say something to me, but he isn't certain now is the time. Or perhaps he's uncertain it is information I can handle. I might be fragile, but it's irritating after what I did for us that he doesn't seem to understand there isn't much I can't handle in this world.

"Where are they?" he asks.

"Napping. Both of them." I nod toward the baby monitor on the counter. "Josie went down twenty minutes ago. Nora said she was going to lie down for a bit."

He nods. He pours himself a coffee and stands at the counter, and we are quiet for a moment.

"No word from Marcus," he says, knowing me well enough to know that Allison is at the forefront of my mind.

"I've been thinking about it all night. I could barely sleep," I reply.

"Not sleeping isn't going to change the situation. You need to find a way to put your mind at ease about these sort of things, or eventually, it will start to impact your health," he says, and all I can think about when he does is how it never made sense to me that he could compartmentalize so easily.

"That's easy to say to me, but it's not how I'm wired."

"Fair enough," he says. "So what conclusions did you come to from your restless night?"

"None." I wrap my hands around my own cup. "I don't know what the empty car means. I don't know if we should be more afraid or less afraid than we were before."

He nods slowly.

"I think," he says, choosing the words with care, "that the most useful thing right now is to not let it become the only thing. We watch. Marcus watches. We stay alert. But we don't let the uncertainty of it—" He pauses. "We don't let the not knowing become its own burden on our minds."

I look at him.

"You're very good at that," I say.

"At what?"

"Not letting things become a burden on your mind." I say it without edge, but his expression tells me he's unsure how I intend the statement. "I mean it as a genuine observation. That's all."

He is quiet for a moment. He looks out the window at the lake.

"Reese," he says.

"Yes."

He doesn't say anything for a long moment. I watch his profile, the familiar geometry of him. He's working up to something.

"I've been watching you," he says. "The changes in you. The painting, the therapy, the—" He stops, then starts again. "You're more yourself than you've been in over a year. It's like something that had been compressed has had room to expand again. I'm really proud of how hard you've been working to find yourself again."

I wait. He turns from the window and looks at me. "Thank you," I say with a small smile tugging at the corner of my mouth.

"I've been thinking about something," he says. "And I need you to hear it the way I mean it before your mind builds the version of it that it's afraid of."

I laugh. "Okay, that setup doesn't cause me to worry at all."

He lowers his gaze, letting me know this isn't a joking matter to him.

"What is it?" I inquire, trying to hide the fact that the muscles in my shoulder have tensed as if I'm bracing for impact.

"I love you."

"I know. And I love you too."

He nods once. He takes a breath. And then he tells me.

He says it carefully, measured and deliberate with his words. He tells me how happy it has made him to watch me building a friendship with Nora. The conversation takes a turn when he brings up Joe. He says that when we loved Joe, he could feel that I didn't love him any less. Then he explains that his love for Joe didn't take anything from his love for me.

"Why are you saying all of this?" I ask.

"I don't want to stand in the way of something bringing you back to me. I want you to be happy."

"I am happy."

"Reese." He looks at me. His eyes tell me he doesn't want to discuss it and that this is more for informational purposes.

I look at my husband.

I want to ask him if he's thought about what happens next. Not in the abstract but in the specific. The specifics of Nora in this house, of Josie growing up in the particular atmosphere of it. There is more to consider now. The three of us building something that will have to be managed and navigated and held with both hands every single day won't be as easy with a child in the home. I want to ask him if he's thought about what it cost us last time.

Instead, I say, "Adam."

He says, "I know."

And we sit together at the kitchen island while the lake moves outside, and Josie and Nora sleep.

TWENTY-TWO

REESE

I'm awake before anyone else.

In the morning, the lake is the color of pewter. The way it transforms itself depending on the time of day or the season is one of the things I love most about painting it. I sometimes think I wish I could transform myself as easily.

I lie still for a long time, and I don't reach for the day. I stare out at the lake through the large window in our bedroom. I practice what Dr. Carver has been calling receptivity—the difference between meeting the day as an adversary and allowing it to arrive on its own terms. She suggested it after I described mornings feeling like ambushes, and the feeling that consciousness carried with it the full weight of everything that came before it. She said, "Let the day come to you. You don't have to meet it halfway. The day will happen either way, but when you start greeting it on your own terms, it can feel like yours again."

I've been practicing. Today has been easier than most days.

The first thing my mind goes to is warmth.

I lie with that. I don't try to explain it or interrogate it. I have spent too much of my life doing both of those things, circling every feeling until I've worn a groove in it. I am starting to learn that some things are simply true before they are understood. The warmth is one of them. It lives in my chest, and I give it permission to be there without requiring it to justify itself.

I think about Adam.

Be happy. Two words carrying sixteen years of everything behind them. I think about what it cost him to say them—not the generosity of the gesture, which I don't question, but the specific quality of love that can see what someone else needs and step out of the way of it. He could see that I needed to find my own way through the dark. He loves me enough to let me find it.

I close my eyes, and I hold that.

By eight o'clock, the house is in its morning motion.

Nora is in the kitchen when I come downstairs, Josie in the crook of one arm, moving along the counter with efficient multitasking. She looks up when I appear.

There is a moment. Not long—a fraction of a second, shorter than a breath, the kind that would be invisible to anyone not looking for it. But I'm looking. What I see in that fraction is not the warm professional expression she produces for regular mornings. It is something less managed. Something closer to the surface.

Then it settles back into the warmth, and she says,

"Good morning," and I say, "Good morning," and the morning proceeds.

Even as I work to quiet my overthinking, it surfaces. I'm questioning whether that fraction of a second actually happened or if I invented it. I carry the thought with my coffee and do not answer it.

Adam comes home at noon.

He looks good. He looks rested, which is something neither of us has managed reliably for the better part of a year. He sets his keys down and crosses to me, kissing the side of my head with the unhurried ease of a man who has nowhere else to be. Then he goes to Josie, the way he always does, like a doting father. Those thoughts I am learning to quiet resurface. Doting father. Josie has Joe's eyes. Does Adam see them too? If he does, is he just choosing not to say anything? I focus on quieting the thoughts that lead nowhere good, reminding myself that even with Joe's eyes, Adam is her father.

He takes her face in both hands, and she grabs his nose immediately. He lets her have it with the expression he reserves only for her—fully unguarded. His delight is contagious when he is around Josie. He wears the face of a man who cannot account for his own luck.

"Hi, you." His voice drops into the register that belongs to her. "Miss me?"

Josie grabs his nose with both hands and delivers her verdict.

"I'll take that as a yes." He kisses her forehead and looks over her head at Nora with a smile of a man who is pleased with the room he is standing in.

"Good morning," he says.

"Good afternoon," Nora says, the gentle correction landing with a warmth that makes it feel like affection rather than a rebuke.

Adam looks at Josie with exaggerated gravity. "So, Josie. What do you say—should I tell them about the surprise dinner I planned?"

Josie renders her opinion.

"Keep it a surprise? That's exactly what I thought." He laughs. "I couldn't agree more."

"You're making dinner?" I ask.

"Josie has spoken," he says with finality. "You'll simply have to wait."

An involuntary smile spreads across my face. And I know the ease of these ordinary moments is the source of the warmth in my chest that I didn't attempt to name this morning.

Later in the afternoon, Adam appears in the living room doorway with Josie on his hip and the expression of a man executing a plan.

"You two need to leave," he announces.

Nora looks up from the book she has been reading. "Excuse me?"

"Josie and I are making dinner. It's a production. There are—" He pauses for effect. "Ingredients. And processes. And it is categorically a surprise, which means neither of you can be in this house."

I look at him.

He looks back at me with the particular expression he knows only I will understand. It's saying, *Take the time. I'm handing it to you. Be happy.*

Something moves through my chest.

Nora is already uncurling from the couch where she was busy making her shopping list for the grocery store on her phone. "What are we supposed to get?"

Adam shakes his head again as if he has no answers for us. "The two of you will just have to figure that out. It's out of my hands, Josie insisted."

Josie grabs his ear in confirmation.

I get my jacket, and seeing me, Nora does the same. I kiss Adam, then Josie, and walk to the door, Nora following close behind.

"Well, that was different," Nora says, a small laugh in her voice.

"That's Adam."

"So what do we do now?" she asks. Nora likes a plan, and I can see that at this moment, the lack of one is making her uncomfortable.

"How about a walk?" I suggest.

"A walk would be nice," she replies after a moment of contemplation.

"The beach can get pretty windy this time of year, but the waves are beautiful. You up for it?"

"Sure," she answers, shoving her hands into her pockets as she walks along next to me.

The path to the beach is steep.

It begins at the back of the property, past the garden and the edge of the lawn, where the landscaping gives way to something wilder. I take a deep breath as I walk through the scrub grass and around the exposed rocks, welcoming the smell of the lake rising through the trees in gusts. The path itself is narrow, cut into the bluff sometime before we bought the house. The wooden steps are weathered to a soft gray that feels like they grew here. You have to go single file, and a rope railing guides you.

Nora goes first.

I follow her down. By the time we reach the bottom, and the path opens onto the beach, she turns back to check that I am behind her. The expression on her face is something I haven't seen there before.

She is delighted.

The wind off the lake is cold, her hair is blowing in three directions, and the beach stretches in both directions. The private beach is shared with the other houses along the shoreline, and I'm not surprised to find it empty this time of year. Most residents prefer to only come down to the beach in the summer. It has never made sense to me that you wouldn't want to enjoy all the lake's personalities, but the peacefulness of the empty beach is a gift I am thankful for.

She looks at it, and she looks like a person who has just been handed something they didn't know they needed.

"How have I never been down here?" she says to herself more than to me.

"Adam comes down to run sometimes, but we honestly don't come down enough," I say.

"I would come down every day," she says.

I believe her. When we first moved into the house, I came down every day. In fact, I walked the beach every day until what I did to Joe.

We walk. I practice pushing the thought of Joe out of my mind.

Now that we are close to it, the choppy water has

shifted from pewter to a gray-green. We pause and look out at the body of water. It's enormous, with the horizon line very far away.

The sand shifts under our feet as we begin to walk the length of the beach. We walk close enough that our arms occasionally touch.

Neither of us mentions it.

"Do you paint it from life?" Nora asks after a while. "Or from memory?"

"Both," I say. "I used to set up on the bluff above the beach and paint the water directly, but I haven't done that in a long time. Other times, I paint it from inside the house, looking through the glass, which changes it."

"It does?"

I nod, "The light is different, more filtered. And sometimes I paint the version of it that lives inside me."

Nora is quiet for a moment, looking at the water.

"The one that lives inside you," she repeats. "I like that version."

"Me too. Photographs lie," I say. "They catch light correctly and everything else wrong."

She laughs.

"Do you miss it?" she asks. "When you can't paint?"

"I used to miss it the way you miss a limb," I say. "While I was pregnant with Josie, the gray came in, and I stopped being able to access it. I started to think I lost it, that maybe I didn't deserve it anymore." I watch a wave break close to our feet, and we both step back at the same moment.

"Why would you think you didn't deserve it?" she asks, and there is genuine concern in her voice.

I can't answer her honestly. I can't tell her about the guilt I carry every day for what I did to Joe. Or that as much as I want to believe Adam's version of Josie being a gift from Joe, all I can think is what if she is instead supposed to be a constant reminder of what happened. I shrug. "I don't know, I guess that's for my therapist to figure out," I joke, attempting to avoid the question.

"It's come back, though. But I won't pretend that year it was gone didn't scare me."

"What scared you most about it?"

The question is from someone who is genuinely asking, not from someone building toward something else.

I think about it honestly. "I suppose that it might have been permanent. The only version of myself I have ever known is the one that could make things. If the making was over..." I pause. "What would be left? If you lose the thing that makes you who you are, is there really much point to life?"

Nora is quiet.

"No," she says. Just that.

Something in the way she says it tells me she understands this not as an abstraction but as something she has encountered herself. I want to ask about it and give it the same space she always gives to what I say.

We walk a little farther. The beach curves slightly, and the bluff above us is higher here. The path back is invisible from this angle.

"Where did you grow up?" I ask, desperate to shift the conversation's focus.

She takes a breath. "We moved around a lot, but Chicago was where I spent most of high school."

"I see. Did one of your parents have a job that made you move around a lot?"

She nods. "My dad, but then his circumstances changed my freshman year in high school, which is why I got to stay in one place for so long."

"That must have been such a relief for you," I say, looking at her profile. A part of Nora comes a little more into focus as I realize my assumption that she has not been broken was quite wrong. What I hadn't understood about her was that she was broken and had reassembled herself. I couldn't see it because she didn't let that define her. She simply carries it the way you carry anything true about you.

"I'm sorry," I say.

She looks at me. "Don't be. It's what made me good at this job."

"How so?"

"Because I understand what it means for a child to need someone who is simply—present," she says. "Not perfect. Not performing. Just present and consistent."

I think about Josie. About the way she reaches for Nora with the full-body trust of someone who has learned that the reaching will be answered. My throat tightens, and I am suddenly more grateful than I realized that we found Nora.

"She's lucky," I say. "To have you."

Nora is quiet for a moment. "We're lucky to have each other," she says.

We stop walking eventually.

There is a shelf of flat rock jutting slightly above the waterline, smoothed by years of waves into something almost comfortable. Without discussing it, we sit on it, side by side, and look at the lake. The light is changing, the late afternoon starting to go golden at the edges.

"Do you ever get lonely?" Nora asks.

It catches me off guard at first. I am a wife and a mother, and on the surface, it feels like an odd question to ask someone with those titles. Then I consider the question a little more. "I suppose sometimes. After Josie was born, the loneliness I felt was the strangest kind. I had someone in my life who loved me and cared about me, but I couldn't be reached. I knew Adam was there, and he was trying, but it's like being behind glass. Everyone could see me, and I could see them, but there was no way through." I pause. "It's less like that now."

"What changed?"

I consider how much of the truth is mine to say and how much to hold.

"Therapy," I say. "The painting coming back to me helped. Adam, of course, helped me in many ways. And—"

Nora waits. She does not fill the silence.

"You," I say at last. "You changed it."

She looks at the water.

I look at the water.

Nora picks up a flat stone and turns it over in her hand.

"Thank you for sharing that with me. I haven't had this in a long time," she says quietly. "A place. People." She looks at the stone. "I've been a nanny for other families, of course, but I'm not talking about just being around people." She stops, and I can tell she's uncomfortable with being the one who's vulnerable.

"Nora."

She turns.

I reach over, and I put my hand over hers on the rock between us. She looks at my hand. She looks at my face. She doesn't move her hand away. "I'm glad you're here," I say.

She turns her hand over so that she is now holding my hand in return.

"I'm glad I'm here too," she says.

We sit with our hands together on the rock until the cold makes sitting impractical, then we stand. We don't discuss what just happened. We don't need to.

We begin the climb back up to the home that has the lights already on like a beacon, warm and yellow in the early dark. I climb toward the people I love who are inside waiting for us. Nora talks about a documentary she has been watching—something about migratory patterns, the long, improbable journeys birds make on instinct alone, and the way they navigate by starlight. She describes it with the same concentrated attention she gives to everything. Josie watches her face with the focused interest she gives to moving things and to Nora's voice specifically. I watch Josie watching Nora and feel the warmth layering itself over the warmth that was already there.

TWENTY-THREE

ADAM

I hear them before I see them.

Their voices carry up the path from the beach, arriving through the back door before they do. I hear Reese's laugh first, the real one, and then Nora's underneath it. There is the particular warmth of two people who have found the frequency of each other.

I stand at the stove with a wooden spoon in my hand and Josie on a blanket behind me, engaged in a serious inspection of a wooden block she has apparently decided deserves her full attention.

The back door opens.

They come in together, wind-cheeked and slightly disheveled from the bluff path. Reese looks like herself. Not the person who had been doing a Reese impression, but truly Reese.

"It smells incredible in here," she says.

"All Josie's doing," I say.

Josie, from the blanket, endorses this.

Dinner is for the four of us.

The table is set properly for the first time in longer than I want to calculate. We aren't gathered around the kitchen island, shoveling food in to simply get through the meal as quickly as we can. We are gathered at the table, a place designed for us to connect.

Once Josie is in her high chair, and Reese and Nora are seated, I set the pasta on the table.

"This looks beautiful," Nora says.

"Josie supervised," I say. "She had very clear instructions on where everything goes."

"Well then," Reese chimes as she looks at Josie. "Thank you for doing such a marvelous job, my beautiful girl. It's all so divine."

Josie bangs the tray, clearly impressed with herself.

We talk the way we have been talking more frequently in the evenings, the four of us. A conversation between people who are comfortable enough with each other that no one has to worry about entertaining anyone else.

Nora has been watching a documentary series. It is about deep-sea ecosystems and the particular strangeness of life at pressure, in the dark, where the rules of the biological world above the surface don't apply. Creatures that generate their own light. Relationships between organisms that have no equivalent anywhere else on earth.

"The part that gets me," she says. "Most of it has never been seen by human eyes. We've mapped less of the ocean floor than we've mapped the surface of Mars. Did you know that there are entire ecosystems down there that have existed for longer than our species and that will exist long after we're gone?"

"That's either comforting or terrifying," Reese says.

"Both," Nora says. "Definitely both."

Josie offers an opinion on the tiny pieces of food on the tray in front of her.

"She thinks it's comforting," I say.

"Well, we all know she's very wise," Nora says.

I tell them about the book I have been reading. It is about decision-making under uncertainty, specifically how human beings misread risk. I have been finding it, unexpectedly, one of the more personally relevant things I have read in years.

"We overestimate visible threats and underestimate invisible ones," I say. "We are much more afraid of things that have a face, such as a person, a creature, a storm we can watch approaching. Human beings are very bad at gauging long-term risk assessment, but very good at short-term threat response."

"That tracks," Reese says.

"We consistently underestimate our own capacity for adaptation," I add. "Which I will say has been the most enjoyable part of the book for me to read so far." I look at the table, at the food I made, and the people eating it.

Reese looks at me.

I look back at her.

Nora reaches over and refills Reese's wine without being asked.

Reese tells us about a show she has been tracking. It's a museum exhibition coming to the city in the late spring, a retrospective of a painter whose work she has loved since graduate school. She describes the specific qualities that make this artist's work significant, and as she talks about her face lights up."

"I want to see it twice," she says. "Once on my own and once with someone who will ask me questions about it."

"I'll ask you questions," Nora says.

Reese smiles and nods. "It's a date then."

I watch this and examine the way it makes me feel. I can confidently say I am glad. I wasn't sure how I would really feel as their relationship deepened, but as I watch them, I am now certain. I am glad.

After dinner, I do the dishes, despite both Reese and Nora trying to step in. Nora pushes until I finally agree to let her dry the dishes that I wash. Reese says she is going to put Josie down for bed and disappears a moment later. Nora and I talk about nothing in particular—the kind of conversation that exists to fill the comfortable space of shared activity. When Nora finishes drying, she says good night and takes her book to her room, and the house settles into its evening quiet. Reese comes back downstairs and finds me sitting on the couch with the rest of my wine.

"What are you thinking?" she asks as she sits down next to me, tucking her feet under her.

I think about how to answer honestly.

"I'm thinking about what it looks like," I say. "The life we're making."

"And?"

"And I like what I see." I look at the table. "There was a moment tonight when you were talking about the exhibition, and Nora was looking at you, and Josie was doing the thing she does with her spoon..." We both laugh at the mental image of Josie. "And I don't know, the only word I could think of was that it looked like enough."

Reese is quiet.

She looks at her wineglass.

"That's the thing about enough," she says. "You only recognize it when you're in it. You can't see it coming."

"No," I agree. "I guess you can't."

Later, after Reese has gone up to bed, I sit in the dark kitchen.

I sit with my thoughts about Allison. The thoughts I keep to myself. The ones I hide from Reese. She's still out there. This is the fact I carry underneath every other fact. The car in the ditch. The empty seat. No sighting. No resolution. She's out there somewhere with her anger and whatever she has been building toward. We don't know where she is or what she intends or when she intends it.

I think about the table tonight.

I think about Reese's laughter on the path, and Josie's face when I lifted her into the high chair, and Nora refilling the wine with the ease of someone who has decided to belong here. I think about how hard it was to get here.

And then I think about how I will not let anything destroy it.

I think about Reese.

About what she did and what it cost her and how hard it has been on her to carry that burden. I think about the nightmares she doesn't tell me about, but that wake me up. She did the thing I told her had to be done, and she has never once said it was my fault or used it against me. She has simply carried it. Every day.

As much as I wish I could take it from her, I cannot. That is one of the facts I have had to make my peace with. In the dark of this kitchen, though, I can make a promise and then keep it.

If Allison comes, if she arrives at our door with the intention of dismantling what we have built, she will find the price is higher than she calculated.

Reese did what had to be done once. I will not ask her to do it again.

My wife loves the water. One day, Josie will be old enough to take a walk with her down to the beach. She will frolic while Reese takes a mental image of the scene to paint later. I want her to have that. I will make sure she has it. I turn off the kitchen light. I go upstairs to my wife, knowing exactly what needs to be done if I ever see Allison again.

TWENTY-FOUR

REESE

I have been trying not to overanalyze the entire evening with Nora, as Dr. Carver instructed, but the more I try not to, the more I find myself stuck in an endless loop. As I drive to my appointment, I decide today is the day I open up a little more. I will ask questions that the honesty of has scared me up until now.

Once I am seated, I don't wait for Dr. Carver to ask me anything.

"I want to talk about something I haven't talked about enough," I say.

"Oh?" Dr. Carver adjusts slightly in her chair. "Okay," she says.

"Do you remember the man? The one I've mentioned," I begin.

"The one you and your husband had a romantic relationship with, but it ended abruptly?"

I hesitate, fear gripping for a moment. What I did, what we did, has to be a secret that remains buried forever for Josie's sake. I think about my words before I say them, careful not to say something that could reveal too much. "The dynamic of what we had. All three of us. I haven't described it to you accurately because I didn't think I was ready until now. But I think I need to now."

"I'm listening," she says.

I tell her. More than I have before. Not everything—never everything, that is simply not available in this room or any room—but more. I describe the way the three of us worked. The particular equilibrium of it. The way the house felt when he was in it. Then I describe the way Adam's love for him was different from mine. I tell her there was never a feeling of competition. That there was always enough of everything to go around. That it was the happiest I had been in years and that the happiness was not a guilty thing but a genuine one. I also tell her that the loss of it was one of the things I have been grieving.

I tell her that now, looking at where I am, I think some part of me has been trying to find my way back to that particular quality of happiness and that I've been afraid to admit that because admitting it feels like saying that what I have with Adam isn't enough.

Dr. Carver writes several lines. Not her usual word or two.

"And then it ended," she says.

"Abruptly." I hold her gaze. "He died." I can't believe that the two words left my mouth. I know instantly that it is more than I should have said, but as much as I wish I could grab the words out of the air and put them back into my mouth, it's too late. They live here now. Out in the real world.

The room is very still.

I watch Dr. Carver's face for some indication of what she is thinking, but like usual I have no idea what is going through her mind.

"Why do you think you are only just now telling me that the sudden end to your relationship was due to his death?" Dr. Carver asks.

I don't know how to answer. If I were telling the truth, I would say it's because I couldn't tell you. I couldn't tell you because we killed him. I killed him.

"I think because I didn't feel like I was entitled to grieve him."

"Why is that?"

Because I killed him. "Because as far as the world was concerned, he was just a sexual partner. You grieve someone you love, and maybe somewhere in my mind I thought I wasn't allowed to love him because I love my husband."

"From what you have told me, both you and your husband loved him," Dr. Carver's words make me wonder if she is questioning the honesty of my answer.

"I didn't say it made sense," I reply, hoping it's enough. "It was sudden," I continue. "Unexpected. There was no warning and no preparation. We had no chance to say the things you'd say if you knew it was coming. No goodbye. No—" I stop. I breathe. "No resolution."

"That's a particular kind of grief," she says. "The unfinished kind."

"Yes."

"And Adam?"

"What do you mean?"

"You said he loved him as well. Do you think your husband has actually grieved the sudden loss?"

The truth is, I don't know the answer to her question. Sometimes Adam decides that something is over and closes the door on it very quickly. "Honestly? I have no idea." I answer truthfully.

Dr. Carver's pen moves. She looks up.

"You haven't discussed him since he died?"

"Just mentions in passing," I say.

"I see. Do you think maybe the reason Adam wanted you to go to therapy was because he was scared of losing you too?" I'm surprised at how much insight Dr. Carver has about Adam, considering she has never actually met him.

"I could see that being a thought for him," I agree.

We sit in quiet as she jots down a few more notes in her notebook. And then she asks the question that takes the air out of my lungs, "How did he die?"

I feel it. A tightening in my sternum. A sense of the floor being very slightly less solid than it was a moment ago. My mouth makes a decision before my mind has finished its deliberations.

"An accident," I say. "On the water."

I sit with them, and immediately, with a cold, detailed clarity, I understand what I have done.

On the water. Not a car accident like a normal person would say. Not simply an accident, which would have been vague enough to move the conversation in a new direction. I fucking said the words "on the water." It's specific. It's foolish. It's dangerous.

I have been so careful. I have been so careful for so long, and in three words, I have handed someone a thread that, if she pulls it—I can't let my mind go there.

Dr. Carver writes something.

I watch the pen move, and I wait.

She puts the pen down.

"I'm sorry," she says. "That kind of loss being unresolved and then on top of that, it being circumstances outside the ordinary, it can make processing the grief very difficult to navigate."

I exhale.

"Thank you."

Hope blossoms in my chest when she doesn't ask a follow-up.

I do not let my relief show, because showing relief would itself be a kind of evidence. I have spent too long in this room to make that mistake. I can't afford any more mistakes.

"So what about this relationship that made you want to discuss it more today?" she asks.

"Oh, yes—well, I guess I've been a little worried. I think when Adam offered me the chance to pursue something with our nanny, maybe he saw it as completing a circle. Giving me the thing he had. But what if this new thing makes him feel excluded? I guess I just don't want to entertain the idea of something more with Nora unless I know it won't hurt him."

"We can't know these things in advance. I think it's okay that you want to proceed with caution, but just as you were unaware of how your husband having a relationship with this other man would make you feel, he can't possibly know how this would make him feel. That being said, you two do seem to have very open and honest communication, and I don't get the impression he's trying to lay a trap for you or something if that is what you are worried about."

"Oh God, no. Never." I reply instantly.

"In any relationship that involves more than two people," Dr. Carver continues, "communication isn't optional. It's structural. It's the load-bearing thing." She looks at me steadily. "He's doing his part. He's telling you what he needs. You have to give him the benefit of the doubt, and take what he says at face value."

Her words slam into me as I realize what I have been doing. I haven't been giving Adam the same trust he gave me. When I told him I was okay with Joe, he didn't question me. He simply accepted it. Dr. Carver is right. It's time for me to accept Adam's gift of me, Nora, exploring a connection, and to quit allowing my mind to create problems where none may exist.

"Thank you, Dr. Carver," I say, and I mean it. I also try to practice not overthinking the fact that I revealed Joe died or that I said on the water as the session ends.

TWENTY-FIVE

REESE

I tell Nora that Adam and I have a date planned for the evening and need her to watch Josie. I want to tell Nora that I think she's beautiful and that my husband has told me he just wants me to be happy, but before I do, I need to have one final conversation with him. I need to see in his eyes that he is okay with this.

Nora has become a part of this home. I know the sound of her footsteps on the stairs. I know the particular way she hums when she's doing something that doesn't require her full attention. I know the three different laughs she uses for Josie and what each of them means. I have learned her the way you learn the things that are present every day.

She turns, and Josie is on her hip. She looks at me with the directness and warmth that is so immediately and entirely Nora. I feel the flutter.

"Wait, is this a proper date. Like dress up and dinner?" she teases.

I smile. "Maybe even a movie first." I pause. "I think we need it."

"I think that's really good," she says. "You two should do that." She shifts Josie on her hip. "He'll love it."

"You think?"

"Reese." She says my name with the particular tone she uses when she thinks I am undercutting something that doesn't deserve it. "That man lights up when you walk into a room. Yes. He'll love it."

When the evening approaches, I dress carefully, wondering if Adam will notice before the thought quickly disappears. He always notices. Before Josie there was a version of me that dressed for things. That spent time in front of the mirror not from vanity but from the particular pleasure of making a deliberate choice about how to present herself to the world. I'm not sure if it was motherhood or the grief about Joe that caused this version of me to retreat, but something is exciting about seeing a glimpse of that version of me.

The blue dress. I bought it before Josie, before any of this, when I still had the instinct to buy things. I have not worn it. I never had the opportunity before—before everything changed. It hangs in the back of the closet.

I pull it out and put it on.

It still fits. A little differently than when I purchased it, but it fits nonetheless.

I stand in front of the mirror, and I look at myself for a moment. I feel the thing I have been feeling more frequently in the past few months. It's the thing that has been arriving with less effort than it used to—recognition. The sense of a self returning from wherever it went. I look at the woman in the mirror, and I think, with a surprise that still has not entirely become ordinary, there you are.

Adam stands at the bottom of the stairs. He looks up when he hears me coming down. He looks at me the way he looked at me when I walked down the aisle sixteen years ago, and the way he looked at me the day Josie was born, and the way he looks at me in the moments when I am the only thing in the world he wants to look at.

"You look beautiful," he says.

"You say that every time."

"You look beautiful every time." He says.

I reach the bottom of the stairs, and he puts his hand on my face briefly. Then he steps back and looks at me with a tender smile planted firmly on his face.

Nora comes out of the kitchen. She's bouncing Josie on her hip, who is wearing her duck pajamas and who has recently developed an unfavorable opinion about bedtime.

"You two look amazing," she offers, and I can hear the warmth in her words.

We all chat for a moment about our plans before Nora adds, "Okay, you two. Go. Have fun. We'll be perfectly fine."

Adam looks at his watch, realizing we are cutting it close to making it to the movie on time. "Oh shit, we'd better get going if we are going to make it on time." A moment later, he's at the door, keys in hand.

Nora reaches out and grips my arm. I pause and look back at her. "I mean it," she says, words meant just for me. "You look amazing. Have fun, okay?"

I smile and nod before I step back and turn toward the door. I am almost through it when Adam stops. He turns back. His hand is on the frame, and he looks at Nora.

"Nora," he says.

"Yes?"

He glances at me and then back at Nora. "If Allison shows up tonight—"

Nora's expression doesn't change. "She won't," she says.

"If she does." Adam's voice is even. "Call the police first and then call me immediately."

Nora looks at him.

"I understand," she says. "She won't come here. But if she does, I know what to do."

"Good," he says. He places his hand on my back, and we step out into the evening.

The door closes behind us.

Adam puts his hand in mine, and I take it, and the contact is warm and certain.

We walk to the car, hand in hand, and above us the sky deepens. For the first time in longer than I can remember, I am simply here. In this moment. With this man. Going on a date.

TWENTY-SIX

REESE

The movie is something neither of us would have chosen on our own.

A thriller that is fast and loud, with relentless tension. Under ordinary circumstances, this would not be what I want from an evening. Under ordinary circumstances, I prefer the slow films, the ones that trust you to sit with something unresolved.

But ordinary circumstances are not what tonight is.

Tonight, I want exactly this—to be in the dark, in the noise, thinking about nothing except what is on the screen in front of me. Two hours where the only thing required of me is that I keep my eyes open.

Adam's arm comes around me, and I lean into his side. He pulls me slightly closer without breaking his attention from the screen, a small instinctive adjustment.

On the screen, someone is running. Someone is always running in these films. I'm content at this moment. I'm happy.

After the movie, we walk to dinner through the cool of the evening.

Adam's hand is in mine, and the street is full of the specific Saturday-night energy of the neighborhood. Restaurants have their doors open, and a dog on a leash is straining toward something interesting at the base of a parking meter. The ordinary theater of other people's lives.

As we continue walking, Dr. Carver's words settle in my head. *Communication isn't optional. It's structural. It's the load-bearing thing. He's doing his part. He's telling you what he needs. You have to give him the benefit of the doubt and take what he says at face value.*

His thumb moves against my hand. It's a small motion that stirs big feelings. I am here. I am in this. This is the living.

The Italian place on the corner has been there for thirty years. With dark paneling and white tablecloths, it has never tried to update itself and is better for it. We have been coming here for ten years, and the host knows us by name. He seats us at the corner table without being asked because that's the one we always want, and he understood this sometime in year three and has never needed to be reminded since.

We sit. We don't look at the menus. We have been ordering the same things here for years. There's the specific comfort of a choice you don't have to make.

"I've missed this," Adam says.

"Me too." I reach across and put my hand over his. "I'm sorry it took me this long."

He turns his hand and holds mine.

"Don't apologize." He shakes his head slightly. "What you went through would have leveled most people. You got through it, and you're getting better, and you're here."

The wine arrives. We order. We talk about the movie and the particular preposterousness of the third act. Then we move into other conversations about a book Adam has been reading, about Josie's developing opinions on bedtime, and her latest favorite food.

Eventually, Adam thanks me for suggesting the evening out. I'm about to bring up the reason I wanted us to go out in the first place, but he beats me to it.

"I can tell that your connection with Nora seems to be getting even deeper," he says at last.

"Actually, I was hoping to talk to you about that," I say, relieved he was the one to bring up her name first. "I know what you said about you just wanting me to be happy."

"And I meant it."

"I just wanted to talk to you one more time to see if anything had changed."

"Reese, what's this all about?"

"Well, the night you made us dinner, it was amazing. Thank you for that."

"I wanted to."

"I know, but I just wanted to check in with you and see how you were feeling about the whole Nora situation." He doesn't say anything in response. "I just think that communication is important, and I wanted to check in to see how you are feeling about it before—"

"Before what?"

"Before I tell Nora how I feel about her," I say.

He laughs. "I'm pretty sure she already knows how you feel."

"I mean, yes, but she also is very respectful of us and our marriage. I don't think she would do anything about it unless she understood that you were really okay with it," I explain.

"And I told you that I am. I just want you to be happy."

My instincts tell me to push and make sure he's being honest, but then I hear Dr. Carver's words in my head, and instead, I take his words at face value.

We are halfway through our entrées when my phone buzzes against the table. With the reflex of a parent, I glance at it before I can decide not to. A name I don't expect.

Dr. Carver.

My therapist does not text me in the evenings. She communicates through her office and via scheduled appointments. She has a careful framework for a professional relationship. A text on a Saturday evening is outside the frame.

I read it once.

I read it again.

> Dr. Carver: Reese. I am sorry to bother you on the weekend.

I was at my office this evening getting caught up on paperwork when a woman showed up. She was asking questions about you and your husband. She kept mentioning a man named Joe. I don't mean to worry you, but she didn't seem stable. I wanted you to be safe and aware.

The table goes very far away.

"Reese? What's wrong?" Adam's voice cuts through the noise in my head briefly.

The room tilts, and I can't find the words to explain what Dr. Carver just texted to me. I hand him the phone and watch him read it.

He reads it twice. He hands it back.

"Text her back."

"What do you want me to say?"

"Ask her if the woman told her a name and then ask her what she told her."

My thumbs move, doing as I was instructed.

Dr. Carver's response arrives in two messages.

Dr. Carver: She didn't say her name, but she was very scary. You need to take this seriously.

Dr. Carver: I told her that I was your doctor, and I would never share what a patient tells me. She kept pushing. She said your name, Adam's name, and she kept talking about some man named Joe. I told her that I could honestly say you had never mentioned anyone named Joe to me.

I sit with that sentence. *I could honestly say you had never mentioned anyone named Joe to me.*

She said it because it was exactly, technically, completely true. I never said his name. Not once, not in any of the sessions. I always referred to him as a man or him or the person.

> Reese: Thank you. Are you okay? Did she threaten you?

> Dr. Carver: She said some things. I've already called the police. I wanted you to know first. Please be careful.

I put the phone face down on the white tablecloth and look at Adam. Adam looks at me.

"Nora," he says as he picks up his phone, worry spreading across his face. My heart thuds in my chest.

He dials, and then he waits. The response arrives.

"Nora, it's Adam. Is everything okay there?"

Something in his shoulders releases by a fraction.

"Good. Okay, just make sure the doors are locked, and we will be heading home shortly," he adds. Nora says something else before Adam adds, "No, we're still at the restaurant, but we should be leaving soon."

After he hangs up, he says, "They're fine. Josie's down." He puts the phone in his jacket pocket.

"Why didn't you tell her about Dr. Carver's text?" I ask.

"Because scaring her wouldn't have done any good," he replies.

"Adam," I say.

"I know." His voice is quiet and direct, and in those three words, we have an entire conversation in which I tell him I'm scared, and he tells me he's scared too, but not to worry, because he will make sure nothing happens to our family.

When I look at this man, I understand why we have survived through everything. We know each other, the good and the bad, in a way nobody else does, and we simply accept it as part of each other.

He flags the server for the check.

We drive home through the dark.

Lakeshore unspools in the headlights. The curve after the park where they found Allison's car abandoned in the ditch. I have driven this road hundreds of times, and I know every feature of it the way I know Adam's face and Josie's laugh. This is the life I have built, and the text from my therapist is a message that someone is trying to take it away.

Adam's hands are steady on the wheel.

Mine are folded in my lap.

Neither of us speaks.

I think about Allison.

Could she really have gone to my therapist's office, and if so, with what purpose? Was she trying to create some sort of doubt in Dr. Carver's mind about me? Did she tell Dr. Carver that I was a killer? Was she trying to make my therapist think that I was a killer? If so, why? Was she no longer trying to convince us to be with her, and instead was she now trying to ruin us? None of it made sense.

If she wasn't trying to make Dr. Carver see me as a murderer, maybe she thought I told my secrets to the good doctor. Perhaps Allison went there trying to obtain proof from my therapist that I did, in fact, kill our boyfriend. Did she hate us so much that it was all she could think about? Destroying our lives?

Allison is somewhere right now, having not found what she was looking for from Dr. Carver, and I do not know what she will do next.

The lake disappears between the trees.

Appears again.

Disappears.

Adam turns down our long private driveway.

The lights of the house come into view through the trees.

I press my hands flat on my thighs, and I look at them, and I breathe.

We are almost home.

TWENTY-SEVEN

ADAM

I'm in my office with the door closed.

On the desk in front of me is a manila folder that my attorney sent over. The paperwork inside it is for our will. We've needed to do this since the week Josie was born—the specific and nonnegotiable adult reckoning with the fact that you have created a person who depends entirely on you. I have handled the financial structures, the trusts, and the accounts. But I have been avoiding the will itself in the way I avoid very few things: completely and with intention.

There of course is the piece where I have had enough death in my life in the past year. But underneath that is the question of what happens to the people I love after I'm gone. Joe was in the foster care system, and the stories he told us are enough to make anyone's heart break a little. I don't want that for Josie, but what if something happens to us? Who would take her? Who would raise her? Reese and I do not have relationships with anyone from our families, and in no world would I place my daughter into the care of any of those monsters. So who? Who cares for Josie if something happens to us?

Unable to find the answer to the question that has been haunting me, my mind shifts to another question. Allison. Where is she? What is she planning?

What were her intentions when using Joe's name at Dr. Carver's office? What information did she have about Joe that gave her that particular confidence? If she had evidence she could actually take to the police, why would she have gone looking for information from Dr. Carver? So many more questions than I have answers.

Mostly, I have been thinking about Josie and Reese.

About what it means to love two people so completely that the thought of something happening to them is not a fear you manage but a weight you carry in your chest at all times. I think about Josie on the blanket in the other room, examining her wooden blocks with the focus of someone for whom every object in the world is still new and full of information. I think about Reese in the studio, the painting that has been building on the easel for months.

I have been careful about what I share with Marcus and more careful about what I share with Reese. Marcus knows what I have asked him to find. He has not found everything I need, which set me on a mission to find some things on my own. What I have found, in the hours between Reese going to bed and sleep becoming possible, is where Allison is from.

I know the town. I know her parents' names and that they still live in the house where she grew up. I know she has a brother two years younger and a sister who moved to the coast but comes home for holidays. I know the particular geography of a life I have been assembling from the fragments available to a careful man with time and a reason to look.

I need to understand her, though. That is the information that perhaps only the people who loved her can give me. I need to know what would make a woman obsess over the ending of a three-week relationship. A relationship that really ended long before it ever began.

The problem that hangs in my mind is the trail.

Once I go there, I am seen. I'm a man asking questions about a woman who has been stalking his family. If I do the thing I have been allowing myself to consider—the thing I have not yet decided to do but know I am willing to—her family will speak to the police. Her family will describe a man who came around. Her family will, if pressed, describe me well enough.

There will be a trail.

Reese and I have been careful to leave no trails. To be careful not to give investigators a single thing that can't be explained away. I have been that man every day since the night in the carriage house, and I am good at it. I believe in it, and I understand that the single greatest threat to our safety is not Allison's certainty but our own departure from the careful.

And yet, Allison is out there.

I sit with the math of it, and the decision is one I have no other choice in. The only thing left is what to tell Reese.

I think about this for a long time. I think about it with the care I give to everything that involves Reese. If I am going to keep her safe, safer than I did when it came to Joe, she cannot know what I am actually doing.

Not because I want to deceive her but because I will not add to what she carries.

Once I make the decision, I waste no time. Reese is in the studio.

The door is open, and she stands in front of the painting, with a brush in her hand. I knock once on the frame. She blinks and comes back from her faraway place.

"Hey." She turns. "Sorry, I was—"

"Don't apologize." I lean against the doorframe. "I need to talk to you about something."

"Okay," she says.

"I know I just went to Chicago not too long ago, but I spoke to the board this morning," I say evenly.

"Is everything okay?" Her concerned look causes a pang of guilt that I have to push past."

"A situation has been developing for a few weeks. I can't really say much about it other than I probably should have stayed and handled it while I was there. I need to go to the city. Maybe two nights, possibly three." I pause. "I'm so sorry for the timing."

She searches my face.

I hold steady.

She nods.

"Okay," she says. "I understand. Don't worry about us. We'll be fine." And then, because she is Reese and she has always read me, she asks, "Are you okay?"

I cross the studio. I take her face in both hands the way I have taken it a thousand times, the gesture that has always meant I see you, and I am here, and I am not going anywhere, which is true in every sense I know how to make it true.

"I'm fine," I say. "Take care of our girl."

She puts her hands over mine.

"Always," she says.

I kiss her forehead.

I leave her in the studio with the painting and the light and the particular quality of the work she has been building for months, the unnamed shape in the center that is almost ready to be what it has always been becoming.

I go upstairs to pack a bag. I do not let myself think about what I am going to do. I only let myself think about why.

TWENTY-EIGHT

REESE

The house is different when Adam is away. Not in a good or bad way, just emptier.

He left this morning with one bag and the look on his face that means a decision has already been made. I don't envy the other members inside that boardroom. Whatever is going down, it's clear that his mind is made up.

The morning proceeds as mornings do in this house despite Adam not being there. I suppose with a child, this is how things are. As far as Josie is concerned, she is at the center of everything and requires attention accordingly.

Nora gives her a bath. I make coffee. I stand at the kitchen window, and I look at the lake, and I wonder what it was that Adam didn't tell me before he left. There was something in his eyes. The way he looked at me told me there was more on his mind than just this business meeting. I considered asking but decided he would tell me when he was ready.

Nora comes downstairs with Josie clean and pleased with herself, and the morning continues.

The morning is full of routines. I help with the laundry before heading in for some studio time. Later in the day, Nora puts Josie down for her long afternoon nap. She then finds me in the studio.

"Hi," she says.

"Hi."

She doesn't tend to come into my studio when Adam is around. I wonder if it's because Adam treats my studio time as sacred that she assumes she should, too. She comes to stand beside me. We look at the painting together.

"It's almost there," she says.

"I know."

"What's stopping you?"

I look at the unnamed shape in the center. The dark below it, the light above it, and the shape itself that is reaching.

"I still don't know yet what it is," I say. "I have to know what it is before I can finish it."

She is quiet.

"What do you think it is?" she asks.

I study it for a long moment.

"Maybe something that is about to cross from one place into another. The moment just before..."

Nora observes the painting.

I watch Nora.

After looking at the painting for a long time, we end up in the kitchen. The room seems to be the house's center of gravity, the place everything returns to. Nora makes tea without asking whether I want any because she already knows the answer. I sit at the island with my hands around the mug and the late afternoon light.

The monitor on the counter is silent. Josie is still sleeping.

Something is present in the room with us, and it has been there for months. It's in the brief encounters, in the space between us on the couch and on the beach and in the studio just now. I have been careful, waiting for a moment that was its own. A moment that there would be no mistaking what brought it about. It would not be a reaction to anything. It would be a moment when this thing came into existence with intention.

This is that moment.

I know it the way I know most things that matter—by a feeling before I have ever made a decision.

"Nora," I say.

She looks up from her tea.

"There's something I've been wanting to say to you." I hold her gaze. "I don't entirely know how to say it because I've been not-saying it for long enough that now it feels awkward." She is listening with her whole body.

"I have feelings for you," I say. "I know what I am, and I know what you are in this house, and I know all the reasons this is complicated. Trust me, I've thought about all of them, and—" I stop. I breathe. "I just needed you to know. That's all. I just needed to say it out loud to you, instead of carrying it around and pretending it isn't there. I want you to know your job won't be affected by your response. This is nothing like that. I just—"

"I know," she says. "I've known for a while." A pause. "I have them too."

The kitchen is very still.

"But," she says.

"I know," I say, understanding all the reasons she will give why this shouldn't work.

"Reese." She sets her mug down. "You're married. And Adam—" She stops. "I don't know how to say this without sounding like I'm making an assumption about your husband that I have no right to make."

"Then say it anyway," I say. "Say the assumption."

She takes a breath.

"Adam loves you. I can see that clearly. And I think he genuinely wants you to be happy." She pauses. "But wanting someone to be happy and being able to actually share them—truly share them, without resentment—those are different things. I don't want to be something that hurts your marriage. I don't want to be something that comes between what you and Adam have spent so long building."

I look at her.

I think about how to say what I need to say.

"What if I told you pursuing this wasn't my idea?"

She stills.

"What if I told you that Adam was the one who said it first. He saw it before I'd admitted it to myself. He told me that he thinks you're good for me, and he wants this for me."

"That's—" She shakes her head slightly. "That's not something men usually—"

"I know."

"How can you trust that he means it?" The question is genuine. There is no skepticism in it. She is simply asking the thing that a careful person asks when something sounds too good to be true.

"Because we've done it successfully before," I say.

She waits.

"There was someone. Before you. Before Allison. I don't like to talk about it, but we were in a relationship, the three of us. Adam and I and someone else. And it worked. I've seen what it looks like when Adam actually means it, and I believe him."

"What happened to him?" she asks gently. "The guy?"

"He's gone," I say. "It ended. And I think that's part of why Adam is doing what he's doing now. He had something special with that man, and I think he's trying to give that same gift back to me."

The kitchen is quiet as I look at Nora.

"I'm choosing to believe him," I say. "That's the honest answer. I'm not certain. But I know this man. I have loved this man through everything, and he has loved me through everything, and I am choosing to take the thing he is offering me and believe that he means it."

Nora is looking at me.

"Okay then. I'm choosing to believe him too," she says.

Relief floods me, warm and dizzying. I reach out, my hand trembling just a bit as I cup Nora's cheek. Her skin is soft, warmer than I expected, and I lean in, closing the distance. Our lips meet—tentative at first. Nora responds immediately, her mouth opening slightly, inviting me deeper. The kiss builds, Nora's tongue sliding against mine, tasting faintly of the tea she was drinking. It's electric, a spark that shoots straight down my spine, making my thighs clench.

I pull back just enough to catch my breath, my forehead resting against Nora's. My red hair falls forward, mingling with Nora's dark strands. "Would you... do you want to go to my room? I mean, only if you're comfortable. I'm kind of new at this, but I want to be with you."

Nora's eyes darken, a hungry glint in them, and she nods, standing and taking my hand. "Yes, I want that more than you could ever know."

She leads me down the hallway, her fingers laced with mine, firm and reassuring. We climb the stairs to my bedroom, the door creaks open, and we step inside. She faces me, her hands on my waist, pulling me close. "First things first," she murmurs, her breath hot against my neck. "Let's get these clothes off. I want to see you—all of you."

I nod, my pulse racing. She starts with my shirt and tugs it over my head. My bra follows, simple black lace that Nora unhooks with practiced ease. Cool air hits my skin, my nipples hardening instantly under her gaze. She traces a finger along my collarbone, down to the swell of my breasts, and I shiver.

"You're so fucking beautiful," she says in a whisper.

I arch into her touch, my hands finding her waist. "So are you," I whisper back, my voice barely more than a rasp.

She pulls back just enough to meet my eyes. "I want to taste you," she says, her voice low and rough.

A shudder runs through me at her words. I've never

had a woman talk to me like this—so direct, so hungry. It's intoxicating.

Her gaze drops to my breasts, her tongue darting out to wet her lips. Her hands are cupping them, her thumbs brushing over my nipples. I gasp at the contact, my back arching into her touch.

"You like that?" she asks, her voice a dark purr as she rolls my nipples between her fingers.

"Yes," I moan, my hands tangling in her hair as she leans down, her mouth replacing her fingers. She takes one nipple between her lips, sucking gently at first, then harder, her tongue swirling around the sensitive peak. I cry out. An involuntary tremor ripples through my body.

She laughs against my skin, the vibration sending a jolt of pleasure straight to my core. "You're so responsive," she murmurs, switching to my other breast, her hands gripping my ass to pull me closer.

I'm panting now, my thighs pressing together in an attempt to ease the ache between them. She pulls back just enough to meet my eyes, her hands sliding down to the button of my jeans.

"Take your pants off," she says as more of an order than a request.

I don't hesitate. I kick off my shoes, then shimmy out of my jeans and panties in one motion, leaving me completely naked before her. Her gaze rakes over me as she quickly removes every stitch of clothing that she's wearing. I take in the sight of her beautiful body, and that's when I notice that her eyes linger on the wetness between my thighs. She licks her lips again.

"Reese," she says, her voice thick with desire. "You're perfect."

"You are too," I say, clearly uneasy about finding the words to tell a woman how beautiful I find her.

Before I can respond, she's on her knees in front of me, her hands gripping my thighs as she leans in. Her breath is hot against my pussy, and I whimper, my fingers tangling in her hair as she finally laves a slow, wet stripe up my slit.

"Oh fuck," I gasp, my knees nearly buckling at the sensation. She does it again, her tongue circling my clit before dipping lower to fuck me with shallow strokes.

I moan, my hips rocking forward, trying to get more of her. She groans in response, her hands gripping my ass to hold me steady as she feasts on me like I'm her last meal. Her tongue is relentless. Her lips seal around my clit as she sucks, her fingers joining in to stretch me open.

She guides me to the bed, pushing me gently onto my back. The mattress dips under our weight as she climbs over me, straddling my hips. "Relax," Nora whispers, her hands roaming my sides, thumbs brushing the undersides of my breasts. "I'm going to take it slow. Tell me if you want to stop, okay?"

"I won't," I breathe, arching up as she leans down to kiss me again. This time, it's deeper, her body pressing against mine—skin on skin. The heat of her is seeping into me. Her mouth trails from my lips to my jaw, then down my throat, sucking lightly at the pulse point that makes me gasp. "Oh God, Nora..."

She chuckles softly against my skin. "I love hearing

how good I make you feel," she says. Wetness builds between my legs, a slick ache that demands more.

Shifting lower, Nora kisses a path down my stomach, her breath fanning over my skin. She parts my thighs with her knees, settling between them. I feel the first brush of her fingers against my folds. I'm soaked already, and she hums appreciatively. "Fuck, you're so wet for me." Her fingertip circles my clit, slow and steady, building pressure that makes my hips buck.

Her thumb stays on my clit, rubbing in tight circles while her fingers thrust, the rhythm picking up. The sounds are obscene. Wet slides. Ragged breaths. All of it only heightens the heat pooling in my belly. She watches my face, adjusting based on my reactions, and when I whimper, she leans down, replacing her thumb with her mouth.

Her tongue is magic. It's flat and broad at first, lapping from my entrance to my clit, then flicking the sensitive nub. I cry out, gripping the sheets. "Nora, yes—fuck, don't stop." She doesn't. Nora sucks my clit between her lips, humming vibrations through me, while her fingers keep their steady in and out. It's overwhelming, the buildup coiling tighter, my thighs trembling around her head.

I'm close, my breath coming in short, sharp gasps. "Nora, I—fuck—I'm gonna—"

She pulls back just enough to look up at me, her lips glistening with my arousal. "Come for me, baby," she purrs, before diving back in, her tongue swirling over my clit in tight, demanding circles.

That's all it takes. My orgasm crashes over me like a

wave. My back arches as I cry out, my fingers gripping her hair so tightly I'm sure I'm hurting her. But she doesn't stop. She rides out my orgasm with me, her tongue lapping at me through every shuddering aftershock.

When I finally come down, my legs are trembling. Nora presses a final kiss to my thigh before standing, her hands sliding up my body to grip my waist.

"You taste incredible," she murmurs against my lips before kissing me, letting me taste myself on her tongue.

I whimper into the kiss, my body still thrumming with the aftershocks of my orgasm. But I'm not done with her yet.

I push her back onto the bed, straddling her hips as I kiss my way down her body. Her skin is warm beneath my lips, her muscles tense with anticipation as I work my way down.

"Fuck, Reese," she gasps, and I can tell she is shocked by my aggressiveness. Her pussy is glistening, already wet and ready for me. I don't hesitate. I lean down, my tongue flicking over her clit in the same rhythm she used on me.

She cries out, her hips jerking off the bed. "Fuck, yes —just like that—"

I grin against her, my hands gripping her thighs as I feast on her, my tongue working in slow, deep strokes before focusing on her clit. She's already close, her breath coming in sharp gasps, her fingers gripping the sheets.

"You're gonna make me come so hard," she pants, her voice rough with need.

I moan in response, my own arousal building again as I feel her getting closer. Her thighs begin to vibrate around my ears, her hips rocking up to meet my mouth as she chases her release.

"That's it," I murmur against her, my fingers sliding down to circle her entrance. "You know what I want, don't you?"

She does, her back arches as she cries out, her pussy clenching around my fingers as her orgasm slams into her. I don't stop, riding out her pleasure with her, my tongue lapping at her through every shuddering aftershock.

When she finally collapses back against the bed, her chest heaving, I press a final kiss to her center before crawling up her body to kiss her deeply. She moans into the kiss, her hands sliding up to grip my waist.

"You are so fucking incredible," she murmurs.

Without warning, Nora positions herself once again between my thighs.

"What are you doing?" I ask, confused by what is happening.

She doesn't answer with words. Instead, her fingers slide back into me as her wide, wet tongue massages my clit.

"Fuck," she groans, her hips snapping forward as she fucks me with slow, deep thrusts. "You feel so good—so tight—I can't get enough of you."

I can't form words. All I can do is grip the sheets, my body trembling as she sets a punishing pace, her fingers slamming into me with every thrust.

I'm close again, my body coiled tight with need. "Nora—I—I'm gonna—"

She's relentless. Her motions demand another orgasm from me, and my body is helpless to resist. My pussy clenches around her fingers as I begin to twitch wildly. She collapses on top of me, her chest heaving as she presses a final kiss to my shoulder.

We lie there for a long moment, our bodies slick with sweat, our breaths slowly returning to normal. Nora presses a kiss to my collarbone before pulling back just enough to meet my eyes.

"That was incredible," she murmurs, her fingers tracing idle patterns on my skin.

I grin, my fingers tangling in her hair. "Yeah," I agree, my voice rough with satisfaction. "It was."

Nora grins, kissing my nose.

TWENTY-NINE

ADAM

I have been doing this for two days.

The town Allison is from is the kind of place that hasn't changed much since the seventies. There's a main street with a diner, a hardware store, a pharmacy with a soda counter, and a post office that closes for an hour at noon. I have been moving through it carefully with business nearby. A man asking about a woman he is trying to reconnect with, an old acquaintance.

The diner is where I start both mornings.

The woman who works the counter has been here long enough to know most people who grew up here by first name and family association. She is not a gossip in the malicious sense. She is simply someone for whom the accumulated knowledge of a community is a form of currency. I am polite. I tip well. I mention the name on the second morning, casually, between the coffee and the eggs.

She knows the family.

"The Harmons. Sure. Kathleen and Dale. They still

live out on Fir Street." She refills my cup without asking. "You're looking for the daughter? Allison?"

"Yeah, we worked together years ago, and I was out this way and thought I'd look her up while I was here," I say.

She makes the particular face people make when they know something and are deciding whether to reveal it. "Honestly, I haven't seen Allison around in a long time. She moved away after the divorce."

"The divorce?"

"Mmm." She lowers her voice. "Her husband. They were married—oh, six or seven years maybe. He was from out of state. He came to town to work at the plant for a season and ended up staying for her." She wipes the counter. "Turns out, he had a whole other situation before her that she never knew about until it was too late. Allison found out the hard way."

"The hard way?"

"Turns out he was already married before he met Allison and had two kids with that wife. She found out when the woman showed up looking for the deadbeat," she adds before excusing herself to wait on a new customer.

I was so angry after I found out Allison had tried to run Nora and Josie off the road that I could have ended her life right then and there had she been in front of me. I'd be lying if I said this new information hadn't changed the way I looked at Allison. Despite the pity I might have felt for her, though, it didn't change what she had done or the danger she posed to my family.

My next stop is the family home on Fir Street. It's a

green split-level with a metal lawn ornament in the shape of a heron that has weathered to a dull gray. I knock on the door. Allison's mother answers. She is a small woman in her late sixties, with the particular wariness of someone who has received difficult news. I give her the old-friend story. She studies me for a long moment.

"She doesn't really have old friends anymore," she says. Not unkindly. Just as a fact.

"Well"—I force a laugh—"it has been quite a while. When did you last hear from her?"

She looks past me at the street. "Christmas. Maybe. She called." A pause. "She doesn't visit."

"I see. Well, I'm sorry if I disturbed you," I say.

She nods. She does not ask me inside.

It doesn't take long after I leave the mother's home before the brother finds me, which I did not expect. He is two years younger than Allison. He comes into the diner and sits across from me without being invited, which tells me his mother called him after I left.

"Who are you actually?" he asks.

"Just who I said, an old friend," I say.

"Well, she's not here," he says. "She hasn't been here in two years, at least. She calls sometimes." He wraps his hands around his coffee. "After that shit with her husband—" He shakes his head, as if he has decided better of speaking negatively about his sister. "She's not here, and she's not coming back, okay?" he says as he prepares to stand and leave.

I grab his wrist and look into his eyes. I need to know more. I have to understand what I have allowed into our lives. "I'm not exactly an old friend," I explain.

"No shit," he grunts.

"Look, I'm sorry, I'm not trying to upset you or your family's lives," I say. "My wife and I met your sister some time ago, and—well, I know this might sound crazy, but she's been harassing my wife. I'm just trying to understand why she's doing this."

He sighs a heavy breath, looking down at the diner table in front of him. He shifts back into the booth before looking up at me and says, "I'm sorry to hear about Allison and your family. I can't say I'm surprised to hear it. When the shit went down with her husband, she got—fixated. That's the word the therapist she wouldn't keep seeing used. Fixated. She had a hard time letting go of the idea that someone had stolen her life. When she left, she said she wasn't coming home until she got it back."

"I didn't know," I admit.

"She's been through a lot," he says. "She moved around a lot. Got into—situations. Things my mom and I really couldn't help her out of." He looks at me again. "If you find her, tell her to call home. Tell her Mom would like to hear from her."

I nod. "I will. Thank you for telling me all that."

"I'm sorry she's been a problem for you and your wife," he offers before leaving.

I sit in the diner after he leaves.

I came here to find answers.

I came here to find the threat and understand its dimensions and do what I needed to do to ensure my family was safe.

What I have found is a woman who was hurt a long

time ago. She didn't have a husband to protect and love her like I do Reese.

I sit with that.

She isn't our enemy in the way I needed her to be. She's simply someone who has been broken by someone else and who had the bad fortune to come looking for the missing piece of herself in a direction that led her to us.

I leave money on the table.

I go to the car.

I drive north, back toward the lake, back toward my family, back toward the life I've built that is damaged in places, but real and mine and worth protecting.

I do not find what I came for.

I find, instead, a sadness I was not prepared to carry.

I carry it anyway.

At this point, it's not the heaviest thing I carry.

THIRTY

REESE

By midmorning, I'm in the studio. I stand in front of the canvas for a long time, longer than usual, and I look at what is there. The dark at the bottom, and the light at the top, and the shape in the center that I have been building in layers for months, and that I now understand with a clarity I did not have yesterday. It is a threshold. Two figures in a small boat.

I mix my colors without second-guessing. I paint for two hours without looking at the clock.

Adam calls after lunch.

I take my phone, and I go outside onto the back porch, which overlooks the path that leads down to the beach. I sit on the top step, and I answer.

"Hey," he says.

"Hey." I pull my cardigan tighter. "How's it going?"

"As expected," he says, which means he will tell me more when he is home and not over the phone. "How are my girls?"

"Josie is asleep."

"And you? How are you doing?"

After last night. After Nora. I intended to tell Adam in person. But at this moment, it feels like I should tell him. "Adam," I say his name softly.

"I'm listening."

I look at the lake. I think about the way Adam said be happy in the studio doorway with his bag over his shoulder. I think about what Dr. Carver said—that he is communicating and doing his part. How when someone tells you what they mean, the respectful thing is to take them at their word and not construct a more complicated version of their intentions out of your own fear.

I have been practicing that too.

"Nora and I—" I stop. "We were...intimate. Yesterday."

A pause.

Not a long one. Not the pause of someone receiving a surprise.

"Good," he says. The word is warm. "I hope you enjoyed it."

"You're distracted," I say.

"A little," he admits. "Work. Sorry. I mean it, though, Reese. All of it."

"Okay," I say.

"Okay?"

"I believe you," I say. "That's all. I'm choosing to believe you."

"That means more to me than I know how to tell you right now."

We are quiet for a moment, the comfortable kind. "Adam," I say. "I've been thinking about something else."

"Tell me."

"I miss my life."

He is quiet. Not confused—waiting. He knows there is more.

"Madison," I say. "I miss Madison. I miss having a best friend. I miss having someone I can call about nothing, who already knows the whole story of who I am, who I don't have to explain myself to." I explain the weight of what has been on my mind.

"So why not reach out to her?" Adam's answer seems so simple, but also so far from it.

"I can't. It's been too long. I've been avoiding her for so long that if I just reached out to her out of the blue, she's going to hate me. I think it's too late to fix it," I explain.

Adam is very quiet for a long while. "If we have learned anything over the last year, I think we can both agree it's that nothing is guaranteed in life. If you miss Madison, reach out."

"Really? Do you think she would even talk to me?" I ask, unable to imagine a path forward that would allow Madison and me to salvage our friendship.

"You're kidding, right?"

"What do you mean?"

"Madison adores you. If I had to guess, she has missed you as much as you have missed her. Besides, you have Josie now." He laughs. "She won't be able to resist her."

I laugh as well, "Everyone does love Josie," I say.

"Well, Josie is pretty damn lovable, just like her mother."

"Go be with your girls," he says. "I'll be home as soon as I can."

"Be safe," I say, relieved at how well he took the news about Nora and me.

"Always."

I hang up, my mind on Madison.

Madison, who had been my best friend since we were twenty. I have avoided her since Joe, terrified the woman who always seems to see right through me would figure out what I had done within ten minutes. The woman I have missed every day for the past year in the low-key, constant way you miss a limb you have learned to compensate for.

You're ready.

You need her.

I open my phone.

I look at her name in my contacts for a long moment.

And then I type.

Reese: Surprise. I'm alive.

Reese: Okay, not funny. I'm so sorry it's been so long. I was going through some stuff, and I handled it like a little bitch by disappearing. I know you deserve better than that from me. I hope you can forgive me. The past year without you has been hell.

I stare at it.

I press send before I can revise it into something more managed.

The typing indicator appears almost immediately. My stomach twists into knots as I wait.

Three dots. Three dots. Three dots.

Madison: Took you long enough.

I laugh.

Madison: Yoga class in an hour?

Of course that's how she replies. So much for me learning to stop overthinking things.

Reese: See you then.

I text Adam that he was right and I am meeting Madison for yoga in an hour.

Adam: That's my girl. Have fun.

I race up to my bedroom, time slipping away quickly, and get dressed in workout clothes. I'm rushing and have no time to explain to Nora that I am meeting a friend. I decide I will explain when I get back. I find her in the nursery, changing Josie's diaper. I tell her I'm going to a yoga class, and I'll be back after.

She kisses me. It's soft, and tender, and makes me question if I really want to leave for the class or stay here with Nora and get naked again.

I sigh.

"I mean, I suppose I could stay here."

She laughs, turning her attention back to the diaper changing.

"Go. Have fun. Get all sweaty and then come back here so we can take a shower together."

"Even better!" I exclaim before giving her another kiss, but this time on the cheek, and then turn to run out the door.

Madison looks exactly the same.

This is the first thing I think when I see her in the parking lot of the yoga studio, standing in the bright morning light with her mat under her arm and her hair in the same knot she's been wearing since we were in our twenties. I feel something crack open in my chest.

"Hey, you," she says.

"Hey." I close the distance between us, and she hugs me, and I hold on for a moment longer than I intend to.

"I'm so glad you called," she says, into my shoulder.

"I should have called sooner."

"Yeah, you should have." She pulls back and looks at me with the direct affection that has always been her particular gift. "But you're here now."

We attend the class where she whispers about all the craziness she has been getting up to over the last year. I save my news. Afterward, we head over to grab a smoothie at the shop next door.

We sit and Madison says, "Tell me everything."

"Well—" I hesitate, unsure how the woman I have called my best friend for my entire life will take the news that, after accepting I would never have children, my dream came true, and she wasn't there to see it. I feel my chest grow tight as the familiar weight of guilt settles in it. "I had a baby."

She says nothing for a long while, and my heart beats faster as the anxiety grows. "I guess at least it's good that I finally heard it directly from you."

"Wait, you knew?"

She nods. "I even came to your house after you had her with a gift, but I never made it past the driveway."

"How did you know?"

"Really? Do you understand how small this town is? Hell, I even saw you at the grocery store just before you were about to pop."

"Seriously? And you didn't say anything?"

"Really? Is that what you're going with?" Madison asks, furrowing her brows as she takes a long sip of her smoothie.

I laugh and lift my hands in surrender. "Okay, fair enough."

Then I tell her what I can. The version of my life that I can tell. Josie's arrival, the difficulty of the early months, the slow return. I don't tell her about Joe, or Allison, or the carriage house, or the things I have said in a therapist's office that I have had to manage like a controlled burn. But I tell her about the painting. I tell her about Josie's dark, serious eyes and the way she has opinions about her rattle. I tell her I feel more like myself than I have in a long time.

Madison listens the way she has always listened, with her full body, her chin in her hand.

She says it simply, as a fact. "Fuck, I missed you so damn much, girl."

"I missed you too." I mean it in a way that costs me something to admit. "I'm sorry I disappeared."

She shakes her head. "You're back. That's what matters. But please don't ever have a crazy freak-out meltdown and abandon me again or I will kick your ass."

"Deal."

THIRTY-ONE

REESE

The house smells extraordinary when I walk in.

French toast casserole. Butter and vanilla and the particular sweetness of bread that has been soaking overnight. It hits me in the doorway, and I feel it in my chest before I have even taken off my shoes. There is something about coming home to a smell like this, made by someone who thought about what it would be like to arrive to it, that lands differently than I would have expected. Like being received.

"Hi," Nora says from the kitchen. She looks up from where she is bending to check something in the oven. "How was yoga?"

"Good," I say. And then, with the particular honesty of a person who has been practicing it: "Really good, actually. Better than I expected."

She laughs. "I mean, I'm happy for you, but it was just yoga."

"Actually—" I hesitate for only a moment. "I went with my old best friend."

"Really? The one you told me about?"

I nod, looking over to see that Josie is in her walker in the middle of the kitchen floor, navigating with the determined inaccuracy of someone who has recently discovered mobility. She sees me and makes the sound that is not yet a word, but that I know means there you are. "Yeah," I say. "Madison. I was so nervous, but it was like old times."

"That's amazing. How did that happen? Did you just run into her?"

"No. Adam called earlier and I told him how much I'd been missing her, how I'd been thinking about reaching out. He told me I should." I cross to Josie and crouch down so she can grab my face with both hands, which she does immediately. "I guess I just decided"—I make a small gesture—"fuck it."

Nora smiles. "I'm glad you reconnected." She turns back toward the stove.

I reach out and catch her arm.

"Nora."

She stops and turns to look at me.

"I need you to know something," I say.

She waits.

"You're the reason I finally did it." I look at her to show her that I mean my words. "The things you said to me. On the beach. About not holding things at arm's length. About what it costs to live like you're waiting for the worst to happen. It's been on my mind since you said it, and I want you to know what you have given back to me."

"Reese," she says, softly.

"I'm serious." I stand from Josie's level, keeping one hand on the walker so she doesn't navigate into the cabinet again. "I had been telling myself the story that I was protecting Madison by staying away because I was so broken. But what you said made me look at it more honestly, and when I did, I realized I wasn't protecting her. I was protecting myself."

"From what?" Nora asks,

The real answer is that I was afraid Madison would ask the wrong question at the wrong moment. That she would look at me with the specific attention of someone who has known me since I was twenty, and she would see the thing I have been carrying since the night in the carriage house. She would ask about it, and I would not be able to lie to her, not to Madison, not fully, not without her knowing I was lying, and then what.

That is the real answer.

But the real answer is a door I cannot open. "I guess it was the postpartum," I say. "Madison tried. She was calling, and I wasn't answering, and then enough time passed that answering felt impossible, and I convinced myself it was rational to stay away because I didn't want to burden her with how bad it was." I pause. "But it wasn't rational. I was scared. And the scared part of me invented reasons to stay scared."

Nora nods slowly.

"Depression can do that. It makes the world feel like something to be survived rather than lived in. And one of the things you do when you're in survival mode is let go of the things that feel like too much to hold." She looks at me with her dark eyes and says, "Madison was too much to hold."

"Madison was the thing I missed most and the thing I was most afraid of," I say. "Which tells you something, I think, about how bad it was."

"It tells you something about how much she means to you," Nora says.

I look at her.

She is standing at my counter in her gray sweater, with an oven mitt on her hand and a casserole to check on, while Josie bangs gently against her walker behind me. Nora has taken the evidence of my fear and turned it into evidence of love. She does not seem to know that she has done it.

That is the thing about Nora that I could not have explained six months ago and that I understand now with complete clarity.

She makes things make sense.

Not by explaining them. Not by analyzing them. Just by the specific quality of how she looks at them.

"Thank you," I say.

She tilts her head. "For what?"

"For all of it," I say. "But specifically right now."

She smiles. The unguarded one.

"Go play with your daughter," she says. "The casserole has eleven minutes."

I do as she says. Josie grabs my fingers and pulls herself to standing with the full-body determination of someone who has decided that uprightness is the next milestone and intends to achieve it before dinner.

I look at my daughter's face. For now, that is everything I need.

A little bit later, the timer goes off. Nora pulls out the casserole, then closes the oven and straightens. "Oh, I almost forgot. Someone called for you while you were gone."

"Who?" I ask, still playing with Josie.

"Umm...Natasha, I think."

My stomach drops when she says the name. I look up from Josie.

"I'm sorry? Who?"

Nora looks mildly puzzled by my reaction. "Natasha. She didn't leave a number. She said she'd try again. I wrote it down because it's not a name you hear very often." She crosses to the counter and picks up a yellow sticky note. "Natasha..." She looks at it. "Carver. Natasha Carver."

Natasha Carver.

I think about Joe. About the things he told us, the glimpses he gave us of a life before ours, careful and selective the way people are careful and selective about pain. He told us about the foster home. He told us about a sister. A foster sister—whose name I heard exactly once and stored in the part of my memory that holds the things you don't know you'll need.

Natasha.

And Dr. Carver. My Dr. Carver, whose first name I have never known, whose office I have been sitting in for months, into whose careful silence I have been feeding the architecture of my guilt in small and calibrated pieces.

"Reese?" Nora is watching me. "Are you okay?"

"Yes," I say. My voice sounds normal. I don't know how. "Sorry. I just—I don't think I know a Natasha Carver."

"Oh, well, it was crazy when she called. I had eggs all over my hands. Maybe I got the name wrong," Nora says, though she glances at the sticky note again with the expression of someone who does not think they got the name wrong.

I stand from Josie's level, and I cross to the island, and I sit on a stool. I put both hands flat on the counter and focus on breathing in through my nose and out through my mouth, the way Dr. Carver taught me.

Dr. Carver.

Natasha Carver.

It can't be. I was referred by my primary care doctor, a routine referral, the most ordinary possible chain of events. There is no possible way. It is a coincidence. It is nothing. It has to be nothing.

But Joe's foster sister was named Natasha.

And the woman I have been telling the shape of my guilt to, in careful and calibrated portions, for the better part of a year—

I hear the front door.

Adam is home.

THIRTY-TWO

REESE

He says it the moment the bedroom door closes behind us.

"Marcus heard back from his detective contact about Allison."

I'm still holding the shape of what Nora told me downstairs, still turning the name over and over in my head, struggling to concentrate on what Adam is telling me. Natasha. Natasha Carver. I make myself put it down and force my attention onto the man in front of me and the sentence that requires all of me to be present.

"She's..." He looks away and then back at me, hesitating before he finishes. "She's dead."

Dead. The word loses all meaning for a moment because it cannot be possible that she no longer exists. I don't know how to process the fact that this complicated woman, this woman with whom we had a sexual relationship, this woman who tried to run my child and her nanny off the road, no longer exists in the world as we know it.

I shake my head. "What do you mean—dead?" The word feels heavy on my lips.

"He said the investigation is ongoing, but they found her body. They're waiting on her mother to travel in and confirm the identity." His voice is steady and quiet, in the register he uses when he has already processed something and is now simply transferring it.

"So there's a chance it's not her?" I ask.

"Marcus said the police seem pretty confident that it's her. There was a license with the body," he explains.

"Oh my God." I cover my mouth. The horror of it is more than I had expected when we walked into this room —the same room where we once had an encounter with this now-dead woman.

"How did it happen?" I ask, desperate to make sense of everything.

I sit on the edge of the bed, my knees threatening to buckle.

"Marcus said they aren't releasing many details while it's under investigation."

"Investigation?" I look up at him, eyes wide. "Do they think she was murdered?"

"I don't think they're ruling anything out. It's too soon."

Suddenly, I am thinking about Dr. Carver's text. The evening of our date—the restaurant, the candle between us, Adam's hand over mine—and then my phone buzzing against the white tablecloth. *A woman came to my office this evening. She was asking questions about you and your husband. She kept mentioning a man named Joe.* Could something have happened to Allison as she left Dr. Carver's office? Dr. Carver. My mind wanders. Natasha Carver.

"There's something else," he says. The expression on his face tells me I'm not going to like it. I suck in a deep breath and brace myself as he sits beside me.

"What is it?" I ask, looking at his hand on my leg rather than into his eyes.

"I lied to you." His words make my stomach sink immediately. "I hate that I lied, but I couldn't stand the idea of adding to your worry. I hope you understand why."

"What did you lie about?" I force myself to look up into the eyes of the man I fell in love with, the man I thought would never lie to me.

"I wasn't out of town on a business trip." I have as hard a time processing his statement as I did the news about Allison. Adam doesn't lie. He doesn't cheat. He loves me. These are things I have never questioned. "I couldn't stand not knowing what Allison was planning. I had to find her. I had to know she would stop all of this madness."

Allison is dead. Adam lied to me and went looking for her. The two facts collide in my mind, and the next words out of my mouth are ones I never thought I would say to this man. "Did you kill her?"

He looks instantly hurt, but I don't regret asking. He just told me he lied about where he was and that he was searching for the very woman the police found dead.

"Did you?" I ask again when he stays silent.

"God, no—is that really what you think of me?"

"What do you expect me to think? You just told me

that you lied to me about where you were and that you went looking for her."

"And I never found her," he explains. "But that doesn't mean this isn't going to come back on me."

"How in the hell could this come back on you if you never found her?"

"Reese, I promise—I was just trying to talk some sense into her. I thought maybe she'd gone to see family, so I remembered her mentioning where she grew up. I spoke to her mother and her brother and—" He stops, looks up at the ceiling as though tallying something. "A lot of people in that town know I was looking for her."

"And?" I press, fear tightening my throat.

"And I don't know yet, but I'm sure it will come up that some stranger was in town looking for her when the detectives go to tell the family about her death."

"Did you tell them your name?"

"No, but we have a restraining order in place against her. It wouldn't shock me if someone looks a bit closer at us based on that alone."

"So what do we do?" I ask, a tiredness in my voice.

"I told Marcus everything."

"When you say everything—"

"Not about Joe," he says, irritation at the edges of his words. "I mean about me going to look for Allison. He said he'll find out as much as he can about the investigation and get back to me. And that if he hears something, we just need to try to get ahead of it."

"This is a nightmare."

"Tell me about it," he grumbles. "Can you imagine if

I get arrested for a murder I didn't commit instead of one I did?"

"Is that supposed to be funny, because it's not." I scold.

"I'm sorry. I'm not trying to be funny." He pauses. "I'm just saying—the irony isn't lost on me."

"Do you really think they'll suspect you had something to do with it?" I ask, the reality of what he's telling me finally settling in. After everything I did for us with Joe, and now that Josie is here—I can't lose him. We are finally starting to figure things out. Josie needs her father, or at least the only version of one she has left.

"I mean, even I can see how it doesn't look good that I was in her hometown asking questions about her, and then she turns up dead. I think it really depends on what the coroner says, though."

"Adam, there's something else we need to talk about," I say, looking away.

"What's wrong?" he asks, and I try to think of the best way to tell him that I believe my therapist may actually be connected to Joe.

"I'm sure I'm overreacting."

Just as I begin, Adam's phone rings.

I pause as he glances down, then holds up a finger asking me to wait. "Hang on just a minute, babe," he says, swiping across the screen and lifting it to his ear. "It's Marcus—I've been waiting for him to call."

I nod, and he answers.

"Hello . . . yeah, hi, Marcus. No—I'm here with her now. Yeah, I already told her. Is there any news?" I listen, holding my breath, waiting to find out whether my husband is the prime suspect in the murder of a woman we slept with and who then stalked us.

The two of them go back and forth, exchanging information. I feel myself move from hopeful to worried to hopeful again as I listen and try to piece it together.

"No, man...I appreciate it," Adam says finally, and I can tell he's wrapping up. I might finally get some answers. "Yeah, we will. Let me know if there are any further developments."

"You're not going to believe this," he says as he hangs up.

"What is it?"

"Apparently, based on the decomposition, the coroner thinks Allison has been dead for a while," Adam says.

Decomposition. The word turns my stomach as my imagination supplies a mental image I immediately push away. "What's 'a while'?"

"They won't know for certain, not until the coroner finishes, but according to Marcus, the detective thinks it could have been around the time of the accident."

"Wait, are they saying she died from wounds sustained in the accident?" I ask, more puzzled than before.

He shakes his head. "It doesn't sound like it. Marcus said they have to wait for the official ruling on cause of death, but from everything at the scene, it looks like it could be a suicide."

"Oh my God. Adam, that's terrible."

"I know."

"You don't think she did it because of us, do you?" I

ask, my head beginning to throb at the thought of more blood on our hands.

"You can't do that, Reese."

"Do what?" I say. "Don't you see the pattern? Every person who crosses our path ends up destroyed."

"That's not true. You're just struggling with the news, and that makes sense. This is overwhelming. But it wasn't our fault." His voice is firm but quiet. "She was the one who was wrong when it came to our relationship. People can't behave the way she did and expect no consequences."

"Maybe all she needed was a little kindness."

"Jesus, Reese—we weren't unkind to her. She's not entitled to a relationship with us. She stalked you and our baby at the grocery store. That's not okay."

"She didn't deserve to die," I say

"And had Josie been hurt when she tried to run her and Nora off the road?"

My eyes burn at the thought. I let out a long breath, a heaviness settling in my chest. "I don't even want to think about it. I just can't believe Allison has been dead all this time."

"I know. It's strange to think I was speaking to all these people who knew her. We actually knew very little about her. Apparently, she was divorced."

"She was?" I ask, unsettled that I never bothered to learn that about a woman we slept with. Is that who we were? Did we treat people like objects to be discarded? I push the thought away, unwilling to entertain it.

"Mm-hmm. Her brother told me she wasn't really over it. I guess another woman showed up in town looking for him and found Allison instead. That's when she realized her husband had another family."

"That's awful."

"That's my point, though—about not blaming ourselves for what happened to her. It sounds like she was spiraling long before she ever met us." He tilts his head as though a thought has struck him. "What I don't understand is if Allison was already dead, who threatened Dr. Carver the night we were at dinner? If it wasn't Allison, someone else was in that office—someone who knew enough about Joe to use his name. It just doesn't make sense."

"Adam, I need to tell you something." I blurt it out. Instinctively, I stand and begin to pace. I can feel his eyes on me, but I keep my gaze fixed on the floor.

He stands too and grabs my arms, stilling me, forcing me to look at him.

"Reese. What's going on?"

I tell him. All of it. The message Nora mentioned. The name written on the yellow sticky note. I remind him of the name Joe gave us one evening when he talked about the foster home—the girl who came to live there when she was eleven. Natasha. And then I tell him that Dr. Carver, my Dr. Carver, whose first name I never knew because I never thought to ask and she never offered, is in fact that Natasha.

Natasha Carver.

I tell him about the impossible arithmetic of it. The referral from my primary care doctor. The most ordinary chain of events, the most routine transaction. I ask if I'm being paranoid. I lay out how she could have arranged it, but before he can answer, I say, "No, it's impossible." I say the word, then hear myself saying it, and think about all the things I once believed were impossible. I thought I could never love another man—and then I did. I thought having a baby was impossible—and then I had Josie. I thought Adam would never lie to me—but here we are.

Adam is very still while I talk.

I finish.

The room is quiet.

"Did you tell her about Joe?" His voice is careful. Not accusatory. Careful. "About any of it?"

"I never said his name." I hold his gaze. He needs to hear this part. "Not once. I was so careful about the name. I said 'a man.' Or I said 'him.'" I pause. The next part is harder. "But I told her we'd been involved with a man romantically and that it ended suddenly."

"That doesn't mean anything," he says, trying to soothe me.

I sigh. "I told her he died."

Adam's jaw tightens. "You what? Why would you tell her that? How much detail did you give?" He fires off the questions in rapid succession.

I shake my head. "It's fine, okay? I revised the story a little." I look at my hands in my lap. "She asked how he died, and I panicked. I told her there was an accident. But then I panicked again, and I thought about where Joe is now, and I don't know why—I told her it happened on the water."

The quality of the silence changes.

"Reese."

"I know."

"Jesus Christ." He stands. He moves to the window, his back to me, his hand pressed flat against the frame. "What if she tries to look into recent water accidents?"

"Well, he didn't die on the water, did he?" I snap in frustration. "So I guess she won't find anything."

"No, but if she doesn't find what she's looking for, it could lead to more questions. What if part of his body washes up? Have you ever thought about that?"

"You said that couldn't happen."

"Nothing is impossible. That's why I told you that first day that we have to be extra careful from here on out. You might as well have told her we murdered Joe and saved us both some time."

The heat moves up from my chest into my throat.

"Don't," I growl, balling my hands into fists at my sides.

He turns but doesn't say anything.

"Don't you stand there and make this my failure." I hear the tremor in my voice, and I don't try to smooth it out. I'm done smoothing things out in this room. "You were the one who said he couldn't leave. You were the one who said we had no other choice. You said the word protect as though it were a simple thing—something you do once and then it's done, and you move forward and build your life, and you don't have to think about it anymore."

"I didn't mean—"

"No! I'm not done!" I exclaim. "You told me where the gun was. You put that gun in my hands. You told me what had to happen, and I did what you asked, and I have been living in the wreckage of that every single day since.

So don't you dare. I am not going to stand here and let you reduce sixteen years of that to a slip in a therapist's office."

My voice breaks on the last words.

I press the back of my hand against my mouth and breathe. I look at the lake through the window, and I do not cry. I have cried for Joe. I have cried for what we did, for what it cost, and for what it continues to cost every morning I wake up in this house and choose to keep going. I am not going to cry in this room, at this moment, when what I need is to be clear.

Adam is looking at me.

His face does the thing it rarely does. It cracks.

"You're right." He says it quietly. "I'm sorry. That was unfair, and it was wrong, and you are right."

I breathe.

"It wasn't the only option," I say, almost to myself. "I've never been able to make myself believe it was the only option. I've tried. I've spent the past year trying to construct a version of that night in which it was necessary—inevitable—and I can't get there. I can't make it add up. And that is something I have to live with every single day."

Adam listens before he speaks. "I believe it was the only option. I know you can't get there, and I'm not asking you to. But I need you to know that when I told you what needed to happen that night, I believed it with everything I had. I still believe it. Joe was going to destroy everything we'd built. Not because he wanted to—but because of what he knew, and what he felt, and where that was heading. He was a man who felt compelled to do the right thing. I could see it, and I couldn't—" He stops. "I couldn't let it happen. I couldn't let you lose what we had."

I look at him.

"You couldn't let yourself lose it," I say.

He holds my gaze.

"Yes," he says. "That too."

The honesty of it lands in me. He has never said that before—and the fact that he says it now, in this room, at this moment, costs him something.

I reach over and put my hand on his.

"I know," I say.

We sit together for a while in the quiet.

"We need to figure out what we're going to do about Dr. Carver," I say finally.

"I'm on it."

"Adam." I turn to face him. "We can't hurt her."

He looks at me. "If she really is the Natasha who was Joe's foster sister, she knows something. There's no way she found us, arranged to become your therapist through a referral chain, and all of it was just a coincidence."

"Maybe the fact that her name is Natasha is the coincidence," I point out. "Maybe it's not the same person."

"Yeah? And someone who knew about Joe harassed her at her office? Allison was already dead. Does that make any sense to you?"

"No. But at some point, it has to stop." My voice is steady. "We cannot keep being people who solve problems this way—who look at a situation and decide the solution is permanent. I can't live inside that. I've been trying to live inside it since Joe, and I am telling you I can't do it anymore. We are not those people, Adam. Josie needs us not to be those people."

"Josie needs her parents," Adam says simply.

"I won't do it," I announce. "It doesn't matter if we find out she's exactly who she claims to be or if she really is Joe's sister. None of that changes anything for me. I won't hurt her. And I won't let you, either."

"Reese, we need to understand what she's trying to do. Then we'll deal with whatever that is. Okay?"

"No! It's not okay. Deal with it how?"

He doesn't answer immediately. He looks at the window. He looks at his hands. He looks everywhere but my eyes.

"Don't worry about it," he says. "I'll handle it."

I feel cold.

"Promise me," I say.

"Reese—"

"Promise me you won't hurt her." I hold his gaze and don't let him look away. "Promise me. Look me in the eyes and tell me you will not put another person's blood on our hands. I can't carry any more of it. I'm telling you honestly—I cannot carry any more."

He looks at me for a long time.

The room is very quiet.

"If I have any choice," he says slowly, "I won't hurt her."

I hear the qualification. Four letters. "If you have a choice," I repeat, refusing to back down.

"I will always look for the choice," he says. "I promise you that."

I look at my husband. The man who built this house

and this life, and who essentially put a gun in my hand so I could kill a man he supposedly loved. I make a decision, and I say the words.

"If you touch Dr. Carver, I will turn myself in for Joe's murder," I say.

His mouth falls open. He takes a moment. "You'd really do that? After everything? You would do that to Josie?"

We stand facing each other in the room above the lake, and I look at his face and think about Joe. "Josie deserves to grow up with parents who choose to do the right thing. We made a mistake. Prove to me we can come back from it. Prove to me we don't have to take another life. If you can, I will learn to live with what I did to Joe. If you can't, then I promise I will do the thing that will finally give Josie something to be proud of."

"You can't mean that," Adam says at last, and I can hear in his voice that he already knows I mean it.

"Every day of my life, I think about what we took from the world when we took Joe out of it. I think about the particular quality of his laugh and the way he could sit with us for an entire evening and be entirely present. I think about his eyes—the same dark eyes I see every day now in a smaller face looking up at me from the crib—and I hate myself. I will live with what I did for Josie. But I can't let it happen again. Also for Josie."

He processes what I've told him.

"If you do, Josie will grow up just like he did," he warns.

I give him a tender smile that reaches my eyes. "And look how remarkable he turned out."

What I don't tell Adam is that every minute of every day, I think about the fact that I pulled the trigger. I have never stopped thinking about it, and I'm not sure I ever will. Standing here with Adam's hand in mine, I understand that this is the weight I will carry for the rest of my life.

Adam squeezes my hand.

"Okay, if that's how you want it. I promise I won't do anything to Dr. Carver," he concedes, and part of me isn't sure I can believe him. "We should go back downstairs before Nora starts to wonder what's happened to us."

I nod and follow him to the bedroom door. Nora. I'd never stopped to consider how hard all of this would be on her if Adam didn't keep his word. I meant every word. If he harmed Dr. Carver, I would turn myself in. What would Nora do when she found out that Allison's warning had been true? What would it do to her to know she loved a cold-blooded killer?

THIRTY-THREE

REESE

The kitchen smells like safety. Like a life in which we could all be happy—here in this home, with Josie. But knowing the vultures are circling has me thinking about what Josie's life will look like if I do turn myself in. Will she end up, as Adam says, in foster care? And if she does, how many times in her life will she live in a home where the kitchen smells like love? I push the worry from my thoughts, determined to hold to my ultimatum.

The French toast casserole sits golden and fragrant at the center of the kitchen island. The butter-and-vanilla-and-custard-soaked bread looks as though it should grace the cover of a culinary magazine. Nora smiles at us as we emerge from the stairwell. She turns, retrieves the orange juice from the fridge, and proceeds to pour it into two champagne flutes waiting on the counter.

"What's all this?" I ask, smiling at her.

"I thought some mimosas would be fun with the casserole," she replies. After the news about Allison, I'm grateful for Nora's brightness.

Glancing over, I see Josie already strapped into the high chair. She lets out a high-pitched shriek of delight as she picks up one of the crumbs in front of her and pops into her mouth.

Allison is gone. Every sensory detail of this moment is telling me I am safe. That I am home. That the worst is behind us. But in the back of my mind, I keep thinking about Natasha Carver.

Nora watches us settle into our seats.

I notice her watching. I've come to understand, over the past nine months of living with her, that she is always observing.

"Is everything okay?" she asks.

She asks it warmly—with the gentle, open quality of someone who genuinely cares about the answer. What if we ruin her? I think. I know Adam says what happened to Allison is not our fault, but I can't stop thinking that it's a pattern with us.

"Everything's fine," Adam says. "This smells so good, Nora."

Nora nods. "Thank you. It's one of my favorite comfort recipes." She turns back to Josie, cutting something soft into smaller pieces, transferring them across the tray with the efficient tenderness she brings to everything involving Josie.

I take a bite of casserole. It is extraordinary—the kind of thing that tastes as though love is actually baked into it.

"How was your trip?" Nora asks, glancing over at Adam. I chew quietly, wondering whether he will tell Nora about his trip to Allison's hometown. The lie.

I take a sip of the mimosa while Adam answers.

"Good, good," he says. "But, actually, there's something we needed to talk to you about. I got a call from my contact who has been monitoring the search for Allison."

Nora's head snaps toward Adam. "Oh my God, did they finally find her?"

"Well, yes. But apparently, she's been dead for some time," he replies.

Nora's brow furrows. She shakes her head. "Dead? I don't understand."

"The coroner hasn't issued a report yet, but from what I understand, they think Allison died not long after the accident."

I watch as Adam sips his mimosa, and then I do the same, staying quiet.

I watch her absorb the information, clearly shocked. "Do they think she died from the accident?" Her voice is smaller now. Something moves through it that sounds like guilt. "Would she have lived if I'd turned around? If I'd stopped and called for help instead of just driving away?"

"No," Adam says firmly. "There was nothing you could have done. They're actually looking at it as a possible suicide."

"A suicide?" Nora repeats. "That's awful."

She looks down at Josie, who waits eagerly for more casserole.

I eat another bite. I take another drink.

Adam is talking—explaining to Nora what to expect as the investigation moves forward. He tells her she's not in trouble, but the police may want to interview her. She sits there absorbing it. I watch Adam wash down another bite of casserole with the last of his mimosa.

Josie starts to fuss. "Aw, sweetie—are you getting tired?" I move to go to her, but when I stand I feel lightheaded. The champagne has already gone to my head.

Nora stands and lifts Josie from the high chair. Josie goes to her with the ease of the deeply familiar. She settles against Nora's hip and reaches for Nora's collar, grabbing it with the focused intentionality she brings to things she has decided belong to her.

"I'll take care of her. You two finish your meal," Nora says before heading toward the stairs.

I take another sip of my drink.

I pick up my fork.

Adam says my name.

I look at him.

Something is wrong with his face.

Not dramatically wrong. Not the kind of wrong that announces itself. Just slightly off, the way a painting is wrong when one element is a fraction of an inch out of place, and you can't locate the error, but you feel it.

His mouth is open as though he was about to say something.

His eyes are moving in a way that is not the way his eyes move.

"Are you..." he says.

And then I feel it.

Not anxiety. Something physical, arriving too fast—faster than tiredness arrives—with a warmth behind my eyes that I don't recognize. A heaviness in my limbs that is unfamiliar.

I look at Adam.

He looks at me.

His expression tells me he is feeling what I am. The same wrongness. The same arrival of something that has no name yet, but that my body has already recognized.

"Natasha." He manages to say it, but his voice is wrong—slower than his voice should be, thicker, like a signal passing through something that is dampening it.

I turn toward the counter, scanning the room as it starts to shift side to side around me. I'm not sure whether I expect to see Dr. Carver standing somewhere in it, but something in his voice tells me it's a warning. All I can think is that I need to warn Nora. I need to tell her that something is wrong and that she should take Josie and get out of the house.

My body doesn't listen when I tell it to go upstairs and find her.

I look at Adam, who has his eyes fixed on a single point in front of him, gripping the counter as though letting go would fling him into space, to drift forever. I open my mouth to speak—to tell him I can't move—but nothing comes out.

In the single terrible second before the heaviness reaches my eyes, the kitchen begins its slow, inexorable tilt.

And then there is nothing.

THIRTY-FOUR

REESE

The first thing I feel is the cold.

Not the cold of a winter morning or an open window but the cold that comes up through concrete into your spine when you have been lying on it long enough that the warmth has left your body and gone somewhere you can't follow. My back knows it before the rest of me does. The rest of me is still working through the layers of whatever stands between me and awake.

The second thing is Adam's voice.

"Reese."

He says my name with the particular urgency of a man who has already been conscious long enough to understand the situation and is now waiting for me to catch up. I know this voice. I have heard it once before from him—in a car in our driveway, the morning after the worst night of our lives.

"I'm here," I say, or try to say. My mouth is dry, and the words come out slower than I intend.

"Don't move too fast," he warns. "Give yourself a moment."

I do just that, assessing my surroundings as the fog slowly lifts. I am lying on something narrow and firm. The smell of the room reaches me before I have fully opened my eyes—concrete, and beneath it something older, something that lives in the pores of the walls.

I know where I am.

I close my eyes slowly, then reopen them, waiting for the room to come into focus.

The carriage house ceiling. The single light fixture, casting its flat light over the space. I hate this room. I hate the walls. I hate the ceiling. I hate the lies we told Joe. And most of all, I hate that this is where Adam showed me where the gun was.

I try to sit up.

I can't.

Understanding arrives in pieces. My wrists are secured behind me. There is no play in it, no slack, nothing to work against. Whoever did this did not do it quickly or anxiously. They took their time.

"Adam."

"I know." His voice comes from my right. Close, but I can't see him. My head isn't responding to my brain's commands yet. "I'm the same. We can't panic."

"What happened?" I ask, trying to piece together how we arrived here.

The kitchen. The casserole. The mimosas. Nora taking Josie upstairs for a nap. The heaviness arriving too fast.

"Oh my God—where's Nora?" I ask.

"I was calling out before you woke up, but I don't hear anything," Adam says.

"Do you think Natasha did this?" I cry, beginning to pull desperately at the straps around my wrists. I don't wait for him to answer. "Do you think she pumped some kind of gas into the house? Or what if she poisoned our food?"

"Reese, Nora prepared the food."

"Oh my God—Josie and Nora were both eating the casserole. Do you think they're okay?"

"Reese, it's Nora."

"Where?"

"No, Nora was the one who drugged us."

I try, but I can't make his words make sense. "No. She wouldn't do that." I pause, wondering if this could come from jealousy. "Besides, they ate the casserole too."

"But Josie and Nora didn't have the mimosas," Adam answers.

"No—you're wrong. Nora would never do that. It's Dr. Carver."

My head finally begins to swivel in response. I look around the room as much as my position allows. The space is still clean from when Adam emptied it. Two narrow cots—new ones, the kind that fold flat—occupy the floor.

Someone planned this.

Someone has been planning this for a long time.

Then I hear the door.

She stands in the doorway for a moment before she steps inside. A light surrounds her from behind, reducing her to a silhouette at first. Nora enters the space, and relief floods me.

"Oh, thank God," I cry. "I think it's Dr. Carver. Hurry—untie us before she comes back."

Nora walks toward us, her dark hair loose around her shoulders. She rarely wears it down, and it's hard not to notice how striking she is when it frames her face. She looks at us both. Her expression is—I search for the word and can't find one that fits.

She looks at us the way she looks at Josie when Josie does something predictable that she finds endearing.

"Nora? What are you doing? You have to help us before she finds us. Where's Josie?" The final question twists my stomach. My Josie. My beautiful miracle.

"I told you before," Nora answers matter-of-factly. "I put her down for a nap. She's fine."

The statement should relieve me, but the absence of urgency in her voice makes my stomach drop. "Nora, what's wrong?" But she doesn't answer. "Please—you have to hurry. Help us."

She tilts her head a fraction.

"Help you," she says, as though tasting the words. "Hmm. I'm just trying to figure out why I would do that, given that I'm the one who put you there in the first place. It seems like it would make the whole thing rather pointless." She crosses to the center of the room and looks between us with an expression of genuine consideration. "I suppose there's a version where I tie you up and then immediately set you free and we all have a good laugh about it, but that's not quite the energy I'm going for today."

The lightness of it is more frightening than anything else she could have said.

"Where is Josie?" I ask again, fear gripping me.

Her expression shifts completely. Whatever dark amusement was there a moment ago is gone, replaced by something I recognize as genuine. "I just told you. She's safe and sound," she says. "She went down for her nap before I brought you out here."

I believe her. That's the thing I wasn't expecting. I believe her completely about Josie.

"What do you want?" Adam asks, his voice still controlled.

Nora walks to the wall and leans against it—the posture of someone with nowhere to be.

"What do I want?" she says. "That's a big question. In the immediate sense, I want to have a conversation I've needed to have for the past nine months. In the larger sense—well. We'll get to that." She looks at me. "Hi, Reese."

My throat is very tight. "Hi," I say.

"So about the mimosas," she continues, as though discussing a recipe. "I want to apologize in advance for the hellish headache you're probably just starting to feel. That's a side effect of the dosage I had to use to account for the weight difference between you two. I could have been more precise, but I was working with limited equipment."

She delivers it with the mild regret of someone who has slightly overcooked a chicken.

"Who the fuck are you?" Adam asks.

She looks at him. Her expression settles into something more serious.

"My name is Natasha," she says. "Joe was my brother."

THIRTY-FIVE

REESE

She pushes off the wall and walks to the center of the room and looks at us with those eyes I have gazed into while making love to her. I have spent months trying to understand the flutter I felt whenever Nora was near. I thought I understood the qualities that drew me to her—her steadiness, her certainty, her confidence. I had never experienced them quite like that in anyone but Adam. But now I see that those qualities in the person I knew as Nora were one thing. In Natasha, they are something else entirely. They are the qualities of someone who has thought everything through before she acts. A person who has been living inside a mission for a very long time.

"Joe talked about you," she says. "Both of you. Not constantly—Joe was always respectful—but that last time he came to see me, he couldn't stop talking about you both." She pauses. "He was always the one who saw the good in people."

"I don't understand," I say, several pieces of the past nine months still not connecting.

"Don't worry—we'll get there," she says, moving closer to me.

"Stay the fuck away from her, you psychotic bitch," Adam growls, pulling as hard as he can against his restraints.

Nora—Natasha—laughs. "There's that asshole you like to pretend isn't lurking just beneath the surface."

"Let us go, now!" he shouts.

Natasha pulls out a large hunting knife. The single overhead light catches on the blade as she turns it over and over between her fingers. "If you don't want me to carve up your wife in front of you, I suggest you shut the fuck up. Do you understand?"

A whimper escapes me before I manage to regain my composure. I turn my head to look at Adam, whose eyes are fixed on Nora. His stare looks as though he could rip her head from her shoulders with his bare hands, if only he could get loose.

"What do you want?" I ask.

"What do I want?" she repeats before letting out an exaggerated exhale. "I want you both to understand what brought us to this moment."

"What?" I ask, confused.

"I'm not sure how much Joe told you about me. He was always pretty open about his own experiences growing up, but he tended to be protective when it came to me." She continues without waiting. "I was eleven when I ended up in the same foster home as Joe. I'd been in seven different homes before that." She laughs, but it carries no warmth. "It's funny—none of those foster parents had a problem cashing the checks from the state until they found out who my father was. You see, I came into the system under very different circumstances than Joe did. My father—" She stops. Something moves through her expression that is real—an old real. The kind that takes years of practice to suppress.

After a moment, her composure is restored, and she continues with the same tone she'd use to describe a documentary. "My father was arrested when I was nine. The newspapers had all kinds of nicknames for him. The core point to my story is that my father was a killer. A serial killer." She tilts her head and shrugs. "I actually think that term is far too kind, if you want my opinion."

The carriage house is absolutely still.

"I suppose you could say I'm like him," she says simply. Not with shame. Not with pride. As a fact that has been examined and accepted. "I recognized it in myself early. The compulsions. The particular way certain situations present themselves to me as problems with solutions that other people don't see. Joe saw it. He could see what I was before I could name it myself, which was one of the things that made him..." She takes a breath. "He was my moral compass. He helped me understand that the compulsion itself was not wrong. What mattered was the application of it. If I needed to kill something to quiet the need, I would only ever kill something that deserved to die."

I listen as Natasha describes her need to kill the way another person might describe a compulsion to create—as an expression of who she is. Nothing more.

"That is what Joe gave me," she says. "A framework.

A way to be what I am without becoming what my father was. And then you took him."

"We didn't—" Adam starts.

"Save it," she says. Pleasantly. Without heat.

"Listen to me. Joe left. He moved on. We've heard nothing from him since—"

"Shut up," Natasha says. Still pleasant. Still mild, as though Adam is a child insisting on a story that no longer applies. "Joe didn't move on. Joe didn't leave. Joe loved you. Both of you. In different ways and for different reasons, but genuinely. He told me about you—about the house, about the life you were building together. Joe didn't leave the people he loves." She looks at Adam steadily. "You know this. And so do I."

Adam's jaw is tight. He says nothing.

"But I had to be certain," Natasha continues. She sits on the floor now, cross-legged, which is somehow more unsettling than if she'd remained standing. "It would have been wrong to act without certainty. That was another of Joe's gifts to me—patience. Accuracy before action. So I had to confirm it. I made him a promise I swore I would never break. No matter how long it takes, I must have proof that someone is truly bad before I do anything."

"What kind of proof?" I ask, replaying moments from the past nine months, searching for anything Natasha might have taken as evidence.

"Well—there was Allison," she says.

"We didn't do anything to her! She was unstable," Adam yells, his agitation mounting the more helpless he feels.

Natasha laughs a new laugh—the laugh she has hidden from me since I met her. It sends a chill through me. "You're not wrong. That woman clearly needed help. It's sad, isn't it, when people who desperately need it can't get it? After talking to her, it became pretty clear she didn't know anything about Joe."

"Wait—I thought you said she told you we murdered someone," I say, studying her face, trying to find any trace of Nora inside this woman in front of me.

"Oh no—that was to put you both on edge. Honestly, I thought it would be enough to make you open up, Reese. You came close, I think. But Adam, you'd be proud of your girl. She never gave me enough that I could be certain."

"So she didn't try to run you off the road?" Adam asks.

Natasha smiles and waves a hand dismissively. "God, no—I was the one who ran her off the road." She laughs, small and light. "We were never even at the park. I made all of that up. I'd been following her all day. Josie and I made a little game of it. I called it Stakeout. Reese, you would have thought her reactions to the car chase were absolutely adorable."

My stomach lurches at the thought of Josie being there.

"Anyway," Natasha continues in a singsong voice, "when I finally approached Allison and told her my suspicions about the two of you—that I thought you'd murdered my brother—she had the nerve to tell me I was crazy. Then she threatened me. Said she was going to tell you exactly who was watching your baby. Can you believe that?"

"Did you—" I can't bring myself to finish.

"Kill her?" Natasha asks. "The airbag knocked her out, so all I had to do was get her into the trunk. You wouldn't believe how hard it is to do that with traffic picking up in the afternoon. By the time I got back in the car, Josie had fallen fast asleep. She's such a little angel."

"Natasha, please. You can't do this. Think of Josie," Adam pleads.

"Oh, I am thinking of Josie!" she snaps, and her irritation surfaces briefly before she regains composure. "Now, where was I? Oh yes. So I took Allison to a private area in the woods, and—well—I confirmed she knew nothing about the two of you and Joe. Poor woman. All that conviction and nothing behind it."

I think about Allison in the grocery store. The controlled, terrible smile. The empty basket. I had seen her as a monster. Had I been wrong?

"What about Joe's code?" I ask. "Did Allison deserve to die?"

"Allison wasn't innocent. She may not have known what you did to Joe, but she wasn't innocent."

"We didn't do anything to Joe," Adam says again, and Natasha lifts the blade in his direction as a warning without words.

"What does that mean—she wasn't innocent?" I press.

"Did you know she murdered her husband?"

"What?"

Natasha nods. "She promised she wouldn't tell you

about me if I let her go. I explained that would be untidy. She had the idea that if she gave me something damning enough to send her to prison for life, I'd let her go—mutually assured destruction." She clicks her tongue in judgment. "I guess her husband had a second family she knew nothing about. She was so humiliated that they got into an enormous fight and she killed him. She swore it was an accident, but killing someone in a rage doesn't feel much like an accident to me. Does it to you?"

"So you killed her?" My voice cracks.

"I'll admit it's considerably harder to manage those kinds of situations with a baby in the back seat, but I managed." She looks at me. "Reese, I'm sorry—I know you're worried about Josie. But I want you to know she was never in any danger."

I don't know what to say to that.

"Wait, so if it wasn't Allison who called my therapist —" I start.

Natasha's expression shifts. "Ah yes. Dr. Carver." The name sits in her mouth like something being set down very carefully. "After Allison was a dead end—no pun intended—I started wondering if maybe you'd told the good doctor something that would confirm my suspicions." She tilts her head. "I considered being more persuasive with her. But I could tell within about four minutes that even if she knew something, she would not give it up. That kind of person doesn't break—they just shut down. Which would have been useless to me."

"But you let her live?" Adam asks.

Natasha lets out a heavy, annoyed sigh. "Joe's code, remember? I could tell Dr. Carver had no skeletons. I knew she'd tell you that a strange woman had shown up asking questions about you, and you'd likely assume it was Allison. But I also knew it was only a matter of time before the police found Allison's body—so instead I needed to cast doubt on the doctor. It was a gamble, but I figured there was a good chance Joe had mentioned my name to you at some point. It's not exactly a common name. I figured it would stick."

"So there was never a message from Dr. Carver?"

"Nope. But it clearly put you on edge. I still wasn't certain, though," Natasha says. "I needed to hear it. Not from someone else. From you." She crosses to me and reaches into the pocket of the oversized cardigan I'm wearing. She pulls out a small white baby monitor and holds it up.

"I got the idea when I heard you in the nursery, talking to Josie," Natasha says. "You spoke to her as though the two of you were the only ones in the world. Later, when you came home and were in the kitchen, I slipped it into your pocket when I hugged you." She looks at me. "You didn't even notice."

My breath catches. I had noticed—or almost had. Thinking back, I'd registered the weight of it at some point and dismissed it, assuming it was the receiver, which I often carry so I can hear Josie when she wakes. There was no reason to think I was carrying the transmitter.

I think about her arms around me in the kitchen. The warmth of her. The way she held on. I felt so safe. So loved. It was all part of her plan.

"I heard everything," she says. "The conversation

upstairs, between the two of you." She sets the monitor down on the concrete floor between us. "Every word."

The room is absolutely still.

I look at Adam. He stares at the monitor with an expression I have never seen on his face before. It takes me a moment to identify it because it is so rare on him.

He's afraid.

"So." Natasha's voice is even and unhurried. "You killed Joe. You have been careful, and you have been thorough, and you have built your beautiful life on top of what you did. I want you to know I understand that. Genuinely. You are not ordinary people. Ordinary people don't do what you did and then simply—continue."

"It wasn't—" Adam starts.

"Don't," she murmurs, looking at him. The quiet is worse than if she had raised her voice. "Don't tell me it wasn't what it sounded like. Don't construct a version you think I'll accept as truth. I'm not a jury. I'm not interested in the lies you tell yourselves. I heard what I heard."

Adam falls silent.

"Where is he?" she asks.

The question is small and direct and contains everything.

I look at Adam. He is looking at me now—I can see the calculation running behind his eyes, the angles, the possibilities, the ever-present search for the exit.

"The lake," I say. "We put him in Lake Michigan."

"Reese!" Adam's voice is sharp. "What the hell is wrong with you? Why would you tell her that?"

"Because it's over, Adam." I hear my own voice say it,

and I understand—in the moment of hearing it—that I mean it. Not in the way of giving up. Not despair. In the way of a thing one has waited a very long time to end, and whose end has finally arrived.

He stares at me.

Natasha watches us both with the expression of someone witnessing something sad but not surprising.

"The lake," she says. To herself, or to the air, or to Joe, wherever he is. She closes her eyes for a moment, then opens them. "Okay."

She adjusts her grip on the hunting knife—the ease of someone whose hands have learned this motion.

"You won't hurt Josie," I say. "Tell me you won't hurt her."

She looks at me. The warmth is fully real. "Absolutely not," she says. "Joe's daughter deserves all the love in the world."

"She's not Joe's." Adam's voice is sharp and raw, every feeling he has never fully processed about the question of Josie's parentage rising to the surface. "She's mine. She's my daughter."

Natasha moves.

A single precise motion. Without warning, the blade enters Adam's side, and he makes a sound I have never heard from him—but as it fills my ears, I feel it in the center of my chest. She steps back.

"Adam," I cry, wishing I could go to him. Hold him the way I held Joe at the end.

"I told you to shut up," she says, without particular heat. "Everyone in this room knows whose daughter she is. Claiming it loudly doesn't make it true."

"Reese," he says.

"Baby." The tears flow freely now as I look at my husband. The pain on his face presses down on me. "I'm right here. I'm right here with you."

"Reese." He says my name again, but his voice is different now. The controlled version is gone. This is the voice underneath.

I look at him. My husband. The man who built me a house on a lake because I once told him the water was the only thing that made everything go still. The man who dismembered someone we both loved and disposed of the body to keep us safe. The man who was willing to raise Josie as his own without hesitation, even as his eyes told me he had always known the truth of whose daughter she was.

"I love you," I say. "I have always loved you. I know all you ever wanted was to make me happy. And I want you to know you have."

His eyes are very bright.

"Don't," he says. "Don't do this."

I look at Natasha. She is watching me. The knife is at her side. Adam's blood drips from the blade.

"She doesn't deserve this," Adam says. He says it directly to Natasha, and his voice has found something past the fear. "This was me. All of it. I was the one who decided what needed to happen. I was the one who told her what to do. She did what I asked." He pulls in a ragged breath, struggling more now. "Whatever you need from this—take it from me. Leave Reese alone." He pauses. "She loves you, or Nora, or—I don't know what to call you anymore. Let her raise Josie. You could raise Josie together."

Natasha looks at him for a long moment.

"You'd just sacrifice yourself so she could live?" she says.

"If that's what it takes," he says. "I mean it."

"I know you do," Natasha says. "You love her. I believe that. It's actually the most human thing about you." She tilts her head. "And you're right that you're a large part of what happened to Joe. I'm not sure whether you wanted him dead because you were afraid Reese was beginning to love him more than you, or if there was another reason. It doesn't really matter. Adam, men like you need to be the one holding the string. You tell Reese you're giving her the gift of a kite, then you keep the string in your hand and call it love. I see you for who you really are."

I look at my husband. Natasha's version of him holds slivers of truth, but for all the bad in him, I see so much more that is good. He is looking at me. I can see it happening. He is breaking.

"I still pulled the trigger," I say. I say it to Natasha, but also for myself—a reminder that no matter what version she wants to tell, I cannot forget that it was me. I was the one who ended his life.

"I know," she says.

"I know you're going to kill me for that."

"I am."

I nod. There is a resolve in me that I didn't expect to find, and I am not going to waste time explaining it.

"Will you promise me something?" I ask.

"Maybe," she answers, without commitment.

"Promise me she will grow up knowing her mother loved her. Promise me she'll be happy."

Something moves through Natasha's face. She crosses to me and kneels beside the cot. She takes my face in her hands—the way Adam has done a thousand times—and looks at me with those dark eyes. I understand with perfect clarity that she means it when she says, "I promise."

She kisses me.

Softly. Once.

"Don't!" I hear Adam shout. "Don't you fucking do it!"

I stare into Natasha's eyes, and there is love in them as she stares back at me. I feel the cold blade at my neck, and I close my eyes and picture Josie's face. I see her reaching up for me, smiling. Then I imagine another future: Adam, Joe, me, and Josie on the boat on the water. It is so peaceful. My chest is warm with the image.

The last thing I hear is Adam saying my name.

And then the lake.

I have always loved the lake.

THIRTY-SIX

ADAM

I have watched her when she was radiant and when she was diminished and when she was lost to me in the months after Joe's death, after Josie arrived, and I could not reach her no matter what I did or offered or built. I have watched her find her way back. I have watched her in the studio. I have watched her hold our daughter in the nursery. I have watched her fall in love with someone else and told myself it was what I wanted for her—and there was truth in that, and there was also a lie I have been managing for long enough that the management became the truth.

And I watch now.

There is pain on my face as I look at my wife, crimson seeping from her neck, and the only word I can find to describe the expression on her face is peace. She is at peace in a way she has not been since the night Joe escaped from the carriage house.

Not the performed peace of someone who has decided to accept something they cannot change. This is different. This is the peace of someone who has set something down and finally feels what it is to live without the weight of it.

She looks like the version of her I met in the quad all those years ago.

I told her she needed to pull the trigger to protect us. I let her believe that. I even convinced myself for a while. I told her it was the only option, but she was right. It was a lie. The truth is one I haven't been willing to admit even to myself until now.

I was afraid.

Not of Joe. Joe was not a dangerous man in the ordinary sense—I had known that from the first month, and I never stopped knowing it. Natasha was right. I was afraid of what Joe was becoming to Reese. The particular quality of her love for him was different from her love for me. It was not a lesser love. That was the thing I did not know how to hold. It was not a lesser love, and it did not diminish what she had with me. I could see that, yet I still could not—I could not let it continue.

I told myself I was protecting us.

The true word is smaller.

The true word is afraid.

I was afraid she would love him more.

I made a decision based on that fear, and I called it protection. And Reese believed me because Reese has always wanted to believe the best version of what I am.

She deserved better than that.

She deserved better than me.

I watch her face in the remaining time.

I watch the peace of it. The resolve. I watch her make

her request—promise me she knows her mommy loved her—and I hear in the making of it the full weight of who Reese Bradley has always been: a woman who loves without condition and without calculation.

Joe.

I think about Joe. I think about who he was and what he gave us and what I took from the world when I took him out of it. I think about the fact that his daughter is in this house, that she has his eyes, that I claimed her loudly and completely—and she was never entirely mine to claim, just as Reese was never mine to claim.

I think about what Natasha said. *He was my moral compass.*

I understand this now in a way I couldn't have before this room, this moment. A moral compass doesn't tell you what you want to hear. It tells you what is true. Joe would have told me what was true. Joe would have said, "You are afraid, and fear is not a reason, and the thing you are afraid of is not a danger to you."

I know this.

I have always known this.

Natasha watches and waits for Reese's final breath before turning her attention to me. Reese is dead. I'm about to die. I fought Joe and the reality of what we were building, and it destroyed everything. I just watched the woman I love most in the world welcome death with peace on her face. And at this moment, I decide to do the same.

I close my eyes, accepting what is coming. The blade enters my other side, and instead of being withdrawn, it begins to tear. I cry out, squeezing my eyes shut as tightly as I can, hoping the last thing I see will be a vision of her.

I open my mouth and let out a long breath that ends in a gurgle. As the world goes black around me, I manage one final word—the last I will ever say.

"Reese."

It is quiet, barely above a whisper, and mostly lost beneath the sounds of my pain. I say it to the room.

I say it to the lake outside, which will still be there after all of this.

I say it the way I have always said it. Like it is the thing that everything else is oriented around.

And then I don't say anything else.

THIRTY-SEVEN

NATASHA

Josie has been on the swings for eleven minutes.

I know this because I have been watching—the way I watch everything. After all, that is the promise I made. I will keep her safe. Josie swings with the full-body commitment she brings to most things. Her dark hair flies back on the forward arc, her feet pointed at the sky as though she is trying to touch something just out of reach. She is four years old, and she already moves through the world as though she has conquered it.

She got that from her father.

Not Adam. Not the man who claimed her loudly at the end. The other one. The real one. The one whose eyes she has.

Joe would have loved her so much.

I sit on the bench with my hands loose in my lap and the late summer light coming through the trees at the angle that turns everything golden. I watch Josie on the swings, and I feel the thing I have been feeling for four years that I didn't expect. The thing that has made me, in ways I couldn't have predicted, more complicated than I was before.

I have been thinking about Joe a great deal lately. Not with grief—grief has a different shape to it than what I've been feeling, and I worked through mine in the year after. What I feel now is more like the awareness of an absence: the way a room feels different after a piece of furniture has been removed. The room is still the room. The space where the piece stood is still there. And occasionally, in a certain quality of light, you can see the outline of what used to be there.

A woman sits down beside me.

I noticed her when she crossed the park. Her posture was turned in on itself, her coat pulled close despite the warmth of the afternoon—the coat of someone who prefers to go unnoticed. Her sunglasses are there to hide something rather than to shield against the light.

She takes them off, and my suspicions are confirmed. The black eye beneath them is almost healed. Almost.

She looks around nervously before clearing her throat. "I heard roses don't grow here," she says.

I confirm my identity with the agreed-upon response, my eyes never leaving Josie. "Only if you plant them deep enough."

She exhales. I tell her to look forward and keep looking forward while we talk. We sit quietly for a long moment.

"He wasn't always like this." She offers it before I've asked anything. I know she needs to say it. She doesn't want to admit she didn't see it. She's embarrassed. They're always embarrassed, these women, for not seeing what couldn't have been seen. But that's not why I'm here. I don't care about the reasons that led them to where they are. It's not what motivates me. And though Joe is no longer in the room, I still live by his code. "He really did love me, at the beginning. I know that's what everyone says."

"Does it matter whether he loved you then—or whether he still does?" I ask, knowing she won't be able to understand the answer quite yet.

"What do you mean?"

"If a man can do to you what he does, why does it matter who he loved and when? He's a rabid dog. And a rabid dog needs to be put down before he hurts someone else."

She nods. "I suppose you're right. It started when he lost his job. He didn't drink much before then. And for a long time, it was just me. I told myself the kids didn't know and that I could manage it. And then last month..." Her jaw tightens. "He raised his hand to my oldest."

She says it with the clarity that arrives when the thing you have been protecting becomes larger than the thing you have been protecting it from.

"How old?" I ask.

"Seven."

I nod.

She reaches into her bag. She slides something across the bench toward me—a plain envelope, thick with what it contains—and I feel its particular weight against my palm before I slip it into my own bag without looking.

"What do I do now?" she asks.

"You're going to take your children to visit family," I

say. "Somewhere far enough that the trip takes more than an afternoon. Somewhere with people who will remember you being there. You're going to stay for at least a week—longer if you can manage it. You're going to be seen. Go out to dinner, take your kids to the park. Better still if it's somewhere with cameras." I pause. "When you come home, you won't have to worry about your children's safety again."

She is looking at her hands.

"Will it..." She stops. "I don't want to know how. I want you to know that. But will it..."

"It will be handled with care," I say. "And it won't come back to you."

She nods once—a small, final motion—then stands, adjusts her coat, and walks away across the park without looking back.

I watch her go.

Being a guardian is expensive. It requires me to be practical about my particular skill set. Joe would have had thoughts about this. He would have had complicated feelings. But I think he would have understood, in the end.

Getting paid to make the world a better place. That is not nothing.

And it's not as though I'm violating his code.

When Josie spots me watching her, she launches herself off the swing with a complete absence of caution that makes my chest tighten—a feeling I still haven't grown used to.

"AUNTIE NATASHA!" she announces, landing in the wood chips. "I flew."

"I saw," I say. "You were magnificent."

She accepts this as her due and races me to the car. She climbs into her car seat and waits while I buckle her in.

"Auntie Natasha," she says, once the buckle clicks.

"Josie."

"What was Daddy's favorite ice cream flavor?"

I start the engine. In the rearview mirror, I can see her face—expectant, already holding a small smile because she knows this answer and is waiting to hear it confirmed.

"Mint chocolate chip," I say. "Because he was completely insane."

She giggles. "Because ice cream should never taste like chewing gum," she recites, in the tone of someone quoting scripture.

"Exactly. Under no circumstances should ice cream taste like chewing gum. Your father was a wonderful man in every other respect, but on this issue, he could not be trusted."

Then she says, "And what was Mommy's?"

I pull out of the parking lot. The afternoon light is still doing its golden thing, stretching everything long and warm.

"Peaches and cream," I say.

"Because my momma was as sweet and pretty as a peach," Josie says, reciting her practiced reply.

"That's right."

She is quiet for a moment.

"She was really pretty," Josie says. It is not a question. I know she doesn't remember her, but I tell her about Reese. I have kept a few photographs of Reese to show her, determined to keep my promise.

"She was," I confirm. "Very. But she was also brave, and honest, and she loved you before she had ever met you—from the moment she knew you were coming."

In the rearview mirror, I watch her gaze drift out the window with the particular expression she gets when she is processing something—the little furrow, the focused stillness that is pure Joe.

"Guess my favorite ice cream!" Josie demands.

"Hmm . . . Superman?"

"No!" She laughs. "It's salted caramel, silly."

I know this answer. We have had this discussion many times. "And why is it your favorite?"

She takes a moment. This is the part she has been working on lately—the part where she moves from knowing the answer to understanding why it's the answer. She is four years old, and she takes this seriously.

"Because," she says slowly, still looking out the window, "the best things always have a little bite."

I look at her in the rearview mirror, a smile spreading to my eyes.

She looks back at me with her father's eyes.

"Bingo," I say.

I park the car.

The ice cream shop is nearly empty on a Tuesday afternoon. A teenager behind the counter. A couple by the window, sharing something. The smell of waffle cones and cold sweetness. Josie presses her nose against the curved front of the display case and surveys her options despite always getting the same thing.

"One scoop of salted caramel, please," she announces.

"Sure thing," the teenager says.

I order the mint chocolate chip—because as wrong as it is, it somehow seems right.

"That's Daddy's."

"I know," I say.

She thinks about this for a moment. Then she nods, satisfied, as though I have passed a test.

The house is near the water.

It looks nothing like the house Adam built for Reese. It's also on the opposite side of the lake. This house is ours. Josie's and mine. A home for our small, perfect family.

A small town on the lakeshore, north of Chicago. Old houses with long porches facing the water. A school where Josie will go in September—one classroom per grade, a playground backing directly onto the dunes. The lake is not decorative here. It is simply the lake: large, gray, and permanent.

We have been here for two years. The walls know our sounds. The floors know our particular weight. The quality of the morning light through the east-facing windows is one of Josie's favorite things. She calls it the gold show—which is accurate, and which she arrived at without being taught.

The painting hangs above the fireplace.

It has been there since the week we moved in. The moment I saw the fireplace, I knew that was where it belonged. Reese never named it—it was simply a canvas on the easel in the studio. When I took it, the paint was still faintly tacky at the edges. It was the last thing her hands made before the casserole, the mimosas, the kitchen tilting, and the nothing that followed.

The bottom of the canvas is dark—deep blues and blacks, the color of lake water at depth, at night. Above it, the canvas lightens, moving through gradations of gray. And in the center, emerging from the dark water into the light, is a small boat. And in the boat, two figures.

A man and, beside him, a small child. The child is too young in the painting to have the face she has now—she is a baby, small and wrapped against the cold, held in the crook of the man's arm. The man's face is not fully rendered. Reese was not a painter of faces in the conventional sense. She painted emotional truth. But the quality of the man in the boat is unmistakable.

Joe.

Joe and Josie, in the middle of the lake, between the dark and the light. The boat is very small, and the lake is very large, and they are at the center of both.

Josie once asked who the man was, and I told her it was her daddy. She stands in front of it sometimes now and just looks at it. I watch her watching.

He is not gone.

At night, after Josie is down, I stand at the kitchen window and look out at the lake.

This is the hour that belongs to them.

Both of them. Joe has been in this lake for five and a half years now—or the parts of him that could be given to water are. The rest of him is in his daughter's hands and her patience and her dark eyes. Reese has been in the lake for four years, or the parts of her that could be given to the water are.

The same fate that befell Joe also befell those who dealt it. It was an ending I hadn't planned when I first began watching the Bradleys—when I first realized they were hiring a nanny. But it felt deserved after everything I learned during my time with them.

I think about them sometimes. Adam less than Reese. I think about that first meeting and how delighted they were with the reference I had provided—a woman who was happy to say whatever I asked, after all, because I was the reason her children were safe.

I think about how much I came to care for Reese. More than I expected to. She was braver than she knew. She had more honesty in her than the life she was living allowed for. In another version of things, she would have been someone more deserving of Joe.

In this version, she is in the lake, and Josie will grow up on the shore above her. I find this comforting in a way I could not have predicted.

Aunt Natasha will always be by her side, but Josie's mother and father will also be there. Watching over her from the darkness.

ACKNOWLEDGMENTS

Okay, gather round. This one is going to be longer than usual. This is the part where I get sappy and try not to cry into my keyboard. No promises.

Josh, my husband, my partner, my co-parent, my business partner, and somehow also the man who reads my chaotic first drafts without filing for divorce. You have been an active, ride-or-die part of every book I've ever written, including this one. I don't know how I got this lucky, but I'm not asking questions in case the universe takes it back.

Nic, Haley, and Brooke, the women who keep this entire operation upright. **Nic**, my best friend of thirteen years. When life shoved you into a corner and you needed something flexible to land on, we sat down, brainstormed, and decided to expand the author business into merch and open a TikTok shop. The plan was modest: make enough to feed you a few hundred bucks a week while you started your journey as a single mom. Reader, that is not what happened. TikTok had other plans. It blew up, it led to Josh launching a 3D print business that also grew like crazy, and somehow we went from "let's see if we can pay you" in September 2024 to a team of ten employees, a 5,000 square foot commercial space we are moving into May 1st, 2026, and growth that still doesn't feel real. None of this exists without you, Nic. Thank you for being my best friend, for being vulnerable with me, for letting me be vulnerable with you, and for trusting me enough to build something wild together. I had been publishing for over a decade and making a modest living, but it took us teaming up to crack everything wide open. **Haley and Brooke**, when Nic moved over to the 3D print side in the summer of 2025, the two of you walked in and became absolute game-changers for the book business. I rely on both of you more than is probably reasonable, and I am so grateful for everything you do. To all three of you: I cannot wait to see what happens next. The new space, the bigger plans, the chaos still to come — I'm so glad we get to do it together.

Zoe and Penny, my kids, my whole heart. I don't know how I ended up with two humans this capable, but somewhere along the way you started running this house better than I do. You've been independent when I needed you to be, helpful when I didn't even ask, (and sometimes when I asked many many times) and on the days when deadlines swallowed me whole, you've literally jumped in to help with the business. You helped packing books, shipping orders, and keeping things moving when Mom was buried in a manuscript. This career exists because you let me chase it. Thank you for being the very best part of every day.

To our sweet River, we said goodbye to you while I was writing this book, and a piece of every page is yours. You were the best girl, the boss, the queen of this house, and we all miss you so much it aches. **Fig and Juni**, that includes you two — I know you miss her too, which is why you've decided the solution is to pester me every waking minute of the day now that your CEO is gone. I love you. Please let me write. (You won't.)

Jenny Sims, my editor, bless you for catching every comma I tried to sneak past you and for making me sound like the writer I want to be. I'd be lost (and very, *very* unedited) without you.

To BookTok, Bookstagram, every reader who has screamed about my books online, every influencer who raised their hand to read this one, I see you. I love you. You are the entire reason I get to do this for a living. Thank you for shouting about my books into the void until the algorithm listens.

To everyone who let me into their world while I was researching this series, the people who sat with me, opened up, and shared what their relationships actually look like, the messy parts and the beautiful parts, the highs and the hard days, thank you. Polyamory and ethical non-monogamy are something that I needed insight around to write this series. I'm a jealous partner. (Josh, stop nodding.) Wrapping my head around the idea that love can stretch and multiply instead of split was one of the most humbling research experiences of my career. Every person who answered my nosy questions with patience and honesty helped shape these characters, their fears, their joy, and their journey. This story is as wild as it is because of you. Also, please note that this is a work of fiction and none of the people I spoke to have ever locked a man in their basement... that I know of.

And finally, **to my readers.** I already gushed

about you in the dedication, but you're getting a second round because you've earned it. Thank you for trusting me with your time, your hearts, and your e-reader battery. Now go hydrate. I'll see you in the next book.

xoxo, Wendy

LOVED IT? HATED IT? TELL SOMEONE.

If you enjoyed *Couple Seeking Girlfriend*, the kindest thing you can do for me is leave a quick review on Amazon and Goodreads. Even a sentence or two helps other readers find this book — and helps me keep writing more.

Thank you for reading. Truly. 🩶

xoxo, Wendy

NEWSLETTER

Stay In My Orbit

Want first dibs on new releases, sneak peeks at what I'm writing next, exclusive coupon codes for my bookish shop, and the occasional behind-the-scenes look at my chaotic author life?

Come hang out in my newsletter. It's the best place to find me. No algorithms deciding whether you see me, no missed releases, just me dropping into your inbox with the good stuff.

Sign up at wendyowensbooks.com

I promise not to spam you. I also promise to occasionally share embarrassing stories about my dogs.

WHAT'S COMING?

A Domestic Thriller

Four trophy wives. One gated community. A victim everyone secretly hated.

In Meridian Heights, the lawns are manicured, the marriages are managed, and the secrets are buried under Botox and bottomless brunches. When Miranda Calloway is found dead by what looks like a suicide, the women who called her their best friend each have a reason to want her gone. And a story they're not telling.

The truth is hiding in plain sight.

You just have to know where to look.

Big Little Lies meets The Housemaid, soaked in the performative perfection of Instagram culture.

Coming 2026.

ABOUT THE AUTHOR

Wendy Owens is a USA Today Best Selling Author who writes across romantasy, romance, thrillers, dark romance, and erotic thrillers — basically, if it has tension, longing, or someone questionable in a good way, she's probably writing it. Since 2011, she's published 28 novels and written and illustrated two children's books, with several titles landing in the Amazon Top 10 along the way.

Wendy lives in the Cincinnati, Ohio area with her husband Josh, their kids Zoe and Penny, and their dogs Fig and Juni — all of whom are very involved in her workday whether she invited them to be or not. When she's not writing, she's running her online shop full of books and bookish goodies (a labor of love that eats more of her time than she'd like to admit), sketching, sneaking in the occasional painting session, or plowing through audiobooks at speeds that probably aren't recommended.

She's done a lot of things she's loved in this life, but writing is the one that makes her feel the fullest.

Find her — and stay in the loop. 🌐 wendyowensbooks.com — sign up for her newsletter for coupon codes, sneak peeks, and bookish goodness 📸 Instagram: @wendylowens 🎥 TikTok: @wendylowens — catch her live multiple times a week

ALSO BY WENDY OWENS

For a complete list of available books and to find links to all of Wendy's Books visit wendyowensbooks.com

DARK ROMANCE (spicy)

Crimson Ties

Crimson Fate

Crimson Vows

Crimson Sins

THRILLERS

My Husband's Fiancee

My Wife's Secrets

The Day We Died

An Influential Murder

Secrets At Meadow Lake

Affair To Die For

Couple Seeking Boyfriend (spicy)

Couple Seeking Girlfriend (spicy)

COZY MYSTERIES

Jack Be Nimble, Jack Be Dead

O Deadly Night

Roses Are Red, Violet is Dead

YA ROMANCE

Wash Me Away

<u>YA PARANORMAL (clean)</u>

Sacred Bloodlines

Unhallowed Curse

The Shield Prophecy

The Lost Years

The Guardians Crown

<u>ADULT URBAN FANTASY</u>

Burning Destiny

Blazing Moon

<u>CONTEMPORARY ROMANCE (adult)</u>

Stubborn Love

Only In Dreams

The Luckiest

Do Anything

It Matters to Me

www.ingramcontent.com/pod-product-compliance
Lightning Source LLC
LaVergne TN
LVHW021629120826
845149LV00023B/2889

9798991622707